TRACING HOLLAND

THE HOLD ME SERIES
BOOK 2

ALY STILES

TRACING HOLLAND
Copyright © 2016 Aly Stiles (Alyson Santos)
All Rights Reserved

Cover Design by Books and Moods

ISBN: 978-1-961197-01-5

 Created with Vellum

NOTE ABOUT TRACING HOLLAND

Tracing Holland continues the story of Luke Craven, Callie Roland, and Casey Barrett from *Night Shifts Black*. It is strongly recommended that readers begin with *Night Shifts Black* to truly appreciate the growth and interaction of these characters in *Tracing Holland*.

PROLOGUE

"Guide me toward the light, I swear I'll follow.
Forgive me for the man I am.
Fight the hollow ghost I carry.
I've learned to hide the tears,
Though they still break me.

Search for me, the broken wanderer
Find me, deep within my own void
Save me, from my burning lies
Don't believe what I am."

- Luke Craven, Night Shifts Black

1

THE ENCORE: PART I

It's deafening. I close my eyes and listen, absorb. I know I should be reviewing what's next, but my heart is pounding too fast, the blood searing through my body and blocking all coherent thoughts in my head.

"That's for you, man." Casey's voice is barely audible over the roar, and I cast a quick glance in his direction. Casey. Callie. The reasons I'm standing here. The reasons I'm alive. The reasons I'm once again Luke Craven, frontman for Night Shifts Black.

I still don't believe I deserve this second chance, but I've accepted it. Those two stubborn beacons of light didn't really give me a choice. It's a gift, or as Callie calls it, a miracle, and I'm not screwing it up this time around. I'm not.

"So are we doing this or what?" Sweeny yells over the chanting. "I mean, I could listen to forty-thousand people scream Luke's name all day, but I wouldn't mind hitting Saxon before the bar closes."

Casey rolls his eyes and smacks him. "Relax, bro. We'll go back out. Just give him a second. What are you guys thinking?

Do the full three-song set for the encore? It's our first comeback show. I think we can do three."

"Three's good," Sweeny says. "Open or close with 'Greetings'?"

"Close," I whisper to myself. I face my band, my friends. "Definitely close."

There's a sudden pressure on my arm, and I turn to meet a pair of sweet, hazel eyes that somehow manage to cut into me every time.

"You've got this, Luke," Callie says with a smile. God, I love her smile. Love the way she makes me believe there's good in the world. There's good in me somewhere. "You ready?"

I draw in a deep breath and stare back at the entrance to the stage. That's the question, isn't it? Am I ready? Ready for what? The crowd? The music? Or ready for life. Ready to face the reality that what I was will attack the very fabric of who I am now. I'm not naïve. I knew the second I agreed to come back that I was signing up for one hell of a ride. I'm a different person now, but no one knows that. No one knows I'm not a monster anymore. Well, no one except the two most important people in my life, which is why there's a remote chance on God's green earth I can actually do this. I might actually pull off a comeback, not just for my career, but for my life.

Am I ready? No. But I'm ok with that now. I'm ok, because for the first time since I can remember, I'm not afraid of myself. I'm not afraid of tomorrow. I'm not afraid to live.

2

HOUSTON, TEXAS

SEPTEMBER 12-13

The chanting begins to spread into an indecipherable roar as the front few rows of fans notice our shadows emerging from the wing of the stage. I can feel the adrenaline pumping through me now, feeding off the crowd, their passion, their excitement. I hadn't bothered giving my guitar to the tech when we'd finished our earlier set, so it's just a matter of a quick adjustment to the strap and tweak of my mic stand. The stand is set perfectly, but I always hit it with one last grip before the lights. I don't know, maybe it's about the connection. Making the microphone a part of me. I insert my in-ears and tighten the cables behind my neck, allowing the custom monitors to replace the din of the crowd with echoes of Casey's adjustments to his kit and Sweeny's last minute tuning.

I close my eyes and take a deep breath.

We delay another twenty-five seconds in silence. The darkness is almost tangible now, taunting the crowd with its presence since they know we're here. They know we're ready, that we're about to explode on them with one last barrage of epic euphoria. We all feel the tension, the air heavy with anticipation. It's up to Casey how long we torture them.

And there it is.

He taps the edge of the snare three times, our signal that he's ready, and I nod, even though I know they can't see me in the shadows. I take my stance, left hand locked on the neck of my guitar, right hand clutching my pick. I do one last scan of my pedal board to make sure everything seems on and ready to go. And then, the steady tick of the click track jumps to life in my ears. Tick. Tock. Tock. Tock. Tick. Tock. Tock. Tock. Casey gives us two full measures before a live count with his sticks.

1-2-3-4.

Explosion.

"HEY, we're all heading over to Saxon after we clean up. You in?" Casey asks as we hover around the table of snacks in the green room.

"I don't know. Who's going?" I ask, grabbing a bottle of water from the ice bowl. I wipe the sweat from my forehead with the hem of my t-shirt and twist the cap off my bottle.

"Um, just us I think. Maybe some of the others. I didn't ask. Does it matter?"

I shake my head. "I guess not."

"Molly is going to meet us there."

I don't even have to see Casey's face to know there's a giant grin. I can hear it in his voice. I can't help but return it. "That's great, Case. Are any of your other siblings meeting up while we're in Houston?"

He shrugs. "I don't know yet. Just Molly tonight. I might try to set something up for tomorrow with a few other locals while we're here. I want them to meet Callie. At least Nate and Abby."

"Molly's gonna love her."

"Hell yeah, she will. Hey, come though, ok?"

I sigh. I know I should, I'm just reluctant to make a promise I might not keep. I've done enough of that in my life. "Where is Callie anyway?" I ask, changing the subject before he can force an answer.

"I think she's with Holland," Casey replies. "They've started hanging out since the tour rehearsals."

I smile, not surprised. It's hard not to want Callie around once she inserts herself into your life. "Did you catch any of their set?' I ask, finishing off my water.

"Whose? Tracing Holland?"

I nod. "Their rehearsals looked great. She's got a good thing going."

"Yeah, I think Callie stuck around to watch them."

I almost laugh. "Of course she did."

Casey grins. "She's loving every second of this. You should have seen her this afternoon when she first saw catering."

This time I do laugh. "Let me guess, she went all fangirl on the mini quiches and selection of flavored teas?"

He snickers and shrugs. "What are you gonna do? You know how she gets with her tea."

We quiet as the door to the green room bursts open with an explosion of female laughter.

Callie spots us and heads over with a huge smile. "You guys were amazing!" she cries. Casey gets a kiss, and I get a tight squeeze around the waist.

"Thanks. Are you having a good time?" I ask as she lets go and returns to Casey.

She gives me a look, and I can't help but smile. "What do you think?"

"Callie's right. The encore was killer. Love the new stuff."

I glance over at Holland and return her polite smile. "Thanks."

I can feel her eyes on me and look away quickly. I know what she's thinking. It's the same thing all of them think. Now's the part where I act like an ass. I don't blame her. I've never done anything to make them think otherwise. But she doesn't say another word, which comes as a relief. My few interactions with Holland Drake have always been painfully polite.

"Are you coming out with us?" Callie asks, hanging on my arm again.

I sigh. That damn look in her eyes. "I don't know. I'm kind of tired."

"Luke..." Her tone is stern now, and I can't help but smirk.

"What about you?" she asks Holland. "You're all coming, right?"

Holland had been studying the selection of protein bars and glances over. "Um, yeah, probably. Where are you going again?"

"Saxon, right?" Callie asks Casey who nods.

"I'll probably just hit the gym at the hotel for a bit and call it a night. Thanks, though," I say, grabbing another water and an apple.

Callie is giving me her disapproving glare, but I only return a sheepish smile. "Another time?"

"Fine," she grunts.

Even Casey seems annoyed. "Molly's going to be disappointed if you don't go."

I groan. "Low blow, Case. That's not fair."

He grins and shrugs. They're waiting. They know I'm wavering. They know I can rarely resist them when they team up on me. It's not a fair fight. A thousand thoughts race through my head, and I feel Holland watching me again. I wonder which side of the debate she's on. I sense it's mine. I sense she'd be happier if I didn't exist at all. She turns back to the snack table.

"Ok, maybe for a bit. But I probably won't stay long. Just enough to say hi to Molly."

Callie rolls her eyes. "When did you become such a loser?"

I laugh. "Hey, at least I'm not wearing a white t-shirt today."

She grins and tugs at my decidedly not-white shirt. "I noticed! First show in a year and a half. I suppose if there's any reason to dress up..."

Holland is chuckling to herself and seems startled when she realizes she has our attention. "What? Sorry, it's just, I'm always bugging the guys about that, too. Hell, I have to spend two hours on hair and makeup. The least they can do is wear a decent shirt."

"I know, right?" Callie cries. "These two insist on looking like they've just finished a landscaping project."

I grin and shake my head. "Please don't encourage her," I mutter to Holland.

"Well, the girl's got a point. That's all I'm saying."

Her tone isn't exactly sharp, but it's enough to draw my gaze. She meets my eyes, boldly this time, daring me to argue. I feel my smile slipping. I hate that I have to wonder what I've done to offend her, but clearly we have a history.

I swallow and look away. "I'm gonna go back to the hotel and change," I direct back to Casey and Callie. "Meet you at the bus? We can grab a ride from there."

It's Callie staring me down now. I know she can sense the change in my demeanor. She always does, but I don't need her worrying about me at the moment.

"Alright, see you in a few," Casey says.

I offer Holland another quick smile as I pass, hoping I've misread her. I don't think I did.

I DECIDE to take a cab back to the hotel. I'm not in the mood for other people at the moment, and skip the shuttle. I can't stop thinking about Holland's stare for some reason. Sure, she's beautiful. Gorgeous, really, but in a quirky way with her messy blond hair and haunting blue eyes. It's almost like she goes out of her way to hide her beauty, although I doubt she cares enough about that stuff to bother with something so petty. She's too confident to need to make a statement. She has nothing to prove. She's just her own person, and I respect that. Hell, I've always been hopelessly attracted to that, but I don't think that's why I can't get her out of my head. It was the secret behind her eyes, still searing my brain, accusing me of something I can't remember.

We really haven't spoken much since we met for rehearsals a week ago, so I know whatever I did must have been in the past. My crime might not even have been against her. In fact it probably wasn't, since I'm pretty sure we never spoke before the tour. But yeah, I've pissed off enough people over the years that the six degrees of separation axiom pretty much screws me on a daily basis. It's not that I don't deserve it; it's just hard to keep track of all the overdue apologies and corresponding train of grievances at every turn.

I turn on the water to the shower when I get to my room and pull off my t-shirt. It was a hot night, and the lights and frantic pace of the performance certainly didn't help. We're all drenched in sweat by the end of each show anyway, and I'm looking forward to a long soak under the waterfall showerhead. We're doing two events in Houston, three if you count the mini acoustic set at a local rock station tomorrow morning. So our tour manager booked us rooms instead of living out of the bus like we do on some of our day stops. I'm grateful for the space, but more so for the privacy.

I strip down the rest of the way and slip beneath the warm stream of water, not too hot since my body is already on fire. I stretch out my arms and lean against the far wall, head bowed, allowing the water to soak into my sore shoulders. I imagine it washing away as much of the day's tension as it can handle. It feels so good, and it especially feels good to feel good. I close my eyes.

My first show back. There's a heaviness in my chest now that I can't quite define. I'm not surprised, given the exhausting reality of this day, this moment. Sure, it felt amazing to be back. The rush of being on stage, consumed by the music, entrenched in the one thing I can do. For a long time, the only good thing I was. My life has always been a constant battle for purpose. I never found it. Not in a way that stuck, that mattered, anyway. Not until Elena, but of course I fucked that up, because that's what I do. Well, what I did. I never knew what to do with Good so I'd destroy it. I'd break it apart and suck the life out of it until I could transform it into something more comfortable. Something disgusting that I actually understood, I deserved.

I know I'm not that person anymore, but that doesn't make the pain go away. Scars may fade, but you don't get to peel them off just because you finally put the knife down. Still, I'm trying to forgive myself, and I've come a long way over these last few months. The counseling actually helped. I was skeptical at first, but Callie and Casey were right, as usual. I learned things about myself I didn't even know. Old memories I'd thought I'd buried turned out to be parasites slowly tearing at my soul. There were plenty of painful sessions, many downright tense. But most of all, I learned how to recognize my thoughts for what they are. To try to stop the downward spiral before it starts. To break patterns, well, glass as Callie says, and not let myself be comfortable in the familiar slide toward the darkness. They're called triggers and I have a fucking truckload.

The water is starting to feel cool against my skin. I open my eyes and let them adjust to the light. I don't know how long I've been standing here, but I suspect I'll have some annoyed texts waiting for me when I check my phone. It's fine. I'm actually pretty sure I've changed my mind about going out. I'm in no state to handle more of my past right now, and I know for sure I don't have enough smiles left in me to get through a night at a crowded club. But they deserve an update.

I quickly finish my shower and run a towel over my hair as I leave the bathroom. I then wrap it around my waist and smile to myself when I see the stream of messages on the display of my phone. Callie does nothing halfway.

I return a quick apology and let her know I've decided just to stay in. I don't get an immediate response back, which seems strange since I know Callie is glued to her phone, waiting for any evidence of my continued breath. She's probably called the FBI by now and put out a missing persons report. I can see Casey rolling his eyes and trying to reassure her, but I've earned her concern. I know it, and it's endearing in its own way. I toss my phone back on the bed and search through my suitcase for some clothes.

I've just pulled on a pair of gym shorts when a knock thumps on my door. Surprised, I move toward it and peek through the hole. I breathe a curse, but can't stop the resigned smile as I shake my head and invite the intruders to enter.

"What are you doing?" I ask as the parade marches into my room.

"Celebrating the opening of your tour," Callie quips. She

holds up a bottle of ginger ale, and I can see Casey has three glasses.

I stare at them in confusion. "What about Saxon?"

"If you're not going, we're not going," Casey chimes in. "I already called Molly and told her to meet us here instead."

I sigh. There's no way out of this one, but I suspect it's probably good I'm trapped right now. I didn't like the direction of my thoughts in the shower. I need a buffer, and these two have turned protecting me from myself into an art form.

"Well, then I guess I better finish getting dressed," I mutter moving back to my suitcase.

"Don't feel like you need to wear clothes on our account," Callie teases.

"Hey!" Casey cries, and she rolls her eyes.

"Oh, please. Even you think he's hot. Get over it. Pass me those glasses."

I laugh as they exchange mock glares before Casey finally relents and hands over a glass. God, I love them together. It's like watching a rainbow trying to trash-talk a unicorn. Casey would kill me if I ever said that out loud, but it's just so damn adorable.

"Wow. Blanchard Crest Ginger Ale, no less. You're serious about this," I observe, pulling a t-shirt over my head.

"Only the best for my favorite rockstar," Callie sings, earning her another annoyed look from Casey.

"Fine. Second favorite rockstar," she groans.

It's Casey's turn to roll his eyes. "Whatever."

"Love you, hon," she chirps, giving him a quick kiss. He shakes his head, but they exchange a grin that turns me into the intruder.

I clear my throat. "Do the others know we're not going out?" I ask as Callie returns to pouring the fake Champagne and hands me a glass.

"Yeah, we told them we're just going to do something with the gang tomorrow. I let Holland know. She didn't seem to mind," Callie says.

I find my stomach tightening at the mention of Holland. I still don't know why. That look.

"She's really a remarkable person," Callie continues, which is how I know I've done a good job hiding my reaction. She can read me better than anyone. "Did you know she actually has a biology degree? She was pre-med before she decided to pursue music full-time. Oh, and she writes children's books! I think she's published a couple."

"Wow," I say. "That's impressive."

She nods. "She's not arrogant or anything, though. You wouldn't know how smart she is talking to her. She's really down to earth. Gosh, her music is so good, too. Dude, they killed 'Perfect Storm' tonight, don't you think? I mean, killed it!"

Casey and I exchange amused looks at her casual use of our lingo. We're converting her. Uh oh.

She waves her hand. "Ok, anyway, this is about you two, not Holland. So, back to business." She raises her glass and we do the same, holding our breath, preparing for her masterful speech that will go down in the annals of history and be inscribed on monuments. She's probably written us a beautiful ode to friendship and stirring aspirations. We grip our glasses. We watch. We wait. And...silence.

She stares at us. We stare back. Her face scrunches into the adorable pout she does when she's annoyed with us. We shrug.

"Well, is someone gonna say something or what?" she asks.

"I thought you were giving the speech, babe!" Casey says.

"Me? Why would I give the speech?"

"I don't know!" he returns in exasperation. "This whole ginger ale thing was your idea!"

"It's a good idea! I just don't think I should be the one giving the speech."

"Well, why would we toast ourselves?"

"You do it all the time!"

I laugh, I can't help it, and put an end to their argument. "Ok, fine, I'll give the speech," I say, and I can tell they're surprised. Even after all this time, as far as we've come over the last few months, they still seem shocked any time I demonstrate even an ounce of interest in acting like a human being. I try not to be annoyed.

"A dark road traveled is not a dark road lost when light turns dark into a path. Labor on, oh weary one, for the end has come now that the journey's begun."

There's silence as they stare at me, and I almost feel shy.

"What's that from?" Callie asks, her gaze searching mine.

I swallow. "Tuesday night."

I swear there's a glisten in her eyes as she nods. "Well, ok then," she says quietly, clinking my glass. "To the new journey."

"I love it, man," Casey says, touching my glass as well.

We all take a sip.

"That would make one hell of a cat poster."

I laugh as Callie smacks him.

———

MOLLY JOINS us about an hour later, and I get a huge hug. She's a sweet girl, and is one of Casey's closest siblings. She's never blamed me for Elena the way most of his family did, although no one blamed me more than my own aunt. I haven't spoken to her since that day, since the news broke. The day she left me a message saying no one who could do that to an angel like Elena would be family to her.

I guess it hurt at the time. I mean, I was such a mess during those first few months it's impossible to tell which dagger slicing into your gut is the one causing the fatal bleeding. My aunt actually told me it should have been me. She always loved Elena. Thought I didn't deserve her. She wasn't the only one. I still believe that. I'm not sure there's enough therapy on this planet to ever change that.

I'm happy Casey and Molly have the chance to connect while we're in Houston, but family reunions don't work the same for me. Molly looks a little bit like her. Ok, a lot like her, the way her eyes light up when she smiles. The texture of her hair. Her laugh. Of course it's not her fault she's bringing it all back, and I try to stay polite and positive during the visit, but the earlier heaviness returns as a concrete block.

"Sorry I wasn't able to make it to your show tonight," she says. "I bet it was amazing."

"It was," Callie confirms. "I'm Callie, by the way."

"I figured. So nice to finally meet you," Molly responds, exchanging a warm hug with her before smacking her brother. "Thanks for introducing us, jerk."

Casey shrinks a bit with a sheepish grin. "Sorry! You figured it out."

She rolls her eyes and turns back to Callie. "Anyway, thank you for giving my brother a reason to actually call us. Even though all we ever get is Callie, Callie, Callie, it's nice to hear his voice more than once a year."

"Oh, please! I actually went home for Christmas last year!" Casey points out.

"Uh, no. You needed a place to crash when you came home to play that show at the Towne Centre."

"Whatever. I was still home."

"Except you wouldn't even come to dinner at Mom and Dad's."

Callie and I exchange a look as they argue, and she casts me an amused grin. I try to return it, but I'm having a lot of trouble with this conversation, with Molly. I can't stop staring at her hair. I wish she'd cut it. I wish she didn't allow her long, dark locks to flow down her back in gentle waves just like Elena used to do. When she turns her back to continue yelling at Casey, I almost choke.

"So, Luke, how have you been?" she asks, suddenly confronting me. My heart starts racing, something akin to panic mounting in my chest, and I have no idea what to do with it. I don't understand what's happening, just that I can't focus all of a sudden, breathe in enough oxygen. I blink.

"Um, good. I'm doing really well," I force out. She smiles at my lie and squeezes my arm.

"That's great. I'm glad to hear that. We were so worried about you. You just disappeared."

I nod in a numb daze, and can feel Callie's eyes. She has to know something's wrong. She always does. She has to see the walls are shrinking.

She clears her throat. "So, Molly, tell me about working at the animal shelter. That must be so interesting!"

Her redirection works, and I hate how I suddenly want to hide more than anything. I love Molly, but I can't see her. I can't be here. I hate that this is happening, that once again my drama is ruining a moment, dragging down the people I love.

Still, I can't stop it, and a small ember of fear burns low as the evening wears on, panic that it's going to be a hard night when the room quiets and the lights go out. The heaviness grows, pressing on my lungs until it reaches a physical ache. I can sense Callie's attention more and more as I withdraw into myself, and know without a doubt she's aware something's up. She knows I'm starting to shatter again, that I need to be in someone's arms, to be held, but I don't want to let that happen. It shouldn't be her. I know that, and I try to force as many smiles as I can to ease her mind. To temper that vigorous compassion that drives her into other people's pain. I know they love me, but I don't want to be their constant burden. I love them, too.

But I just can't breathe all of a sudden.

"You guys have an early morning, don't you?" Callie asks finally, and I immediately know what she's doing. Rescuing me like she so often does with that grace that disguises it from everyone else. It's her smile, the way it always seems to turn a goodbye into a simple invitation for the next meeting. I'd never really felt like I'd had a choice except to show up again in those early days at Jemma's.

Casey sighs. "Yeah, we do. The car's picking us up at 7 to take us to the radio station."

"Oh, ok! Well, I won't keep you up then. I've got work in the morning anyway," Molly says with an understanding smile as she rises.

We do the same. "It was so good to see you again, Molly," I manage, reaching for a hug. She returns it, a real one, and I start to shake. Oh god. I need them all to leave. Now.

"I'll walk you out, sis," Casey says.

"See you tomorrow?" Molly asks Callie who grins and gives a hug of her own.

"Looking forward to it!"

Then, we're alone. I feel Callie's gaze and draw in a ragged breath. I need her to leave, too. I don't want her to see me like this. I don't want her to comfort me right now. I just want her to be happy and safe and force me to confront my demons on my own for once. But I know she won't, so I don't even try.

She doesn't say anything as the horrible tears invade my eyes. I swipe at them and drop to the edge of the bed, leaning my head in my hands. I don't even know how to start explaining what's going on inside of me, which is why I love her so much. I know I won't have to. She covers the distance between us and puts her arms around me, pulling me against her. I try to breathe. To fight the weight pressing into my chest, clamping down. God, I don't even know what's wrong with me.

"It was a long day, Luke. A difficult one with everything you had to face coming back. You were amazing," she says softly.

I nod through my silent tears, grateful there are no embarrassing sobs this time. I pull away and swat at my face again. Fighting to put myself back together.

"I'm ok," I whisper. "It was a lot to handle...and then seeing Molly again."

She sighs. "I know. It was brave of you to even try."

I let out a harsh laugh. "Brave. Yeah right."

"Don't even think about belittling yourself," she barks with a smile, and I manage to remove the rest of the tears. She grows serious again. "But you're not alone anymore. You need to promise me you understand that."

I blink and meet her gaze. She hugs me again, and I can almost feel the tension start to lift.

"Thanks, Cal."

"Get some rest, ok?" she says, pulling away and squeezing my hand.

I nod and draw in another deep breath. "You, too. Tell Casey I said good night."

She smiles and rubs my arm one last time as she rises to her feet. "I will. You got this, kid. I know you do."

———

THE RADIO SESSION goes well the following morning. We do a brief interview with host Russ, followed by a short acoustic set, which seems to go over well with the station and listeners.

Houston has always embraced us, so I'm not surprised by the outpouring of support. There's something about your hometown, the way they claim you. They raised you, created you, so now you belong to them.

We have to check out of our hotel when we get back from the radio station, since we'll roll out to our next stop immediately after tonight's show. We're supposed to be in New Orleans tomorrow night, so I know they're going to want to move as soon as possible. Our tour manager, Kenneth, runs a tight ship. Even I'm afraid of him.

Casey and Callie leave right away for Molly's house to reconnect with some of his family and friends. After what happened last night, there's no way I'd survive that, so I turn down the offer. I know Callie understands and let her soothe Casey who whines until they're out of earshot at least. I feel badly, but I just can't put myself in that situation right now. It's hard enough being home without shoving memories into the open wounds. I don't really feel like doing anything else, so I hang out in my room as long as possible and then decide to retire to the bus for a while. Eli and Sweeny had left an hour ago after jabbering all morning about some new bar they wanted to check out, and I'm lured by the thought of an empty bus.

I'm surprised to see the door already open as I approach with my suitcase. I guess I was wrong about Eli and Sweeny and am actually disappointed they changed their minds. Still, it's their house as much as mine, so I brace myself for a blast of energy and climb the stairs.

I stop cold.

"Luke! Oh, um...hi. I'm sorry, Callie said..."

I force a smile and wave my hand. "No, it's fine, don't get up," I say.

Shit. I can't retreat now.

Holland returns my smile with a stiff one of her own, but straightens on the couch anyway. She'd been writing something in a notebook and closes it as discreetly as possible. Clearly, not discreetly enough.

"Really, it's fine. I just didn't feel like going out and was planning to watch a movie or something in the back to rest before tonight," I say moving through the open partition into the living area where she'd been reclined. "I'll stay out of your way."

She seems conflicted. "I'm sure you're wondering why I'm on your bus when I have my own."

I smile again and shake my head. "If your band is anything like mine, I'm pretty sure I can guess."

This time her smile is warmer than any of the others I've gotten so far. God, it's breathtaking.

"I love them dearly. I do, but sometimes...you just need a break, you know? And Callie said she was pretty sure yours would be empty since you all were going out."

"Like I said, it makes sense. It's fine. I'll stay out of your way. Stay as long as you want. They keep the fridge well-stocked, too, so help yourself."

"Thanks."

She's watching me again. Studying my every move. Evaluating. I'm pretty sure I'll fail, but there's nothing I can do.

"I'm just gonna grab the key to the luggage bay to load my stuff."

I move to the drawer where we keep the key and can feel her gaze burning a hole in my back. I want to say something, to just get it out there, but I know that whatever it is could make things a hundred times worse. We have a long tour ahead of us and I've done a lot of terrible things.

"Mind if I peek in on your set tonight? Callie won't stop talking about how great it was," I toss casually, trying to dispel the awkwardness as I search through the junk drawer. Where is that damn key? And where did all these stupid rubber bands come from?

"Really? Yeah, of course! That would be awesome. You guys killed it last night. Is it good to be back?"

I swallow. She's just being polite.

"It's great. I missed the music," I manage in a steady voice.

Finally! I grab the key and offer a quick smile as I turn around. "Just gonna load up. I'll be back," I explain. She nods and returns to her notebook.

My heart is pounding as I step off the bus and I have no idea why. Is it because of her question? Is it because she got close to a wound? Or is it her. There's something about her. I suspect she hates me for some reason and yet she's never been rude. Callie immediately clicked with her so I know she's incredible. I'm just so confused at the moment, and if I had any other choice, I would not go back to face her, but it's too late. I already said I'd be returning. I'd look ridiculous if I just disappeared now. Plus, I have to return the key. That damn key!

I load my suitcase with the rest of the luggage and relock the luggage bay. I force myself to convert my death march into something less absurd and begin climbing the stairs again. She's an attractive, confident woman; so what? I've dealt with countless of them over the course of my life, but maybe that's the problem.

"You writing?" I ask, and nearly flinch at the stupid question.

A small smile flickers across her lips and I know she's thinking the same thing. She looks adorable as she bites the edge of her pen and looks up at me. "Yep," she says through her clenched teeth, still smiling.

I return it and shake my head with a shy grin. "Sorry, I

know. Just making conversation, I guess. Ok, I'll leave you alone."

I start moving past her toward the back.

"Luke, wait!" she calls.

Surprised, I stop and turn. Her eyes have changed a bit. The amusement is gone, and I brace myself once more.

"Look, I'll just say this, ok? I know it's awkward, but we have a long tour and will be spending lots of time together. I don't want drama in my life, ok?"

I stare at her. I have no idea what that means. "Um, ok. I don't either," I reply.

She's fishing for words. "I just mean...Crap!" She covers her face, clearly embarrassed all of a sudden. "Wow, ok, you know what? I'm sorry. I don't know what I'm doing. I just say things sometimes." She shakes her head, and I swear she's blushing.

"Holland, I'm so lost right now," I confess, staring at her with what I'm sure is a baffled expression.

She laughs dismissively. "No, I know. I...can we just pretend I didn't say anything?"

"Um..."

"Yeah, ok, so I should just go. Thanks for letting me use your bus. I'll just go to my dressing room or something."

After giving me another weak smile, she's gone.

I stare after her, totally confused by her strange behavior. I have no clue what she was talking about, what drama is concerning her. She didn't seem angry, just sincere in her determination to avoid whatever *it* is. Or could be. Or was? What could I have done that would cause someone to fear me without being angry? I swallow, feeling even more uncertain, more insecure. I'm tired of hurting people, and the thought that I'm still hurting them without even trying is hard for me to accept. Just my very presence is a cancer, apparently. Dammit. Trigger.

I CLOSE my eyes and lean against the partition to the sleeping area. I'm not a cancer. I'm just...I don't know yet, but not that. Not anymore. I draw in a deep breath and continue on to the back of the bus in a disturbed silence.

Time alone with myself is uncomfortable at best, and after only a few distracted minutes of staring at the screen, I know I'm not where I belong. My encounter with Holland is only a small fraction of the weight on my conscience. There's a much bigger burden that's haunted me since the second we pulled into Houston, and the fact that I've been trying to deny it with silly excuses has only been feeding the monster. There's something else I have to do while I'm home, one more conversation that needs to be had, and I can't fight it anymore.

It's a bit of a drive to the large suburb outside the city but the cab driver promises he'll wait for me. I leave him at the curb by the ornate iron gate, and he gives me a somber nod as I take the first tentative steps toward it. Drawing in a deep breath, I glance up at the imposing arch and force my feet to comply with my heart.

My lungs are heavy and my progress slows as the distance shrinks. I can barely breathe, the smell of freshly cut grass mocking me with the scent of life in this place of death. It's a frightening maze, but I know exactly where to go even though I've only been here three times.

That first time. The day I can hardly remember. It should be ingrained in my head, a nightmare that haunts me every time I close my eyes, but it's not. It's just a shadow, lurking in the darkest reaches of my thoughts, reminding me of how far I'd fallen and would have yet to fall.

Then, the second time. The day I almost killed Casey and ruined his life too. The day we lost consciousness beside the shiny stone monument and woke up to a firestorm of press releases and irate Label execs.

And the third. The day I'd determined to join her.

I freeze when I reach my destination, unable to move as I stare at the stunning headstone. I hate that it's so fresh, so new, that in this sea of stone and statues, this one is the most beautiful to me. The tears are gathering now as I finally have the courage to kneel down and face her. To say I'm sorry. To finally make promises I will keep.

In loving memory of Elena Barrett Craven
Wife, Daughter, Sister

A sob echoes through the silence, cutting off the distant sound of birds and insects. It's mine, I know, but I'm afraid I'm not ready for it.

I reach out my hand and grip the stone, letting the chill of death seep into my fingers.

Wife, Daughter, Sister.

First love. Inspiration. Victim.

I close my eyes, the hot liquid searing my cheeks and staining my t-shirt. I rest my head on my hands as the late summer breeze rustles the trees, reminding me of the impossible distance that separates us. So much life in the presence of death. But it's time. I need this. She deserves this. After a long pause, I draw in a deep breath, finally letting the door to her memory crash open.

Her face. Her hair. Her smell. The way her laugh made you want to hold her forever. Her eyes, and that first time she looked at me as though she couldn't live without me.

"I'm so sorry, Ellie." I whisper. "I love you. I love you so much. I should have been there. I'm so sorry. I'm so sorry."

The tears are hers now, seeping into the ground, and I find myself praying they'll come to rest with her somehow. I know it's absurd, but I don't have anything left to give her. I want her to have that. I need her to accept them.

I forget about time, collapsed against her, completely paralyzed. I know it's getting late. I know there's another world waiting for me, but I just can't let her go again now that I've finally come back to her. I don't think I'm sobbing anymore, but the tears are still slipping down my cheeks, soaking my arms as I hold on.

But it's not her. It's not Ellie. It's just a cold chunk of rock on a pile of grass, and deep down I know I don't belong here. Not yet, anyway. What's left of her is the ghost in my head, in my heart, and I start to understand. I finally get it. This hope, this budding strength, this overwhelming sense of who she still is because of who she was. I may have failed her then, but she won't fail me now. I finally believe.

I can get up. I can still live.

I can move on without letting go.

IT'S a long time before I'm able to return to the venue, let alone the buses. I feel the pressure of the clock and know they'll be looking for me, but I have the cab driver drop me off a good mile away so I can recalibrate my head with a walk.

I eventually make my way to the dressing room to prepare for the show and grab a snack there to avoid any awkward encounters in catering. In fact, somehow I manage to stay hidden almost completely, other than a few interactions with our stage manager and crew. My discreet return is so successful

I'm even able to startle Callie with a gentle poke as she watches Limelight perform from backstage. She jumps and spins, then breaks into a giant grin when she sees me.

"There you are! Everyone's been looking for you. You here to watch Holland?"

I nod. "I told her I'd check them out."

"She'll love that! Limelight's really good too. You should try to catch their show tomorrow. Jesse's voice is amazing! They're gonna be huge. Have you talked to him? He's actually a really cool guy. Casey said he worked in a warehouse to support himself until booking this tour!"

I love her enthusiasm. I'm pretty sure I'll never tire of watching her get excited about life. "No kidding," I say, focusing back on the action on stage. She's right. His voice is sick, their energy and sound well-beyond their years and experience. They're going to be a big deal one day, and I can almost feel a small spark of excitement at the memory of what that jump was like for me.

"Luke, hey!"

I turn toward the voice and catch my breath a bit at Holland's entrance. She looks incredible in this light with her stage clothes and makeup. I force a smile.

"Hey. Came to check out your show," I explain casually.

"Wow, I'm honored. Thank you," she replies, and her return smile seems sincere. I'm not sure what else to say, but I'm spared when the rest of her band appears and distracts her.

Callie and I back away to make room as Limelight finishes their set and exits the stage. The crew immediately jumps into action to set up for Tracing Holland. Holland and her band are deep in conversation, most likely reviewing some last minute details before they go out, and I use that opportunity to grab Jesse as he passes.

"Looked good," I observe, and I love the pleased shock that

flashes across his face before he can hide it. I remember being in his shoes. Wanting to play it cool, but totally in awe of the moment, the legends who suddenly become peers.

"Really? You watched?"

"Caught the end."

He grins and nods. "Thanks, man. I still can't believe we're playing a stadium. We just fucking played a stadium!"

I laugh. "Yeah, you did. *And* fucking killed it," I echo, almost laughing again when I catch Callie's disapproving look at my choice of language.

"You were awesome, Jesse. Really, really good. I love your sound," she says.

"Thanks, Callie. That means a lot."

"Jess! Get over here! Are you coming or what?" Parker calls from the stage door.

Jesse gives us an apologetic look. "Sorry, guys. Later?"

We smile. "Sure, no problem. Enjoy the rest of your night."

"Oh, no way. I'll be back in a minute. You guys fucking blew this place apart last night. I'm not missing that."

I shake my head with a smile as he darts off, and Callie gently slaps my arm.

"Hear that? Blew this place apart. You're such a rockstar."

I chuckle. "Yeah, whatever."

It's another few minutes before Tracing Holland takes the stage, and Holland gives me a "here we go" look as she passes to make her entrance. I return an encouraging smile and move to a better vantage point once they're loaded.

The lights flash in sync with the first few drum hits of their opener, and the crowd ignites. When Holland's strong, haunting lead flows as a lonely melody into the vast space around us, I'm completely mesmerized right along with every breathless soul in the audience. Chills spread through me as the drum hits continue; just her voice, the echo of percussion, and that restless anticipation that something spectacular is about to explode on us.

> "I won't be your momma's girl.
> I'm not your daddy's pride.
> So if you want me alone, don't expect to take
>   me home, I'm just not that kind.
> There's no mercy for the fallen, no apologies
>   for my prison.
> Brave boy, sure you're ready for this?
> Last chance, are you ready for this?"

The lights go out and a dramatic silence descends over the darkness.

"Yeah, that's what I thought!" she cries into the void. *"But you'll take it anyway. ...Here we go!"*

I'm not sure I move the entire time I watch Holland's set. The way she commands the stage, her confidence, her authenticity, her incredible music, Callie was right, it's magnetic. I'm disappointed when I have to leave to take care of some last minute preparations before my own show. Well, part of me is disappointed. Another part is grateful. That would be the part that recognizes the emergence of these sudden crackling emotions but has no interest in solving, let alone engaging, them.

There's no denying I've been touched by what I just saw, I just don't have a handle on what that means or what to do with it. Holland Drake is a special talent. It's etched into her very presence that makes you stop and take notice. She deserves every bit of her success and recent accolades, and I almost find it funny that she'd been so amazed and honored by my attention to her work when I'm standing here brimming with questions for insight into her own.

Still, I don't know that I'm ready for a new friend or, more specifically, the effort it would take to cultivate another relationship when I'm really only good at screwing them up. The fact that watching Holland has stirred something deep, something that scares the crap out of me, is all I need to decide it's better to leave that whole thing well enough alone.

It's already been a heavy day for me, and a brutal opening to our tour in general. I hope I'm strong enough to survive the next three months, but it's hard to be optimistic when two days has felt like two weeks. At this rate, there is no chance in hell I make it to November. I'll be lucky to make it to New Orleans.

3

NEW ORLEANS, LOUISIANA

SEPTEMBER 14

According to Kenneth's bulleted, outlined, and color-coded schedule for the day, a continental breakfast will be available in catering until 11:00am. It had been a long night of performance, teardown, loading, and driving, so I'm not surprised when I'm one of the few who dares to venture from the bus before lunch. I'm not even hungry, just in desperate need of a change of scenery. I slip off the bus as quietly as possible and make my way toward the designated food hangout of our latest venue, an arena in New Orleans.

I never did tell Casey and Callie about my trip to visit Elena's grave. It was an important, but difficult, milestone on my journey, and I'm not ready to talk about it yet. Besides, if I know them at all, they'll feel guilty, or something ridiculous like that, for letting me go alone, even though that's exactly what I needed. At some point they're going to have to let me spread my wings and attempt this "life" thing on my own.

I hear voices as I approach the open door and hesitate when I recognize Holland's.

"I'm so sorry to hear all of that, Steven. You take all the time you need, ok?" Her tone is gentle, and I can sense the compassion even from this distance.

"Thank you so much. I hate to leave you right at the beginning, though," the other voice replies. Young, male.

"I know. But your family comes first. We'll be fine. Don't worry about us. I'm sure the NSB crew can help us until we get someone else in here."

"Ok. Well, tell them to call me as soon as they can. They need to make sure they do everything right."

Holland chuckles. "Of course. We'll make sure everything is perfect. Oh, wait, here's my cell number just in case. Let me know if there's anything you need. I told Darlene to cover your ticket home, so stop in and connect with her next."

"What? No, Holland! That's not..."

"Stop! It's not a big deal. Just take care of your family, ok?"

"Thank you. I..." I can hear the emotion in his voice.

"It's nothing. Thanks for all you do. Take as much time as you need and we'll see you when you get back."

"Thank you. Thank you!"

I wait until "Steven" exits the room and shuffles past before making my own entrance. When I do, I also see Jesse, Parker, and Reece from Limelight, along with a few crewmembers, seated around various tables. We exchange some polite greetings and I continue toward Holland who's scanning the table of assorted bagels, pastries, and fruit.

"Morning," I say, grabbing a plate.

"Morning," she replies. Her smile is genuine today, and I relax a little.

"Losing Steven?"

She sighs and shakes her head. "Yeah, so sad. His grandmother just passed. I sent him home to be with his family. Poor kid."

"Wow, that's awful. I'm sorry to hear that." I pause. "Just

tell me what you need. I'll talk to Tess and make sure you're covered."

She seems surprised when she glances over, and I'm uncomfortable at the evidence of her low expectations of me.

"Oh, wow. Ok, thanks. Yeah, we'll need a backline tech. At least for tonight."

I nod. "Done. Gary's great. He'll help you out."

She still seems like she's confused by my generosity, and I look away.

"Great show last night," I continue before it gets more awkward.

"Thank you for checking it out! I'm so honored. It was like having Beethoven sit in on your piano recital," she laughs, following me to the drink table.

I smirk. "Um...yeah right. More like Beethoven grabbing coffee with Hayden. Anyway, I didn't really have a choice. Callie said I'd regret it if I didn't."

Holland laughs. "Callie is awesome. I freaking love her."

I grin. We finally agree on something. "She's the best." I fill my coffee cup and move so she has access. "I wanted to tell you, I love how you transition from 'Perfect Storm' to 'Answers.' It's genius."

"Really? You think so? Thank you," she replies, almost shy. I'm not sure how to respond, so I just watch her as she makes her own drink selection. Callie's ruined me forever when it comes to observing people and their food choices. The term "fruit cup" still makes me smile.

Holland goes for coffee, two creamers.

"We played around with a few different ideas," she continues, and I love her sudden animation when she talks music. The same thing happens to Casey. It used to happen to me also. Maybe it will again one day. "There's a key change, so Wes wanted to just modulate up like normal, but then I thought, why not tie in the 'Acrobat' hook instead? Then we can finish with the full version of 'Acrobat' at the end of the set."

"I love it. It works really well. I couldn't catch all of the end, but I totally see that coming together."

She gives me another smile and moves away from the table. I'm about to find my own when she calls me back with, "you wanna sit?"

Shocked, I pause for a moment before following her. I take the seat across from her at a table away from the others.

"I'm sorry again about yesterday. On the bus," she begins, almost embarrassed. "That was so awkward and totally my fault. You were being nice, so thank you for that. How was your movie? Were you able to get any rest?"

I force a weak smile. "I ended up not watching one. Went for a walk instead." It's not entirely a lie.

She takes a sip of her coffee. "Oh, ok. Well, that must have been nice. Get some fresh air and stretch a bit."

I swallow, unable to look at her. "Yeah. Um...so how's your writing going?" I ask quickly. I used all my tears yesterday. I have no interest in going there again.

She sighs. "Fine, if you count the fact that I have a chorus I love and two verses I despise."

I laugh. "You know it took me a month and a half to come up with a decent verse for 'Forget Me.'"

Her eyes widen. "Over a month? Are you serious? I love 'Forget Me!'"

I grin. "Well, you wouldn't have before, believe me. I could not get the word 'forever' out of my head. I kept wanting to rhyme it with 'never' but it just wasn't working and completely blocked any other possibility. Casey was pissed because the music was so good, but I could not get the lyrics to work."

It's her turn to laugh and shake her head. "Oh man, I totally hear you. I once got stuck on 'cross-stitch.'"

I can't hold in my snort and actually have to set my drink down. "Wait, what? Cross-stitch? How was that even in the running in the first place?"

She grins and covers her face. "I know! I have no idea. I was trying to explore this idea of two souls weaving themselves into a fabric, and after ending the previous line with 'chase it,' my brain insisted on using the word 'cross-stitch' for whatever reason."

I laugh again and return to my coffee. "I mean, it kind of works then, I guess," I offer with another smile. "Guess we're both shitty songwriters."

She returns my grin, her blue eyes making a direct connection with mine. I suck in my breath at the sudden, volatile reaction of my body. Racing pulse, blood rushing to places it hasn't in a long time. Shit. What is happening?

I wonder if she feels it too when she quickly looks away. There's a tangible distance again, and I swallow.

"Is it true you have a '43 J45?" she blurts before things get too uncomfortable. I'm stunned by the random question, but grateful at the same time. We still have food on our plates, and she hasn't given up. I would have.

"How'd you know about that?" I ask in amusement.

She shrugs. "Not sure, actually. Just remember reading it somewhere."

I shake my head with a grin. "Yeah. I've had it for a couple years. She's my angel."

Holland sighs. "I would seriously climb over dead bodies just to touch it."

I laugh. "Uh, how about I just let you play it later."

Her eyes ignite as her jaw nearly hits the table. "Wait, are you serious? You have it here?"

I grin, loving the light in her expression and the fact that my words put it there. "Yeah. It's on my bus."

"I... seriously?"

I shake my head, still laughing. "Seriously. We'll meet up later. Wait until you hear this thing. It'll blow your mind."

She's already drooling which only cements my offer. "I still don't believe you. Nope, you're lying. You're just trying to torture me."

I snicker. "Even I'm not that cruel. I'm serious. Whenever you want."

"Yes! Let's go!" she cries, throwing down her fork, and I laugh again.

"Well, you can finish your food first. We're not on for a while," I remind her. She sighs and picks it back up.

"Ok, fine. I'm not kidding, though, Luke. If you're messing with me, I will gut you."

I grin and hold up my hands. "Whoa, take it easy. I swear. She's all yours for as long as you want her."

Her hard gaze continues to bore into me until she finally seems satisfied with my promise. I'm still grinning as she settles back into her seat.

"Have you played The Mercer Center before?" I ask, resuming the conversation.

She shakes her head and pokes her fork at a slice of pineapple. "No, I haven't. What about you?"

I nod. "A couple times. I love arena concerts. The energy is phenomenal."

"Yeah? Sweet. I'm looking forward to it."

"You may want to keep both ears in the whole time, though. The echo there can be..."

"Can I sit?"

Holland turns around at the new voice, and I glance up at the intruder. I'd seen him coming but was hoping to delay the interruption as long as possible. I've only spoken to him once so far and it wasn't exactly a brotherly moment.

"Oh, hey, Wes! Yeah, have a seat. Just chatting about The Mercer Center. Luke says it's a killer venue."

"Hey, man. Morning," Wes says, and I return his forced greeting.

"We played it on our last tour. It was pretty sick," I explain.

Wes glances at me. "Really? You weren't on the last tour though, right?"

I freeze.

"Wes..." Holland hisses, and I swallow hard.

"No, I guess I meant the one before that then," I manage, my heart pounding.

Wes shrugs, and I swear there's something dark in his expression. "Oh ok. Hey, you know what? Touring gets old. I totally got it when you left."

I stifle my glare and start to gather my trash. "Sure. Thanks," I mutter. "I should get going."

"Hey, man, sorry. Didn't mean to upset you. I just... you know... We all need a break every so often. No big deal."

This time, I don't even bother with polite pretense. He's certainly not as he meets my gaze with a clear challenge.

"Enjoy your breakfast," I spit, rising from the table.

"Luke!" Holland calls after me as I move toward the waste bin. I don't want to turn around. I don't need to see her face. I don't need to know she agrees her lead guitar player is acting like an ass, but has to stay loyal to him anyway. I definitely don't need to see his smug expression. I saw the obvious smirk before I was able to escape. They all love how far I fell. Watching me shatter for public consumption. I know it, I'm not an idiot, but it doesn't mean I have to let them see how weak I still am.

I'm in the hall when footsteps clap toward me. I don't want to turn around but have no choice when a hand grabs my arm and tugs me to a stop.

"Luke, I'm sorry." It's Holland looking up at me with a

sincerity that touches something deep, something forgotten. "I don't know why Wes said that stuff. He didn't mean anything by it."

"No? I'm pretty sure he meant a lot by it." Her face falls, and I sigh. "Look, Holland, I get it. I'm not saying I don't deserve that shit, but I also don't need to sit around listening to it. Besides, I have to go see Gary about a problem with my pedal board anyway. We can do the J45 another time."

"Luke, wait! Just..."

I pause and give her the floor, but suddenly she doesn't seem to know what to do with it anymore. There's that look again. Like she's fighting herself more than anything. After a few more awkward seconds, I force a polite smile. I know she means well and deserves that at least.

"Seriously, thanks for the chat. I needed to laugh for a bit. Good luck tonight," I answer.

She still looks like she wants to say something but doesn't. Or can't. Or won't. I don't know, but it's not my problem.

"Thanks, you too," she returns finally, and we exchange another awkward smile before going back to being unnatural strangers.

I'M in a weird place as I make my way out of the building. Torn between yesterday's emotional reconnection with Ellie's ghost and today's sudden acknowledgement of Holland, I feel the guilt mount, almost anger at my traitorous body that's still reacting to the effect of Holland's penetrating, deep blue eyes. I close my own for a moment, trying to decide what to do next. I'm not ready for the bus and probing gazes of my friends, but I also have nowhere else to go. I kind of feel like writing, but I don't have anything except my phone at the moment, so even that's out. The weariness of the last few days is starting to catch up with me, which isn't helping matters.

I sigh and drop to the steps outside of a service entrance, breathing in the warm morning air. The back of the building is alive with activity at this hour, and I find the din of muffled voices, idling truck engines, and crashing pallets, strangely comforting. There's a pattern, an order to the chaos. An organic relationship between each role and sound that links them to each other and their world. Life makes sense for these people, in this block of time. They know what to do next, how they fit. Meanwhile, I can't even seem to figure out the journey from breakfast to lunch.

I shift when I hear the door open behind me so the employee can pass, but I'm surprised when no movement follows. I open my eyes and squint up, nearly flinching at the blurry silhouette leaning over me, encased in sunlight.

"Took care of your pedal board issue already?" Holland asks with a knowing grin. She drops beside me on the step, forcing me to adjust my position. Her body is close, so close that I can smell the clean, fresh scent of her hair as she brushes against me. It's not her fault, the stairs are narrow, and I swallow. There goes the dam on my blood again. God, it's so annoying, and I'm so not in the mood to deal with it.

"Just enjoying a moment of peace and silence," I respond, trying to sound much more relaxed than I feel.

Her gaze flickers to the line of trucks backed into the loading docks.

"Yeah, it's quite the sanctuary out here," she teases. I cast her a quick grin in spite of myself and shake my head.

I can feel her eyes as I look away again and focus on nothing in particular. Just as long as it's not her. I don't understand what she wants from me.

"So are you stalking me or something?" I toss casually.

"Don't even pretend you're not used to it."

I smile again as she continues her assault on my sour mood and can't believe I'm suddenly shy for some reason. No, I'm not used to being stalked by Holland Drake. I have a feeling I'd never get used to that.

"Honestly, no. It's been a while since I've been properly stalked. I've been in hiding for a long time."

"So I've heard. Lucky for you, I'm not your typical stalker. Definitely just a gateway fangirl."

I laugh and glance over at her. "A gateway fangirl? What does that even mean?"

"Um...I don't know. I think it means I'd go through your garbage, but not steal your dog or anything. I'll have to check with your fan groups for clarification."

I can't stop it, and she grins when I double over in laughter. "Oh my god." I wipe my eyes, drawing in a deep breath.

"You know, you're not what I was expecting," she blurts next, jerking us in an entirely new direction. Nope, not a chance I ever figure out her maze. My gaze shoots back to her at her boldness.

"Really. Well, people usually expect the worst from me, so that's either good news, or extraordinarily bad."

She smiles and cocks her head a bit, studying me. "Good, I think. Which could be bad. We'll see."

I'm not sure what she means by that, but I'm afraid to ask. Whatever it is, I'm not ready for it. She's not either, even if she doesn't know it yet.

"It's just that you're intimidating, you know?" she continues, and I let out my breath, caught off guard again. It's like she's purposely trying to taunt social etiquette.

"Huh?"

She's grinning so I know she likes throwing me off balance.

"What? Like you don't know that about yourself? I'm the first to call you out on the enigma thing you've got going?"

"I've never had anyone tell me that to my face, no. Intimidating, how? Sure it's not just you who finds me intimidating?"

I swear she blushes a bit as she shrugs, but I don't feel badly. She started the "smash all social barriers" game.

"No, I doubt it. You're...I don't know. Untouchable."

I laugh again, I can't help it. Untouchable. Sure. I've been Life's fucking punching bag since the day I was born.

"Untouchable? What does that mean?"

It's her turn to stare off. She's carefully considering my question. I can almost see the spark of intelligence, the depth, flashing across her face as she scans the scene around us.

"What's your middle name?" she asks finally.

I stiffen. "What? Why?"

She studies me again for a second and finally leans back against the railing. "See? That's exactly what I mean. That wasn't even an intrusive question. But your instinct forces you to defend. To hide. Mine's Elizabeth. Holland Elizabeth Drake."

She sighs, and when her eyes change, I find myself getting drawn in all over again. "Like I said, you're an enigma, Luke. You're a dark, beautiful painting locked high on the wall behind a protective shield of glass. We all love to approach at a safe distance, but that's it. We admire, we stare, we even drool, many mock and hate, but none of us can imagine trying to touch it, to solve the mystery and get behind the glass. You wouldn't let us even if we wanted to. You're comfortable up there, out of reach."

I almost snort as I'm finally able to force my eyes away. "Oh yeah? You got all that from two conversations?"

She laughs softly. "Heck, no. I got all that from hours of

listening to Callie gush about you. Our two conversations just reinforce it."

My gaze turns to a glare as the blood starts to boil. "Callie told you all that? She wouldn't do that."

She seems affected by my heated reaction. "Of course not. She only talks about you as a friend whom she loves and respects. I read into the rest on my own, comparing what she says in sharp contrast to your reputation and what everyone else thinks. I trust her judgment, which means it's obvious people don't really know you. That there's something else going on. Am I wrong?"

I stare into the distance again, not sure how to answer that, but positive I don't want to.

"Do you always just say whatever you think?" I counter instead.

She laughs. "If you think this is bad, you should hear all the things I'm not saying right now."

I glance over, and despite the momentary darker mood, can't help but crack a smile at her expression.

"Really? How intriguing."

She shrugs, but doesn't resist my gaze.

"Ok, fine. You want to play this game?" I challenge. "What were you going to tell me on the bus yesterday but didn't?"

Now, she definitely does blush and looks away. "I was right not to say anything. It's not going to come out any better now."

I continue staring at her, determined to throw her off her game as well. I can be a damn stubborn painting when I want to be. Finally, she mutters a curse.

"Ok, ok! I was going to tell you that I don't hook up with other musicians, especially on tour. I just wanted you to know that up front. Nothing personal, just a rule I have."

My eyes widen in disbelief before bursting out laughing again. Her audacity is so funny and so freaking hot I can't help it. "Seriously? You were just going to dump that on me right out of the gate? Do you start off every relationship with that warning?"

I can tell she's embarrassed, but amused at the same time. "No. Only when I think my rule could be an issue for me."

There it is again. The sudden rush of searing blood. Shit. I draw in a deep breath.

She grins. She caught me, knows she got to me. "Come on, Luke. You're an insanely talented, walking, talking Greek god bad boy. You even have the sexy accent, tortured soul thing going on. Is there a woman on this planet who could resist you if you wanted her?"

I smirk to hide my own reaction to her words, and tear my eyes away from her. "I can name a few."

"Besides Callie," she laughs. "And let's face it, Casey Barrett isn't exactly far off himself."

I grin and shake my head. "I'll tell him you said that."

"You better not. I love Callie. She'd kill me."

"No she wouldn't. She'd laugh and tell you you're absolutely right. Then thank you for noticing and ask if you wanted some tea."

Holland chuckles. "She would. It's true." She quiets. "Anyway, sorry if this is just making things more awkward. I just...I don't know. Life's too short to play games with people. I like to be open and just put the truth out there. How else can we deal with it and know where we stand? Our world is complicated enough. Why not simplify what we can actually control?"

I don't look at her this time. She may feel that way, but it's so far from where I'm at that I don't even know how to respond.

"Does that approach work for you?" I manage finally.

Her eyes are on me. I can feel her tracing me, and I'm afraid to look. I'm terrified of what her gaze does to me.

"Does deflecting work for *you*?"

I instinctively glance at her now and go still. She doesn't let me look away this time. She's searching for something but I have no idea what. I doubt she'll find it, whatever it is. God knows there's not much left to find.

"Usually it works pretty well," I respond.

She nods, then softens. "Well, it won't with me, Luke," she explains gently, pulling herself to her feet. "I'm just warning you. I have no idea if we can be friends or not, but you should know that I don't believe in bullshit. I guess that should have been my warning yesterday instead."

And with that, I'm alone again on the steps, staring at a line of rumbling delivery trucks, breathing in warm late-summer air, wondering what the hell just happened.

I DECIDE I want to run my own sound check today. My strange conversation with Holland still has me off balance into the afternoon, and I need to reset before tonight. Besides, I never did get my writing time in, and I could use some relaxed creativity. Casey agrees, and even Eli and Sweeny reluctantly follow when I tell them I have a new song I want to work on. Callie is parked in the front row, her encouraging smile beaming off her face as she waits patiently for us to get our shit together.

"Is this the butterfly song?" Casey asks as we settle into our positions.

Eli and Sweeny nearly choke. "Wait, what? You get clean and suddenly we're doing butterflies?"

I shoot Casey an annoyed look. "Can you not call it the butterfly song?"

He shrugs. "What? Ok, fine. But that's what it's about, right?"

"No. It's about metamorphosis. Working title is 'Meta-morphosis.'"

"So butterflies."

I roll my eyes and can hear Callie laughing from her seat. "It's ok, Luke! I love butterflies!" she shouts up to us. "So do all your teen girl groupies! You just need a four-part harmony and coordinated dance to go with it!"

"It's not about fucking butterflies!" I cry in exasperation, even as I shake my head with a grin.

"Don't get mad! I'm just saying, is there a butterfly in it or not?" Casey asks, and I almost throw my guitar at him.

"Not anymore!" I hiss, and he laughs.

"Ok, ok! Sorry! Go for it. We'll shut up. We're ready."

I turn back to the mic and draw in a deep breath. I grip my guitar pick firmly in my right hand, my left hand positioned for a B minor chord. I wrote this one in D, but I'm thinking I might need to raise it to E. It's not exactly an essential detail at the moment, but suddenly it's all I can think about. Maybe I should just play it in E for their first listening. The higher key will give the chorus more energy, more power. Yes, E. But shit, if I do it in E, I have to raise the bridge too. Not sure I can hit that in E. I should have practiced this more. What was I thinking exposing it so early? I haven't played it for anyone except Casey, and that was so early he won't even recognize it.

My hands are sweating, heart racing. Bm, A, D. No, maybe I should go to the 4 instead. A solid G back into the 6. Dammit. I haven't played anything original since...god, I don't know when. Breathe. I've been doing this my whole life. No, not my whole life. Not at all since I became something else, someone else. What if my music was in the darkness, the filth? I have no way of knowing if I can trust what comes out now.

I'm surprised there's no more ribbing interrupting the silence as I hesitate. I glance back at Casey, and my chest suddenly gets heavy. He knows. I can tell by the look on his face that he understands what this moment means to me, and all the teasing is gone from his expression. He's no longer worried about butterflies, just me.

I suck in my breath and turn back to the audience, finally able to breathe again when my eyes rest on the lone judge seated in the center of the first row. It's Callie. Just Callie, gazing up at me, eyes full, waiting for me to be the person she discovered.

I wrote it in D. I have to start trusting myself at some point. As the music pours out, I can almost feel the suffocating curtain start to lift.

"Crawl in, crawl out
Terrified but moving now
Claw up, slide down
There's no going back, can't go back

Break down, break out
Break down, break out

Brand new day feast on the dark
Shuttered light, reluctant spark
Growing dawn and setting sun
Fight song of the desperate one.
Cocoon shredding
Past, heading straight for the wall
No more regretting, just breathing
Underwater

Too late to choose, too far to fall
Nowhere to go but on
No more excuses, no denial

No holding on to lost time

Break out, I'm breaking out

Brand new day release the dark
A new light, the smallest spark
Growing dawn and setting sun
Fight song of the desperate one.

Break it down, break it
Breaking out, just break it, break it"

I hadn't even realized I'd closed my eyes until the last note lingers in the air, in the darkness behind my eyelids. I open them, and I'm shocked, a little shaken, when I see Holland seated next to Callie. They both are staring at me with grave expressions as I back away from the mic and face my band.

"I mean, I'm still working on it," I explain into the silence. "Just..."

"It's awesome, man," Casey says, cutting off my instinctive apology. "I love it. We haven't done anything that hard in a long time."

"Yeah, dude. That bridge is sick," Sweeny echoes. "Can we run it again? I have a couple things I want to try."

"Yes! Definitely," Casey agrees. "We've got plenty of time. How's it sounding out there, Miles?" he calls to the front-of-house engineer.

"Guitar and vocal sounded great! Love the new stuff. Would also love to get a full check now," Miles returns into our ears.

I swallow, unnerved by the sudden warmth spreading through me. I don't know what to do with it, and turn back to Callie and...Holland is gone.

"LUKE! HEY!"

I stop on my way back to the bus and turn toward Tess, our road manager.

"How's everything? Did you get a chance to grab some food?"

I smile and nod. "Yep. Thanks, Tess."

"What about the bus? Does anything need to be restocked before we roll out tonight?"

"I don't think so. Maybe a few bottles of water. Hey, do you know if Gary is all good to take care of Tracing Holland tonight?"

"Yes! He's all set."

"Did he get in touch with Steven?"

"Steven?"

"Holland's backline tech who had to leave."

Tess waves her hand. "Oh, right! Sorry, I can't believe I forgot his name. I don't know, but I'll check." She quiets, and I brace myself. It's that look I've come to dread. The "you're-a-fragile-little-dandelion-but-we-love-you" look.

"How are you, Luke? How's it been being back?"

"I'm good," I answer. As if I'd say anything else. "It's an adjustment, but going ok."

"You sure? You'll let me know if there's anything you need, right?"

I try to hold in my sigh at the familiar script. She means well. They all mean well. "Yes, of course. I'll let you know, but I'm good," I repeat.

I don't know if she believes me or not, but at least she seems to understand that's the best she'll get. I have this conversation memorized at this point. There are a few versions of it and I'm grateful that Tess is sensitive enough to make it the short one.

"Ok, well, I'll go check with Gary and Holland to make sure they're all set. Kill it tonight, ok?" she says, swatting my arm as she passes.

I manage to return her smile before the resigned sigh escapes. Dandelion Luke. I guess it has a certain ring to it. Beats Train-Wreck Luke anyway.

4

ATLANTA, GEORGIA
SEPTEMBER 15

"Donuts! Coffee if you want it!" our tour manager Kenneth calls, waving in the promoter's assistant whose arms are loaded with provisions. I jump up from the couch to help him set his load on the table in the lounge of the bus. Eli and Sweeny are still in their bunks, and Callie and Casey are giggling in the back behind closed doors. I can tell Kenneth is annoyed at his small audience, but that's nothing new.

"Where is everyone?" he asks, gripping his binder with white knuckles.

I struggle to suppress my grin as I shrug, amused by his abhorrence of all things rocker-living. Kenneth is a fantastic tour manager, but I can't imagine a worse career for the rigid, detail-oriented drill sergeant than dealing with a busload of entitled, Type B artists day-in and day-out.

"I'll fill them in, don't worry. What've you got?" I assure him before his eyes burst from their sockets.

He mutters something and shakes his head in an attempt to refocus on his thick, tabulated binder. I grab a coffee from the tray and lean back, waiting for my instructions. I can sense the young assistant's gaze and glance over, even more amused at his obvious awe as he hovers at the top of the stairs. He knows his job is done but is reluctant to end his brief moment inside the walls of this legendary shrine. I've seen it a thousand times and it still makes me smile.

"Come grab a donut," I call over to the poor kid, half to be nice and half to watch the shocked horror cross Kenneth's face. Breakfast with the help is most definitely not on his schedule.

The assistant has no idea what to do with my comment and just stares at me from the top step. I smile to myself and pull one from the box as if demonstrating the process of eating for my two companions. He's now gazing up at Kenneth who's glaring at me. I don't know why I find this whole thing so funny, but I'm about to egg them on further when we hear shuffling. I turn and see Eli staggering toward us, sleep still in his eyes, right hand rubbing his messy hair.

"Oh hey, Kenny. Coffee? Fantastic," he mumbles, grabbing another cup from the tray. He drops beside me on the couch and takes a sip. Oh god. "Kenny." Kenneth hates that!

"What'd I miss?"

I have to restrain a laugh at the expression on Kenneth's face as he scans his pages with suppressed ire.

"Nothing yet, Eli. Thanks for joining us. We were just about to begin. Now, I know we've had a tight schedule the last few days, and it will continue in Atlanta. We'll have a nice break in Myrtle Beach starting tomorrow, but for now, I need you all to adhere to the plan and hang on for one more day until..."

"Can you book us each a room here?" Eli interrupts. "I need a real shower. Like, a big-ass ginormous one. I'm sick of sharing."

I turn away to hide my smirk. I can't tell if Eli is just trying to get under Kenneth's skin or is really so oblivious. He has that dry delivery that makes it impossible to be sure. Either way, it's hilarious watching the older man's world crumble.

"Not in Atlanta, no. I've booked one for you to share for your cleanup today as usual, but that's it. You will have a few rooms in Myrtle Beach. Perhaps you can hold out until tomorrow? I will do my best at finding 'big-ass' amenities on such short notice."

I almost die. It's everything I can do to hold it all inside. Eli just sighs and closes his eyes. It actually looks like he's gone back to sleep, and I jab him in the ribs. He jumps and glares at me.

"Kenneth is giving us the schedule," I explain, and we have to look away from each other so we don't burst out laughing. Yep, Eli is totally playing him. Shit, I'm about to lose it and Kenneth's fuse is already lit.

"Thank you, Luke," Kenneth continues, thankfully missing my gentle sarcasm. "As I was saying, lunch will be available in catering from 11:30 to 2:30. Please do not ask them to hold it again like in New Orleans. Three hours should be plenty of time and..."

"Hey, that was Sweeny!" Eli defends, and I kick him under the table. "Ow! What? It was!" he cries, and I roll my eyes, before turning back to Kenneth.

"You know what? Here," our tour manager grumbles. "Why don't I just leave this with you, and you all can read it at your leisure." He pops open the rings of the binder and yanks out the schedule. You know he's had it when he parts with any sliver of that binder.

"Thanks, Kenneth. We'll review it. Promise."

"Great. Just don't be late for lunch," he mutters.

"Got it," I assure him, and have to cough to cover my laugh when he spins and collides with the kid still standing on the steps.

"Wha...off!" Kenneth almost screams, pointing toward the exit.

Eli doesn't even try to hide his amusement and snorts so hard, the table shakes. "God, he hates us!" he cries after we're alone, still laughing.

I grin. "You're finding us a new tour manager when he quits. You know that, right?"

He shrugs and wipes his eyes. "I can't help it! It's so easy!"

I laugh and grab another donut.

THE OTHERS HAVE GONE to lunch, so I'm startled at the sound of footsteps on the stairs of the bus. Even more so when Holland pokes her head into the lounge and tosses me a warm smile. I can't say I'm entirely displeased to see her, just surprised.

"Callie told me I could find you here."

"Should I be worried that you're trying to hunt me down again?"

"Only if you were lying about that '43 J45."

I laugh and push myself up from the couch. "I wasn't. Hang on."

I retrieve the case from the back lounge and place it on the table in the main space. She's already exploding with excitement, and I love that she practically forgets about me the second it comes into view. Her eyes are glued to the case like I've just returned with the crown jewels.

I open it and step back so she can access the treasure inside, and she approaches with a solemn reverence. Her eyes are huge as she touches the dark wood, running her fingers along the smooth surface, gently as if it might disintegrate if she's not careful. I love everything about this moment, and I'm filled with a strange pride that she's able to appreciate the magnificence of the gem before her as much as I do.

"May I?" she asks, gazing at me with almost childlike awe.

I grin and nod. "Of course. I promised."

"It's nearly flawless!" she whispers, lifting it from its case. "Almost perfect condition."

I smile. "Yeah, I paid for that, believe me. Everything is original. Bridge, frets, pick guard, even the case. It's the Banner model with the maple."

She shakes her head, still staring at it in wonder. "Um, ok. Can we just get married now so I can adopt her?"

I laugh. "I guess I've had worse offers over the years. Wouldn't that conflict with your rule though?"

She meets my gaze with a quick grin before focusing back on the guitar. "Ugh. Damn rules. Alright, enough stalling. I have to play this thing."

She drops to a seat and balances the guitar on her lap, her arms wrapping around it with a casual grace. She passes a few tentative strums, and I can almost sense her shiver. I know what she's experiencing. I remember the first time I held it and introduced our present to this beautiful piece of history.

"It needs to be tuned, but I'm afraid to touch the pegs!" she cries, glancing at me again.

I shake my head with a grin. "Want me to do it?"

She laughs. "No, I got it." When she finishes, she glances back at me with a sincere expression. "Luke, I'm serious. This is amazing. Thank you."

"You haven't even played it yet."

"I know, but..."

"Here." I reach in my pocket and pull out a pick. "It's a 1mm. Hope that's ok. I think I have other gauges in the case."

"This is fine," she assures me. "Seriously, I'd play with a soda can tab right now."

"Um, not on my baby you won't."

She giggles, then seems to forget about me again. I'm fine with that, loving every second of watching their connection.

When she starts to play, I almost catch my breath.

"Flying high as you watch me fall.
Twisting in your beautiful lies, bravo.
Hats off to your elegant show.
Take a bow, my acrobat.
You've won the crowd, it's yours now, sweet
    acrobat."

I'm captivated by her voice, her fingers on the strings. The effortless flow of her music. I love that even though she's playing my guitar, it belongs solely to her in this moment. When she finishes, I have to fight the urge to tell her just to keep the damn thing. It clearly belongs to her. I take a deep breath and force a smile, not at all sure what to do with the sudden storm raging inside me. She's in love with that hollowed-out piece of wood, that much is clear, and it's turned her face into a masterpiece.

"One day," she whispers, staring down at the instrument, tracing her fingers along the smooth surface. She glances back up at me, as if remembering my presence for the first time and gives me an electrifying grin. "She's gorgeous, Luke. Seriously. Just stunning."

I swallow, managing only a quick nod. She is.

"You're turn," she chirps suddenly. "You play something now."

I stare at her in disbelief. "Huh?"

"Um, yeah. All you, rockstar."

She jumps to her feet and hands me the guitar. I instinctively take it, but can't imagine doing something as intimate as play a song for another soul a couple feet away. I can play a live broadcast in front of millions without breaking a sweat, but this...

"Maybe another time," I say, oddly embarrassed.

"What? No! Please? Just something quick! Doesn't have to be fancy. I have to hear this girl the way she's supposed to be played!"

"You just did! You're a fantastic guitar player."

She rolls her eyes. "Oh, come on. I'm fine, but everyone knows very few can touch you on that thing. Please, Luke! When will I ever have a chance to watch Luke Craven play a 1943 Gibson J45 two feet away? Don't make me beg, because I will, then hate you for it."

I can't stop the shy smile and shake my head. "Ok, ok. Fine. Geez."

She actually does look relieved when we switch spots so I can sit this time. I'm still hesitant, but starting to feel more comfortable now that I have a guitar in my hands. As I search my head for what to play, I can suddenly think of only one song. I haven't played it in ages, but it was one of the first I'd mastered. I'd learned it as a child, then embellished on it over the years, almost turning it into a different piece. My father used to play it all the time, and to this day, I don't know if he wrote it, or it was just a lesser-known favorite in his repertoire. Either way, it always held a special place in my heart.

I start picking out the elaborate intro, almost classical in its styling, and let my fingers and instinct takeover. Nothing else matters when I play, and I forget all about the awkwardness of the close quarters, even the beautiful woman staring at me in awe a few feet away. It's just the music and I, my father, memories of the few brief moments of happiness sprinkled throughout my painful life. I wonder if my face looks like

Holland's had a few minutes ago. I don't dare to look at her to find out.

I sing a few verses of the song, adding to the turns like I always do, playing with each chord, each note, like it might be possible to discover a new one this time. I never do, but I've combined enough existing ones in unique ways to at least create new experiences, new progressions that still give me chills when I find that perfect combination. This is my home, these moments, and the only time I feel safe, like I'm actually ok.

The shyness returns as the song comes to an end, and I clear my throat with an awkward smile. I realize I'd gotten wrapped up in the moment and wonder what she must think of me. I rise from the bench without a word and return the guitar to its case so I don't have to look at her and confront her reaction.

"That was beautiful, Luke," she says quietly behind me. "What was it?"

I swallow and snap the latches on the case. "I don't know exactly. Something my father used to play all the time. He called it the 'Sorrow Song' but I'm not sure why."

"It's amazing. *You're* freaking amazing," she adds, and I have no choice but to look at her now. I almost wish I'd risked rudeness at the expression in her eyes.

"Thanks. I've spent a lot of hours fooling around on a guitar."

"That's pretty obvious. You're mind-blowing when you play. Like, seriously, remarkable. I guess the rumors aren't exaggerated."

I feel the heat start to rise in me and have to look away again. "Well, let's hope some of the others are," I joke, trying to deflect the attention and lighten the mood.

I'm pretty sure she knows what I'm doing, but lets me go with a grin. "I guess we'll have to see."

———

"LUKE."

"Callie."

We exchange a smile at our signature greeting.

"Is this seat taken?" she asks, setting her plate across from me.

I smile. "Does it even matter?"

She grins back. "Nope."

I shake my head and motion for her to sit.

"Where's Case?" I ask, and snicker at her annoyed grunt.

"Who knows. He was in the back working on Penchant stuff when I left the bus, so I doubt we'll see him until call-time. I just hope he at least takes a shower and eats something," she mutters.

I laugh. "Bring something back for him. He can clean up in the sink on the bus."

She gives me a look. "Not a chance. There's no way I'm rewarding this behavior."

"Ok, sorry! It was just a suggestion," I smirk, holding up my hands in surrender. I focus back on my lunch, relieved it's just us and a few crewmembers at the moment. I miss my conversations with Callie. She has this way of looking inside you when she's there, turning the conversation into more than just words. Those first few days at Jemma's...she rewired my life with her piercing engagement. I love spending time with her, being in her calming presence, and we haven't had many opportunities for that these last couple weeks. So yeah, I'm annoyed when she ruins our rare moment alone by bringing up the one topic that can unhinge me.

"How are things with Holland?"

I stare over at her in surprise, maybe irritation. "Huh?"

She rolls her eyes. "Come on. She's like the one person in the universe who can understand every aspect of your being. The spotlight, the pressure, the music, everything. You two must be hitting it off. If you haven't yet, you need to get on that, like, yesterday."

I shake my head in disbelief. "None of your damn business," I return lightly.

She rolls her eyes with a smile. "Whatever. She's hot, too. Like, smokin'. You can't do any better, Luke."

My eyes widen, and she only shrugs.

"What? She is! She's sweet, and smart, and talented, and..."

"Callie, please. It's not happening, ok?"

"What's not?"

"Whatever it is you're trying to make happen. It's not going to happen."

She huffs and glares at her plate. "I'm not trying to make anything happen. You know I wouldn't rush you. I just..." She stops and glances back up at me, all the humor gone from her face. "I just hope you're going to be fair to yourself, that's all."

Her words hit me hard. "Fair? What are you talking about?"

She leans forward and gazes straight into me. "You deserve to be loved. You deserve friends. You deserve to let someone in. I'm not saying it has to be Holland, but if it is, you need to let it happen."

I laugh then. I know it's just a defensive reaction, but it's so absurd. Talking about love after all this time. Talking about loving Holland Drake of all people. And I thought Callie understood me. Crap, if she doesn't, I'm completely screwed.

"Thanks, Cal, but seriously, you can't worry about that."

She looks hurt. "Worry about what?"

"You know what I mean. Me. Love. Dating. All that shit. It's..." I stop. It's what? I don't know. It just feels wrong, pointless.

Now, she's annoyed. "I'm not worried about anything, Luke. I would never rush you or pressure you into a relationship! I just know you. I know how you punish yourself and deny yourself anything that could remotely lead to happiness. I'm calling you out on your self-denial because I'm afraid that's what I'm seeing here. This is a 'get real' moment."

I laugh when the grin spreads across her lips.

"Oh, yeah? Is this Callie Roland Straight Talk?"

She leans back and crosses her arms. "Yep, exactly. Callie Roland Straight Talk time. Just promise me you're not going to push Holland away if she starts to get close. That's all I'm asking. You don't have to date her. You don't have to fall in love with her. Just don't push her away if there's a connection, that's all. You deserve to be understood."

I chuckle at that, I can't help it. I know I'm pissing her off, but she has no clue how ridiculous this whole conversation is. "Callie, I love you, you know that. And I love that you care so much, but please, you're way off on this. Holland is great, I totally agree with you, but there's nothing for me to push away, ok? We've had a couple conversations and might be friends one day, I don't know, but she's not into rockers, and I totally respect that. It's a wise move on her part. She faces enough of a stigma as a woman in this business. She doesn't need that kind of drama or gossip in her life. And let's face it, it doesn't get any more dramatic than hooking up with Luke Craven while on tour."

Callie is actually glaring at me now, and I have no idea how to explain this any better.

"She told you that? She actually said she wasn't into rockers," she challenges, and I laugh.

"Honestly, yes. She did."

"I don't believe you. When?"

"Yesterday."

"What? She just looked you in the face and said, 'nope, not a chance'?"

I shrug. "Sorry to disappoint you, but yeah. Pretty much exactly that, actually. Complete with all the awkwardness and uncomfortable silence you'd expect. Although it was actually kind of sweet in a way. Still, trying to figure that one out."

Her eyes widen. "Holy crap. You're serious!"

I shrug again and nod. "Yep."

"Are you freaking kidding me? Unbelievable." She actually curses this time and grips her fork in a violent fist.

"I'm sure she just doesn't want distractions in her life. I don't blame her."

Callie rolls her eyes and shakes her head. "Yeah, but still. To come out and actually say it? I will never understand you musicians," she mutters. "Seriously! You create so much drama trying to avoid drama!"

I laugh and pity her lasagna as she stabs it in frustration.

"It's fine, really. I'm not looking for a relationship, you know that."

She meets my eyes, and I know I've said the wrong thing.

"I know you're not. And it's ok not to look, as long as you're not closing yourself off from one finding you."

"You mean like a wall painting?" I ask just to test her reaction. She looks appropriately confused, and I find some comfort in that. So Holland had been telling the truth. The whole painting metaphor was original Holland Drake intuition.

"Huh?"

I shake my head. "Never mind. Someone told me once that I'm like a painting. People like to look but no one dares to come near it. That I wouldn't let them even if they wanted to."

Callie's expression changes. I shouldn't have said that. I've just invited a conversation I don't want to have anywhere, let alone at a folding table in catering with crewmembers a few feet away.

"Who said that to you?"

I stare at my plate. "It doesn't matter. Do you think it's true?" I ask, daring to meet her gaze again. It's too late to go back now.

Her eyes search me, the compassion I so admire filling my soul with that strange warmth that's been creeping in lately.

"Yeah, actually, I do think it's true. It's a great metaphor for you, but it's their loss, Luke. It is, for sure, but it's also not fair of you to keep denying the rest of the world the beauty inside you. You're just as much to blame."

My stomach drops. There should be a defensive quip rising to my tongue right about now, but instead I'm locked in stunned silence. I don't know how to respond. Nothing seems to fit.

"Luke, I'm serious. You're ready. I know you're ready."

I suck in my breath. "I am? Ready for what?"

She smiles as she shrugs. "I don't know. For whatever's next."

———

"Hello. Hello. Greetings from the inside. Hello.
Hello. Framed in all your lies..."

THE CROWD IS SCREAMING along with me, twenty-thousand backup singers belting out the now famous chorus as I lean into the mic, emptying my lungs of the music exploding in my chest. I can't actually hear their cries as the click track and mix pour into my ears from my IEMs, but it doesn't matter.

It doesn't stop the adrenaline, the rush of being on stage. Of being transported to that one place where everything makes sense. The only place I don't feel like a stranger.

My muscles tense with each lyric, each strain toward the mic, each violent assault on my guitar.

> "Hello! Hello! How you love to see me cry,
>   always so..."

Sweeny kills his riff on the outro and I jump back to give him the spotlight, letting my body take complete control from my head. It's just raw instinct now. A visceral heat driving me as I dominate the stage, my tiny kingdom. Lights flashing, haze swirling around us. I'm exhausted after the long set, but I don't want it to end. No matter how many times I do this, no matter how many shows, songs, hours of pouring out my soul, I never want to say goodbye. This is my home, my giant family I will never know.

Sweeny nods after a couple progressions, signaling the end of his solo, and I pass it along to Casey who leads us out with a huge fill. Sweeny, Eli, and I join in, hammering the last chord for a full seven seconds as we let our bodies match the intensity of our sound.

It's finally time, the end, and I let go of my guitar to hop back on the mic, grabbing it with both hands.

"We love you!" I cry into the final barrage of music still swelling around us. I pull out my in-ears so I can hear the roar, the deafening air. I raise my hand in salute. "Thank you, Atlanta! Good night!"

5

MYRTLE BEACH, SOUTH CAROLINA

SEPTEMBER 16-19

I am so grateful for my own room again when we roll into Myrtle Beach that I pretty much determine I don't want to leave it until we have to report for the show in three days. I stretch out on the bed, closing my eyes, breathing in the stale hotel air like it's a fresh mountain breeze. I'm hungry, but I can't even imagine leaving this sanctuary in search of food. Three days of privacy. Three days of silence. Three days of protection from the endless looks of pity or disdain. Three days of no inquiries, or probing, or questions about my mental state disguised as questions about water bottles and snack food. I'm so giddy, I almost text Callie to let her know I finally remember what happiness feels like. Almost. I'm pretty sure I know what's happening in Casey's room right now.

The thought makes me smile, then frown as Holland's face ruins the moment. Annoyed, I try to shut it out, but the effort only makes it worse. Now it's her hair, her eyes, her smile, the pen in her mouth as she writes in her notebook. Her lips. Her strong, but delicate fingers as they slide over the smooth wood of my guitar. My body starts to react. Oh god, not again.

I curse into the darkness of my room, pounding the mattress in frustration, but it doesn't help. She's still there, burning in my head, reminding me of how long it's been since I let another person invade my soul. Touch me. Since I've touched. My body is screaming now, my breath coming harder as I clench my eyes shut, trying to make it stop. It's been so long. Too long.

I bolt up from the bed, guilty, furious, the self-hatred knocking hard against the wall of my conscience. I don't even know why or what I've done, I just know I'm sinning against something, someone. I strip off my shirt, my jeans, everything, and move into the bathroom, turning on the water to the shower with a rough hand. I'm terrified as I step under the healthy stream, having no way of knowing if the warm flood will save me or push me over the edge. There's no way to be sure, but after a few seconds I realize she's still here. She's followed me from the bed. I lean against the wall, hot tears burning behind my eyes, my brain desperately fighting against the cries of my body. I can't do this, can I? I can't. I...

I try to shut her out, but the harder I try, the worse it gets. Cross-stich. Cross-stich. Cross-stich. No, there's her laugh. Her brilliance. The captivating magic of her immersion in the music. My hand is disobeying my brain now, desperate as it soothes and stirs, crushing my will, knocking me into total submission to the painful ecstasy.

You're an enigma, Luke. You're a dark, beautiful painting locked high on the wall behind a protective shield of glass.

Is there a woman on this planet who could resist you if you wanted her?

You're an insanely talented, walking, talking Greek god bad boy. You even have the sexy accent, tortured soul thing going on.

Don't even pretend you're not used to it.

I gasp, overcome with guilt, with pleasure. My body

collapses against the wall, thanking me and punishing me at the same time. I don't move, absorbing the chill from the tile as it bleeds into my back and calms the raging fire that just wrecked me. I can feel the anger, the guilt, the longing, start to meld together in a twisted knot as my brain begins to catch up with my young, virile body. I finally push away from the wall, the tears mixing with the water as I let go and turn my face into the stream. I hold my breath, not that there was any air left in my lungs.

Oh god, what have I done?

I SIT on the edge of my bed for a long time, haunted by what just happened. Punishing myself, forgiving myself. I don't know. I'm not sure I've done anything wrong, but it doesn't feel right either. I rest my head in my hands, staring at the floor. I have no idea how to be a good person, what that even means. All I know is I'm trying, but maybe it's not enough.

I also know that I'm actually relieved when my phone lights up with a text from Casey and Callie letting me know they're heading to the beach. Funny how an hour ago I couldn't imagine leaving this room and now I'm desperate for any reason to escape it.

The beach sounds great and I respond that I'll meet them in the lobby in a few minutes. I pull on some shorts and a t-shirt, casting a quick glance at myself in the mirror. It's always fast. There's almost never anything there I want to see. I notice my eyes look tired, but that's to be expected with our brutal schedule over the last few days. No one will suspect anything different.

I take the elevator down to the lobby and almost force the doors back closed. I'd left my room to escape her and there she is, perfect flesh giving life to the dangerous hallucination in my head. They spot me, however, eliminating any chance of a retreat, and I plaster my best smile on my face.

"Hey, guys," I say, approaching the small group, careful to keep my eyes fixed on Casey and Callie. I can't look at Holland after what I'd just done with her in the shower. She'd been engaged in a separate conversation with Wes and her drummer, Spence, when I appeared, and suddenly falls silent.

"No Eli and Sweeny?" I ask, mostly to distract myself from the effect of her intense gaze. I can feel her studying me, searching me, and it's messing with my brain chemistry in a bad way.

"They're coming," Casey answers. "Late as usual."

I snicker, not at all surprised. As if on cue, the elevator doors open, and the boisterous duo explodes into the lobby.

"Let's do this!" Sweeny calls, drawing stares from everyone else in the large space.

Callie laughs and takes Casey's hand, dragging him toward the door. "Yes! Let's go!" she cries, giving us no choice but to follow.

THE BEACH IS NOT AS CROWDED as I would have thought. There are plenty of other visitors enjoying the sand and walking along the surf, but it's definitely not the raucous party atmosphere I'm used to. This crowd is mostly families with young children or retired natives strolling along for their daily walk. Callie is clearly through the roof with excitement, and I can't help but grin as she skips across the bridge over the dunes. Casey just shakes his head in amusement and struggles to keep up.

"Come on!" she cries turning back and waving us on.

"Has she never seen the beach before?"

I stiffen at the voice, my smile faltering. I force another surge of energy into it.

"Callie lives everything in the moment," I explain to Holland. I suck in my breath, and allow myself to look at her but immediately wish I hadn't. She's stunning with her loose, cut-out tank draped over a bikini top and tiny shorts. Her aviator sunglasses hide her eyes from me, but I know they're focused on me as well. I can almost feel the tension in her too. It makes no sense, given how much energy she pours into convincing me she has no interest in me.

"It's pretty hot," she muses, still staring at me, and I can't stop my grin.

"What, the temperature or the view?"

She laughs and shakes her head. "Wow. You are so full of yourself."

I give a playful shrug, and she shoves me as we move down the steps together.

"You know what I meant. Yes, the temperature."

"So that's where we are now? Talking about the weather? I let you play my Gibson."

"Exactly. Which is why we've graduated from the stock market to weather."

I laugh, and cherish her return grin. "Oh, I see. So what does a guy have to do to get to sports scores?"

"I'm not sure you could handle that," she responds with a sly look.

"Oh, really?" I ask, warming to the challenge.

"October is the best month for sports."

And the magic vanishes as Wes steps in.

Spence is up front with Jesse, Eli and Sweeny, Casey and Callie are hand-in-hand several paces behind, which leaves our awkward threesome bringing up the rear.

"Oh, hey, Wes," Holland greets, and I have to admit I like the slight hint of disappointment in her tone. I don't know if he picks up on it, but he clearly has no intention of leaving the two of us alone to explore our gentle flirting.

"Great day for the beach," he says, and we nod.

"Gorgeous," Holland replies.

"Not as many people as I would have expected," I add, desperate for anything to fill the uncomfortable cloud surrounding us. I can see Holland holding in a smile, and I love that she knows how awkward this is too. I'm about to excuse myself to join another group, rather than endure this agony, when Jesse, Spence, Eli, and Sweeny do us a huge favor by ripping off their shirts and plunging into the water. Casey and Callie pull to a stop, and I'm not at all surprised that Casey jumps to join them. He drags Callie after him as she screams, laughing and trying to smack him away at the same time.

"Oh my gosh, they are so adorable," Holland observes.

I glance over, basking in the momentary warmth of watching the happiness of my two closest friends.

"They're for real," I say.

"Almost gives you hope, huh?"

My stomach drops. I can't even respond, and she studies me hard, confusing me with all kinds of emotions. I've completely forgotten about Wes. So has she.

"Hope is a complicated word," I manage finally.

After another long silence, she nods and focuses back on our companions.

"Come on guys! You need to get in here! The water is so warm!" They're calling to us, waving us in from the shore.

Holland laughs. "We should. Let's go!"

She pulls off her top and starts slipping out of her shorts, exposing a body that makes my mouth go dry. I can't stop staring, any earlier reservation completely gone. As soon as she started moving, so did Wes, and he's in the water on his way to the group before she even finishes dropping her shorts and tank a safe distance from the water's edge.

I still haven't budged by the time she returns, and she gives me an annoyed look.

"You're still dressed!" she whines, hands on her hips.

I laugh. "You go. I'll guard our stuff."

She glares at me, making it clear that's not going to work for her.

"Not a chance."

She grabs the hem of my shirt and starts pulling it up my chest.

"Hey! What are you doing?" I cry.

"Stripping you so you have fun for five seconds."

Shocked, amused, and completely turned on, I stop resisting and let her yank it over my head. The humor fades as she stills, inches away, our bodies close, but totally off-limits to each other. She's at the right angle that I can see her eyes through her sunglasses now, tracking every detail of my form, and I'm sure I hear her suck in her breath a bit.

"My god," she whispers. "Seriously?" She searches my eyes and I can sense every ounce of her sudden fascination. My blood pounds, my heart racing. She wants to touch me. It's all over her face, her body language. She even glances at the others, testing her limits, and I follow her gaze. I'm sure I feel the same pain of frustration she does at their attention.

We're on stage.

She lets out an awkward laugh and takes my hand instead, pulling me toward the waves as if nothing had happened. I have to force a smile to hide the volcano erupting inside me, and nearly wince as we step into the surf. The water may have been warm for ocean water, but it feels like ice against my burning skin.

The others laugh and splash in the distance, but my gaze is glued to Holland. I love everything about the joy on her face as she joins in the fun. The fact that someone so deep and intro-spective is also able to let go so completely. It's captivating, magnetizing. I've never been able to do that, not without the assistance of substances that could totally abduct my brain and mask my consciousness. I don't regret getting sober for a second, but I do miss those moments of stepping outside my own saturated existence. It gets exhausting being me.

"Luke, get over here!" Holland yells.

"Yeah, come on, grumpy!' Callie echoes, and I roll my eyes.

"Ok, I'm coming," I concede, fighting the small waves as they crash against my knees. I have to jump to avoid being slapped in the face by a few more, but finally reach the three of them hovering a few feet beyond the breaking point. The rest of our group is a hundred yards away, diving into the ripples, and I understand their position much better when I notice a cluster of bikini-clad women setting up nearby at the water's edge. It's only a matter of time before that party happens.

"Wow, they're pretty hot."

The voice startles me, and I almost jump at the intrusion.

"Huh?"

"Those girls."

"Oh, what? No," I say, shaking my head and focusing back on Holland. She's grinning, so I know she's just teasing me. "Not my type," I add, not sure why.

"Hot girls in bikinis aren't your type?"

"Not unless they're just as hot when they open their mouths."

She laughs. "How can you tell they're not your type then?"

She's close now, way closer than she needs to be. I can feel the heat of her body, the intentional contact that can still be disguised as an accident as she pretends to squint at the gathering on the beach. It's messing with my head again, not that I would have known how to answer her question anyway. I just know from experience and that's not a conversation we need to have right now. Or ever.

"I don't know. Just my gut. They picked that spot to be noticed. They've been studying our boys just as much as our guys are checking them out. There's nothing wrong with the game, it's just not my thing."

"Really? Your reputation says otherwise." Surprised, I glance over at her, and she shrugs. "What? Am I wrong?"

I stiffen a bit, annoyed at her bluntness, at myself for making her right in the first place. "About my reputation? No. About me? Maybe."

"You don't even know what I think about you yet, so how do you know?"

"I know you think I'm hot," I tease, trying to lighten the mood. She laughs and shoves me a bit. The playful contact is enough for my body to react again. Shit. I'm just glad the water is past my waist.

"Everyone thinks you're hot. That shouldn't even count as an observation." She quiets. "What I didn't know was that you were also a little shy, kinda sweet, and so damn intelligent."

"Careful. You're going to ruin my reputation as a badass."

She grins. "Don't worry. I think your bad reputation is safe."

I smile and shake my head. "I said badass, not bad."

She returns it. "I know." She grows serious. "I also learned you're a hard person to avoid. Way harder than I thought."

I glance at her. "What do you mean?"

She shrugs and stares off at the other group again, but I caught her revealing gaze before it fled. "I don't know how to explain it exactly." She stops and shakes her head. "Let's just let that one go, ok?" she pleads, and I'm disappointed I have to accept when Wes spots us and breaks up the conversation anyway.

———

HOLLAND and I don't get another moment alone on the beach, and we've barely even exchanged complete sentences with each other by the time we return to the hotel to clean up for dinner. No one else seems to notice the change in our silence, no one except Wes. I can't help but observe how he seemed to be a constant presence for the rest of the day, always the third wheel, the barrier separating us from any chance of exploring whatever that was by the water's edge, her cryptic comments later on.

Part of me is disappointed, but another part is strangely relieved. These feelings for Holland are confusing at best, and I'm having a terrible time converting them into a reality I can process. Better to make the entire issue a non-starter. I'm very comfortable with my plan to try to avoid her for the rest of the tour when she catches my arm just as the others disappear around the corner of the hall to their respective rooms.

"Hey, um, do you have a sec?" she says. "Can we talk?"

I swallow. "Yeah, sure, what's up?"

She glances around. "Not here. Maybe in your room or mine?"

My heart races, blood pounding violently. The memories of her wet body close to mine is ravaging my brain. Her eyes as they scanned me with that hunger for possession. Even I'm not that stupid.

"Holland, I don't think that's a good idea," I say quietly.

Our eyes meet and she knows exactly what I mean. I can tell she feels it too as she bites her lip and studies me again with a troubling intensity. It makes everything so much worse.

"No, I know. You're right." She seems frustrated and grows quiet for a second. "Come out with me then," she offers.

I stare at her. "What do you mean?"

She shrugs. "I don't know. Let's go do something." Suddenly, her face lights up. "Let's play mini golf! I haven't done that in fifteen years!"

I laugh. I can't help it. "Mini golf? Are you serious?"

She shrugs. "Why not? You're too much of a badass to slap a tiny ball around a pirate ship?"

I grin and shake my head. I have no chance against that challenge. "You *are* serious. Crap. Ok, fine. But I have to warn you, I don't think I've ever actually played mini golf."

"What?" she cries. "Never? That's so wrong! Ok, you're coming. Let's go."

"Right now?" I laugh.

"Yes, right now!"

"Aren't you hungry?"

She shrugs. "We'll grab a hot dog or something from the snack bar. Quit whining and walk, rockstar."

She practically pushes me back to the elevator, and I'm still in disbelief that this girl is getting me to agree to a game that involves golf clubs and pirates.

"You don't even want to change first?"

"Change? What's wrong with my outfit? You don't like it?" she teases.

I roll my eyes. She knows full well how good she looks. "I love your outfit, I just know you women. You have outfits for everything. I can't believe your beach outfit is the same as your golf outfit."

"Ok, first of all. It's mini golf, not golf. There is a huge difference which drastically affects the dress code."

I grin, loving how she can match me at every turn. "Ok, fine. And second?"

"And second, you can just toss everything you think you know about 'women' out the window. It's time someone exposes you to the big secret." She stops and glances around before leaning close. "No two are alike," she whispers.

I offer a shy smile. "Fair enough. I'm sorry."

She's clearly not offended, just being gently honest, and grabs my hand as the elevator doors open back to the lobby. "Let's walk. It's not far."

I like that idea as well, and I'm surprised when she doesn't let go of my hand. Instead, she laces her fingers with mine and falls into a casual stride beside me, as if this is just another walk in our long history of walks. It's almost surreal how effortlessly she fits into my universe.

I want to call her out on her recent behavior, which is completely at odds with her earlier warnings, but her hand feels so good in mine. I don't care if it doesn't make sense. I need it there at the moment and can't risk losing my grip.

"I'm sorry about Wes," she begins as we move out of the hotel complex and onto the sidewalk toward Highway 17.

"What about him?"

She shrugs. "He's being difficult. He's protective, you know?"

"I can see that."

"It's complicated," she mumbles, and something about her tone unnerves me. There's history there, deep history that is going to impact more than I can imagine I think.

I glance away. "It's fine. I get it. I'm used to it," I mutter.

She seems hurt by that for some reason. "You shouldn't be. It's not fair that you have to be."

I try not to react. "Is this what you wanted to talk to me about?"

She nods. "Yeah, among other things. Luke..." She pulls us to a stop and faces me. "I know I don't really know you and you don't know me, but I want to make sure you understand something. I don't, I *won't*, judge you for your past. I know all about the rumors and perceptions of how you were before, but I believe in the present. I want us to be friends." She quiets and meets my eyes. "I respect you as an artist. I'm glad you're back sharing your gift with the world."

I just stare for a moment, not sure how to respond to any of that. I'm filled with so many conflicting emotions I don't know where to start. So, as usual, I go with nothing.

"Thanks. You're very talented too," I manage finally, totally weak, but it's all I've got. She grins and shakes her head.

"Am I now?" she muses, moving forward again, the brief cloud lifting. This time she takes my arm, which still feels completely natural for some reason.

"What? You're not?" I challenge.

"Oh, I am! Incredibly talented, actually." I love her playful expression.

"So what's so funny?" I ask.

"Nothing, just us."

I laugh. "Us?"

She returns my grin and leans against me a little as we walk. "Yeah. Our conversations. The open book talking to a piece of granite. I pour out my soul and get 'thanks,' 'ok,' 'sure.'"

I laugh again and meet her gaze. "Oh, I'm sorry. Did I advertise myself any differently?"

She scoffs. "No, my friend. You are exactly as advertised."

"HOLY CRAP, YOU'RE TERRIBLE!" Holland laughs as I hit the limit on yet another hole. Thankfully, the final one.

"I told you I never played before," I return.

"Yeah, but the 7-stroke max was meant as a limit, not a goal!"

I give her a mock glare. "Oh, really. Then I suppose I should stick to fronting a highly successful rock band instead of smacking a ball through fake alligators."

"Crocodiles."

"Huh?"

"Um yeah, pretty sure those are supposed to be crocodiles."

"Oh, whatever! I'm hungry anyway. Let's grab some food. What's the final score?"

"I have no idea. These tiny cards are way too small to keep track of all your strokes."

"Hilarious," I mumble, following her to the equipment stand to return our clubs. The girl in the booth is looking at us strangely, and I try to ignore it. She thinks she recognizes us. She does, but is too shy to risk being wrong. I'm fine with that.

I buy Holland a hot dog and drink at the snack bar, and we settle onto a painted cement ledge surrounding the tables. We're quiet as we eat, enjoying the warm evening air and rare moment of "normal." A couple of teens strum some rough versions of popular songs on a guitar nearby, and I can see Holland's look of amusement as she watches them. But her smile isn't critical, only content as she takes in these kids' love of music and fearlessness at expressing it. Something strange happens in me as well as I study them. Watching the two boys treat that guitar like it's the answer to something in their lives. That was me once. Hell, that was me most of my life. There was a time when that was all I had.

I jump up from the ledge, startling Holland, startling myself, but my brain has latched onto an idea and won't let go. I move toward the boys and notice their surprise as I approach with a warm smile.

"Hi, I'm Luke," I say holding out my hand.

The boys' jaws are on the ground as they shake it. "Wait, are you..."

"Oh, shit! You're Luke Craven!" the other one cries.

I exchange a smile with Holland across the snack area, suddenly filled with something I can't identify. Joy, maybe? I don't know what it is, but my heart is warm as I turn back to the boys and absorb their awed expressions.

"Mind if I play with you?" I ask, motioning toward the guitar. They don't even move at first, as if my request made no sense to them. Finally, one of them nods, eyes wide, and grabs the guitar from his friend's hands and holds it out to me.

"Thanks," I say, taking it into my own. I already know from listening to them earlier that it's grossly out of tune. The strings are dull and should have been replaced ages ago. It's actually not a bad guitar once I get it balanced in my arms, and for rocking the snack bar at Pirate's Adventure Mini Golf, should do just fine.

We've gained a lot more attention, and I can feel the crowd gathering as I give the instrument a quick tune. The action on the guitar is rougher than I'm used to as I test out some chords, but it reminds me so much of my own beater I've been carrying around since I was eleven that I feel a strange air of familiarity. My "Percy" is in my hotel room now, beside my bed, waiting to hold me and comfort me like it always is. Like it had since the day my father gave it to me and told me to take care of it after he was gone. I had. It was the only thing I ever took care of.

I draw in a deep breath and start to play. I cast a quick look toward Holland and love the moment when her face ignites in shocked recognition. Her smile is priceless, the way her eyes dance as she shakes her head, staring at me in disbelief. I almost lose my rhythm as my grin widens and I have to look away to concentrate.

"Wait, that's 'Perfect Storm'!" Someone in the crowd announces. "Tracing Holland, right?"

"Oh! They're in town with Night Shifts Black later this week, I think! My sister has tickets. Is that..."

"Yes!"

"I can't believe it!"

"Oh my gosh! Look!"

I hear the murmurs as the news filters through the spectators. They're starting to realize who I am, who she is, but I don't let it bother me for once. It's the music that makes it ok. I can never stop it once it starts. My fingers navigate the strings with an expertise that comes more natural to me than eating or sleeping. When I play, it just happens and makes the rest of the world fade away. There's no painful past in my music, no history, no nightmares or baggage, just breathing, just being. I close my eyes and start to sing.

> "You and me, babe, a tidal wave I never saw
>   coming.
> You and me, and that hurricane we can't
>   outrun.
> It shouldn't have been, but there's no fight
>   against the wind.
> It all blew in, too fast, too hard, the Perfect
>   Storm."

Then, there's another voice. A beautiful, edgy harmony layering with my melody. It gives me chills in its perfection, the way it wraps itself around my notes and turns them into something entirely different, something breathtaking.

> "You and me, babe, still afraid but locked into
>   fate.

You and me, losing all the reasons to run.
Oh sweet ecstasy of defeat, forgive me now.
It all blew in, too hard, too fast, the Perfect
  Storm."

We continue the song beyond its expiration, taking it in new directions, even improvising a stunning bridge that shocks me in her ability to read my lead. She's always there, every note, every rhythm change, every incidental I throw in to add that extra spark of magic to a song that's already stolen the hearts of the crowd; her own talent and brilliance catch me off guard. I knew she was good, but you never really know how good someone is until you strip away the show, the performance, and see what music is actually in their soul. Hers is full, like mine, and together we've just uncovered an entirely new level of beauty.

"And I will fight through the waves
To get to you, to get to you
And I will scream through the dark
Against the lies, against the lies that overtake
  me"

I don't want it to end, I sense neither of us does, but there's only so much time you can spend in another place before the dream dumps you back in the present. The small crowd erupts with applause and cheers when we finally bring the show to a reluctant close. Still, we barely hear them as we exchange a smile, our eyes speaking volumes about what just happened. An inexplicable protectiveness and warmth is washing over me as I force my gaze away and hand the guitar back to the boys. They are still in shock, but no more so than I am as I try to make sense of these new, tender feelings seeping into my darkness. I'm not sure I'm allowed to feel this way. For so many reasons.

I swallow hard, actually grateful for the cloud of mini golf scorecards that are suddenly shoved in my face for autographs. Nothing distracts from reality like playing the rock idol.

Holland grins and follows my lead, immediately transforming into her celebrity role. I find myself watching her every chance I get, admiring her casual grace as she interacts with her fans. Her authentic smile and sincerity is addicting, and there are several times I have to force myself to tear my eyes away to satisfy my own fan obligations. She's mesmerizing.

IT'S a good hour before we're finally able to make a clean break and head back to the hotel.

I open the door to the lobby for Holland when we reach the entrance, but she doesn't go inside. Instead, she hesitates, looking up at me with an expression that tugs at my heart.

"Can we not go in yet?" she asks quietly.

Confused, I nod and follow her to a bench near the entrance. She grasps my hand as we sit, pulling it close to her in a protective embrace.

"Is everything ok?" I ask, concerned by her sudden mood shift. I'm pretty sure her sad smile is supposed to soothe my fear, but only causes me to brace myself.

"It's great, actually. That's the problem," she explains, confusing me further. She leans her head on my shoulder and studies the passing cars. "I just want to pretend for a few more minutes before we return to reality."

Disturbed, I glance over for a better read. "What do you mean?"

She sighs. "You know what I mean. Pretending that what

just happened today was real. That '*this*' is real," she explains, holding up our intertwined fingers.

I quiet. She's right, I know exactly what she means. Today was a fantasy. Everything about this is a dream.

"Luke, I'm sorry. I know I'm not making this easy for you. I'm a hypocrite and contradicting myself. I know..." She pulls away and buries her face in her hands. "I just don't know what it is with you. You're this magnet for me. You break all my rules," she whispers, finally looking back at me. "But my rules are there for a reason."

She leans back, crossing her arms as she gazes back at the street. "And you have rules too, you know? You have so many rules, so much baggage, you don't even know what to do with me and my rules. Today was fun, amazing actually, but it wasn't real."

She's right, of course. I hate how fucking logical she is.

"I get it," I say finally, and she turns to me abruptly.

"Do you? Really? Because I'm struggling really hard with this. I can't get you out of my head and it terrifies me."

I'm not sure how to respond to that. She doesn't know what my head's already done to her. But this isn't about sex, and that's the problem. We understand sex all too well. It's the rest that's keeping us apart, the fear of what we don't understand, the part that's ripping up the little we thought we did.

But it does make sense. It makes a hell of a lot of sense, even if the truth is killing both of us right now. I've done too much damage in my life to risk this magnificent soul beside me, and she's fully aware of the kind of destruction that surrounds me. She's too smart for that, too strong, and I wasn't just speaking out of my ass earlier. I do get it. I understand. I don't want to hurt her as much as she doesn't want to be hurt by me. Neither of us trusts me with something so precious. I certainly don't.

"I want to be friends, though," she adds, and I almost laugh.

It's such an absurd statement and we're both smirking at the cliché.

"Sure," I answer, following the script like a pro. I start to get up from the bench, pretty certain our journey back to reality is brutally complete at this point.

"Luke, wait," she says, grabbing my arm one last time.

I do, and give her my attention.

"You're an amazing person. Just know I truly believe that."

I force a smile. "Thanks," I manage. "So are you."

She doesn't respond. She also doesn't seem any more content than I am about my return to the lobby, alone.

MY PULSE QUICKENS as I approach my room and see a figure seated against my door. I immediately tense when I recognize him and brace for the inevitable. I'm in no mood for it, not when Holland and I just had this same conversation a second ago.

"What are you doing, man?" Wes hisses as I reach my door.

"Going into my room," I toss back casually, slipping my key into the slot. I'm beyond pissed when he follows me inside and lets the door clatter behind him. "What are *you* doing?" I spit.

"You know what I'm talking about!" he returns, ignoring my question.

"No, actually I don't. Get out of my room," I snap, angry but trying to stay calm. I'm not going to let an asshole like Wes Alton goad me into a stupid battle over a woman. After every-thing I've been through, there's no way in hell I'm going down like that.

"She's a big girl. She can make her own decisions," I say. I know that's not helping, but I'm not the type to back down.

"Yeah, maybe, but she makes bad decisions. You know

why? Because she's good, and trusting, and wants to believe other people are like her. But they're not. They're fucking animals, and I'm not going to stand by and watch them tear her apart!"

My glare turns hostile. I can feel the old rage burning, that destructive fire that will leave us both in ashes. "Get out of my room, or I'm calling security. I'm not kidding, Wes! And if they're not fast enough, I'll remove you myself!"

His eyes are just as hot, but he begins backing toward the door. "I know what you are," he hisses. "*You* know what you are. Everyone knows what you fucking are and knows you have no business breathing the same air as her. If there's any shred of decency left in you, you'll leave her the fuck alone and go prey on some needy fangirl instead!"

I freeze. I'm glad he leaves on his own right then because I can't move. I stare at the door for a long time, my heart racing, pulse pounding, nausea coursing through me.

I'm devastated by his words, furious, but mostly because he's right. Because deep down there's the part that agrees with him and is always waiting to claw its way back up into my consciousness. Triggers. Triggers. Shit! Fuck!

I drop to the edge of my bed and rake my hands into my hair. Triggers. It's just a trigger. It's just...I'm not.... I am! God, I am! I'm a disease. I'm going to destroy Holland, like I destroyed Elena, like I destroy everyone else. Callie, Casey, I'm going to erase them all with my insidious infection.

I'm pulling at my hair so hard now I'm having trouble focusing on anything but the pain. It's so beautiful, the pain. I love how it takes away from the worse pain that I can't handle. I clench my eyes shut and focus on that for a moment. Pulling harder when my brain starts to adjust to the agony. So hard, I actually think I pull some out. Then, it all stops, transforming into something else.

I draw in a ragged breath and collapse on my bed, staring up at the ceiling. My phone is buzzing with texts. Probably Callie or Casey asking about dinner. Holland making sure we're cool after our conversation. Kenneth reminding us about some minor bullet point on an appendix no one saw or remotely cares about.

I take my phone and shove it in the drawer of the nightstand. Tonight, I'm alone. Just me and the pain. Just the brutal quarantine of this vile infection.

THE BATTLE with myself does not go well. By the following morning I'm exhausted from my fitful sleep and tormented thoughts. I had ignored a few knocks on the door since locking myself inside, and turned off my phone when the constant buzzing finally pushed me over the edge.

I'm actually somewhat surprised no authorities were called, or at least a hotel manager to come inspect the room for a body. But Holland must have assured them I was very much alive and stable when she released me back inside.

I don't feel like getting up, I don't feel like doing anything, which is why I know I absolutely have to do one thing. I retrieve the phone from my nightstand and brace myself as I turn it on. Sure enough, the display floods with texts and missed calls, but I don't bother with them. That's not what I need right now. I search through my contacts, find the name, and place the call. It's a little early for her, but I'm hoping she'll be willing to take my drama anyway.

She does.

"Luke, I'm glad you called. How are you?" she asks, and the concern in her voice dissolves every bit of strength left in my own.

"Not good," I manage, the tears filling my eyes as I try to blink them away. God, I'm so pathetic. The anger returns, and I'm grateful for that at least. I'd rather hate myself than pity myself.

"What's going on? Tell me about it."

I suck in my breath. I don't know exactly. I just know whatever it is can't continue or I'll lose myself again. I slid far last night and I'm still spiraling.

"I had a really bad night," I whisper. I hate that it comes out in a whisper. "Fucking awful," I add, firmer this time. It sounds forced, and I know she'll know I'm trying to cover up my weakness. She's really good at what she does.

"I can hear in your voice it was a bad night. Are you able to identify any..."

"Triggers. Yeah, a fucking train-wreck of a trigger."

"Ok, that's a start. Why don't you tell me a little about that. Can you see that maybe you're using some exaggerated language?"

I clench my fist. I like my train-wreck metaphor. I hate when she takes them away from me. "Fine. Not a train-wreck, but it was pretty damn close."

"What happened?"

I sigh. "I don't know. It's a long story."

"I have time," she says, and the gentleness in her voice soothes some of the resistance inside me.

Closing my eyes, I draw in a deep breath. "Maybe some of it is worth talking about."

"Then let's talk about it."

I HATE to admit that I feel a lot better after my impromptu counseling session with my therapist, Dr. Flynn. If you would have told me a year ago, hell, at any point in my life, that I'd not only call a shrink to help me through a crisis, but actually be glad I did, I would have laughed. No, I would have punched you. But man, it works sometimes. Talking. Having someone understand without judgment. Letting them give you perspective because god knows your perspective can get so screwed up you can't even see a straight line let alone walk it.

I'm interrupted by knocking again, but this time, manage to roll out of bed and make my way to the door. It's Callie, with a bag of something and a hyper-concerned look on her face. I still don't want to leave my island, but I've been a dick long enough over the last few hours and open the door.

"Oh my gosh!" she cries, throwing her arms around me. I know she has dozens of questions loaded to fire at me, but I'm grateful she holds off. Instead, her embrace tells me everything I need to know about how worried she was and relieved she is to be here now. "I brought you breakfast," she mumbles into my chest.

I force a smile. "Thank you. I'm ok," I assure her. She pulls away and looks up at me, searching my eyes. I can't tell if she believes me, but she at least accepts my answer. She pulls out her phone.

"Ok. I'm going to let Casey know you're all right. We were all really worried."

"I'm fine. I was just tired," I lie. I'm fixed now. No point reliving the whole thing again. Ok fine, not fixed, but fixed enough. By the end we'd traded the word "train-wreck" for "setback." That's a freaking miracle in itself.

"The hotel had these cute breakfast-to-go bags. Since you missed dinner, I was pretty sure you'd be hungry."

"Yeah, I am a little. Thanks."

She's still staring but I don't want to invite her in. If I do, I'll have to talk, and that's not happening.

"Hey, I was just about to jump in the shower," I lie again. I feel badly, but it's more for her sake than mine. "Catch up with you later?"

She gives me a weak smile. She knows I'm in one of my "moods," I can tell. "Sure, yeah. We're all going over to the outlets. You should come."

I cringe at the thought of another group outing with Wes and the gang. "Thanks, but I think I'm just going to hang around the hotel a bit today. The pools and hot tubs looked pretty sweet."

"They are. We were down there last night. We tried to get you to join us."

"I know. Thanks for thinking of me."

She scrunches her face. "Thanks for thinking of you? Seriously? Ugh, you drive me crazy sometimes," she mutters, and I grin.

"Sorry."

"Of course we think of you, silly! Ok, well, I'll let you shower and do your thing...although, really? Shower before going in the pool?"

I shrug, and she shakes her head. "Whatever. You better do dinner with us tonight though, ok?"

"I will," I assure her. She seems to relax a bit at that.

"Fine. Call us if you change your mind about the outlets. I think they want to head out in an hour or so."

I'M PRETTY COMMITTED to my idea of not going to the outlets, and head down to the pools instead once I'm sure it's safe. There isn't a lot of activity around the pools yet, which works nicely for me as I lower myself into an unoccupied hot tub. I close my eyes and rest my head on the concrete edge, loving the sound of the waves and feel of the warm water embracing every part of my body. Even better is the way the peace of both transports me out of my head to a place where I can get some much needed relief from the constant storm.

It doesn't last long.

"Fancy meeting you here." The voice crashes into my serenity, and my body reacts like it always does when she's close. Oh shit, especially in that bikini.

"Morning. You didn't want to go to the outlets?" I ask, somehow managing not to sound remotely as unbalanced as I feel.

She laughs and descends into the water with me. The struggle intensifies as she brushes past but she mercifully sits across from me, far out of reach.

"Nah, we're at the beach! I can shop anywhere. What about you?"

I shrug and close my eyes again. "Same, I guess. I was afraid I'd be as bad at outlet shopping as I am at mini golf. My ego can't handle another blow."

"Not possible," she snickers, and I can't stop the grin that spreads across my lips.

Even without looking, I can sense her watching me. I feel her eyes all over my body in the saturated silence, exploring me the same way I've explored her in a constant, exasperating loop. I've seen it several times over the last couple days, suffered the effects, but I can't be critical. I'd be doing the same if I weren't using all my energy to keep mine closed.

"Patrick," I blurt against the silence, finally letting go and looking at her.

Her expression is about what I expected, and I smile. "My middle name. Luke Patrick Craven."

She doesn't respond at first. I can tell that one word means a lot to her, and I feel good about my gift.

"I like that," she says finally, her eyes connecting with mine.

I nod, and lean back again. "It was my father's name. Patrick."

"Were you and he close?" she asks. "You mentioned him the other day with the guitar."

I take a breath. "Yeah. He died when I was eleven."

"I'm so sorry, Luke," she says, and I can hear the compassion in her voice. It scares me a little, what her empathy does to me.

I just shrug. "It was a long time ago."

"Yeah, but still. I'm pretty close to my parents. That had to be hard."

I focus on her again. My heart is racing at the direction of this conversation, but for some reason, I'm still here. I haven't run yet. Maybe I won't for once.

"It was. I was very close to my dad."

"What about your mom?"

A harsh laugh escapes before I can stop it. "Yeah, right. No. Not my mom."

She's studying me with a disturbing intensity, and I sigh. I've invited this. It's my own fault.

"She was a junkie," I explain. "Not much interest in kids."

I look away again. I can't handle her expression, and I'm not surprised when she doesn't respond. It's my stupid sob story, I know. There's a reason I hate talking about my past. It does nothing but make all of us regret the conversation in the first place. I didn't even get to the bad part.

"Anyway, what about you?" I ask before things get too awkward.

She shakes her head. "We're talking about you. So how'd you end up here?"

I stare at her in disbelief. Even Callie doesn't push this

hard. "Trust me, you don't want to know any more than you do."

"Oh, trust me, I do," she returns. "Actually, I can't think of anything I want to know more at the moment." She's not flirting. She's completely serious, and my stomach drops. There are precious few people on this planet who know more than what I've just told her.

"What do you want to know?" I manage finally.

Her smile softens me in ways I'll never understand. "How about we start with what you're willing to tell me, and work our way up from there."

I return her smile and shake my head, knowing my walls are in for the assault of a lifetime. "You're optimistic."

"And you're stalling. Talk. How'd you end up here?"

I draw in a deep breath. "Ok, fine. My mom hooked up with some other junkie loser after my dad died, they made my life a living hell for a few years, then finally decided even that was too much, and shipped me off to her sister in Houston."

"Houston? Wow, that's far. Aren't you from Johannesburg or something?"

I glance at her in surprise, unable to stop my grin. "You did your research, I see."

"Well, when your manager says you're touring with Night Shifts Black, yeah, you do research. You didn't look me up?"

I'm actually a bit embarrassed and give her a shy shrug. "Sorry."

She only laughs and shakes her head. "Wow. Thanks."

"If it makes you feel any better, I believe my exact words when our manager told us we'd be touring with you were, 'Sweet. They're legit,'" I offer in exchange. "Bringing you on board was actually Casey's idea. He's been impressed with you guys and told TJ to make it happen."

Holland looks pleased, and I love that I've made up for my

previous disappointment. "Really? Wow. I'm honored. Casey is extremely talented."

"And has excellent taste," I add, but regret it when her direct gaze and grateful smile shred my shield again.

"And, now you're back to stalling. Keep going."

I sigh. "You got the story. There's not much else."

"Yeah, right," she smirks. "You've barely started. I want to hear the rest. All of it."

I grunt. "Really? Come on." My tone was too dark. I immediately know my deflection has failed, which only makes me defensive.

"Yes, really. I want to hear about your childhood, your dad, your junkie mom."

"No, I guarantee you don't. No one wants to hear about that shit."

"It's not 'shit' to me."

"It doesn't even matter anymore."

"Of course it matters! And the fact that you refuse to talk about it shows how much."

She's being way too pushy, and I hate that I can't hate her for it. I especially hate the fact that she's so genuine, part of me feels like she's earned the question. And all of that just makes the other part want to punish her with the answer. I feel my muscles tense, my heart harden as my grimace spreads into a glare.

"Really. So you want details about what it's like to be an eleven-year-old kid forced to take care of yourself and two adults who hate everything about you and wish you didn't exist? About getting pushed around, going hungry, being told you're a worthless piece-of-shit who should probably just disappear. That's how we're going to spend our afternoon at the beach?"

I stop. Suck in air. Something just happened and I can't look at her. I know I won't like what I see.

"Yeah, I do," she replies quietly after a long silence, and I glance up. Her eyes reach deep inside of me, and before I can fight it, I feel something softening. It's almost painful as the strength in her gaze mixes with what I think might be tears in her eyes. It's hard to tell in a hot tub. "I really do, Luke," she whispers.

I swallow, terrified of the fact that I might actually share my story with her. Most of that part was off limits even to Dr. Flynn. I think she senses my hesitation, that she's losing me, and moves to close the physical distance between us. My stomach is in knots, from her, from the memories. The ancient pain. When she takes my hand, I'm not sure what to do with the war raging inside me.

"Why Houston? How did your mother's sister get to Houston?"

We're compromising. I sigh, grateful. That one's much easier.

"That's where she's from."

"Who?"

"Both, really. My mom and her sister."

Holland straightens in surprise, and I almost laugh at her look. "Wait. Your mom is American?"

I grin and nod. "Yes. So am I."

"Um...ok, I don't remember reading that. But your dad wasn't, obviously."

I shake my head. "No. They met in Johannesburg while my mom was modeling, so we lived there."

"Is your mom still alive?"

I shrug. "I have no idea. I doubt it."

She settles against me, still grasping my hand, and once again I marvel at the effect of her touch. "Wow. I guess that answers my questions about immigration and work visas. And why you're so damn beautiful."

I laugh. "You're not even kidding about that are you."

I can feel her grin. "Maybe." Then she grows serious again. "Ok, so now you're what, thirteen, fourteen? And in Houston with your aunt. Tell me about the music."

"The music, huh."

"It's in you, Luke. Deeply embedded like no one I've ever met. I've seen it a couple times now. It takes my breath away. Do you not get what it does to people when they witness it?"

I stare at the palm trees lining the pool area as I consider her words, strangely touched, uneasy. "The music..." I repeat to myself. Facts I can do.

"Ok, well, I guess it started with my dad actually. He was a musician. He knew he was dying and gave me his guitar. He told me it was so that I'd take care of it, but I always knew it was supposed to be a lifeline for me to hold onto after he was gone." I quiet, my chest getting heavy again. I close my eyes and draw in a deep breath. "He knew what would happen next," I continue quietly. "He fought as hard as he could for as long as he could. Somehow, even as a kid I sensed he didn't want to leave me alone with her." I stop again. I can't do any more with that part and draw in a ragged breath before I lose myself. I only agreed to facts. "Anyway, so yeah. It was just me and my guitar most days. When I was scared, lonely, hungry, in pain, Percy was always there, pulling my head back above water. I guess that's where the music came from."

"Percy?" she asks. I glance over at the wavering in her voice and now I'm certain I can see a glisten in her eyes.

I swallow and quickly look away. "Yeah, I named my guitar Percy. I have no idea why. It was my best friend, often my only one. Too important not to have a name, I guess."

She nestles closer, and I can feel my own guard slipping. I'm not crying in front of her. It's not going to happen.

"What? You've never named one of your instruments?" I ask before I get lost back in that horrible place.

She chuckles. "No, but I am now. I think my guitar would be Sam."

I grin. "Sam? Boy Sam or girl Sam?"

"I don't know. It doesn't matter. That's why I like Sam."

"Ok, that's fair. Sam it is."

"Where's Percy now?" she asks.

"In my room."

She pulls away again, and I love the look on her face. "Really? You still have him?"

I laugh. "Of course. He goes with me everywhere."

"I want to meet him!" she cries.

My eyes widen in disbelief. "What, like right now?"

"Yes! Right now! You need to introduce us." She jumps up from the seat and moves toward the stairs. "Come on!"

It's all so funny, so sweet, I can't even argue with her. "Ok! Geez. I'm coming."

She tosses a towel at me as I reach the deck, and this time doesn't even pretend not to study me as I dry off. It's fine. I've given up pretending I'm not captivated by her.

"God, you're pretty much perfect, aren't you," she mutters, and I glance at her, then laugh.

"Um...did you not hear a word I just said? I'm a fucking disaster."

She doesn't smile, which surprises me. "Maybe, but we're all disasters. Perfection is finding that one disaster that makes sense with yours."

I don't know what to do with that. She's confusing me again with her maddening push and pull. "I thought we agreed my particular disaster wasn't good for anyone."

It comes out more bitter than I intended, but her "honesty" is starting to grate on me. We can't be together. Got it. So then why are we still pretending? Why is she still sending these cryptic signals? And why the hell is she looking at me like she wants to shove me against the wall and rip my shorts off? My pulse is attacking my will again.

"I'm sorry. You're right. I'm not being fair," she admits quietly, and I feel badly for hurting her. She wasn't being fair, but I can tell she truly understands her offence and regrets her lack of control. The thing is, I understand it. I can't control myself around her either. We're playing with fire, we both know it, and we're both dangerously addicted. It's all right there in the pulsating tension between us. The looks, the stolen touches, the simmering flame just waiting for us to show weakness and explode into something we can't restrain.

"Look, maybe we should just cancel this whole 'friends' thing," I say after a long pause. Her eyes shoot to mine, and I soften. "I just don't know how to be friends with you, Holland. And I think you're having the same problem."

"Luke..."

I give her a sad smile and sling the towel over my shoulder. "I'm not upset. I have complete respect for you and your rules. I even agree with them. I'm not sure I'm ready for a relationship anyway. I may never be, and even if I was, no one would be ready for one with me."

"Luke...stop..."

"No, it's ok. Seriously, thanks for the time we've had. It really has been amazing, but we're not helping ourselves by doing this." I start toward the door of the building.

"Luke!"

I know I owe her a chance to speak as well, but I don't think I can handle it. She has this way of cutting through my walls, and I need them as strong as possible right now. I keep going.

"Luke, please! Just stop for one second!"

I close my eyes. I can't, can I? But god, I want to so badly.

I sigh and turn, immediately regretting it. She's there, inches away.

"No," she says. "No, it's not ok." And her lips collide with mine.

My body erupts in an immediate rush of fire I know I'll never contain. I let her push me back against the wall of the pool deck, her fingers locked in my hair, mine in hers, pulling ourselves into each other. I can feel my skin absorbing hers with a desperation that's knocking the air from our lungs. Minutes, hours, days of starvation explode on us, finally unleashing that reckless exploration of the forbidden. Our mouths, our hands, fight for every inch they can control, struggling to connect in an impossible union that will lead to the one place we both agreed we can't go. We won't go.

And suddenly, I'm terrified. How much of this is her? Me? How much is my need to be close to someone again? Her getting sucked into my deadly vortex? How much am I going to destroy her when this all crashes down? Because it will. It's going to crash so hard and I'm going to have another victim I care about on my conscience.

I groan and push her away. "Stop! Wait." My body is screaming. It's never going to forgive me for this. I can see the hunger in her eyes as well, just ravaging us as we stare, breathing hard.

"This isn't what you really want," I whisper, searching her eyes with an anguish she returns.

"It is, Luke. I do. Please." Her lips find mine again, her fingers sliding down my chest, circling my waist in a grip that sends my blood pounding to every cell, every recess of my being. She's tugging at my suit now, lower, oh god. She's so close, I know she can feel every hard inch of how much I want her too. She positions herself perfectly to invite it all, and I swear I hear the slightest groan as she pulls my hips into hers in an impossible invitation. Her intoxicating form is totally surrendered, her mouth denying me any arguments as she breathes me in. I'm going to lose if I don't stop this. We both will. Oh shit. A couple years ago I wouldn't have thought twice and now...

It takes every ounce of self-hatred I have left to force her hands away and gently push her back. "No. No!" I search her eyes. "You're about to hook up with me. You don't hook up with musicians, especially on tour."

She shakes her head and closes the gap again, taking my face in her hands. "I know, but I don't care about the rules anymore. The rules are bullshit!"

I flinch and pull away. "No, they're not. They're important to you. And they're good. So good... Don't you see what's happening? This is what I do to people, Holland! This is how I hurt them! I infect them and turn them against themselves. I'm not doing it anymore. I'm not doing it to you!"

I know she's hurt, but I'm completely gutted as I remove her hands from me and launch toward the lobby. This time, I'm running from myself as much as her.

"Luke, stop! Wait!"

She's coming after me, but I don't stop. I can't. I'm not strong enough to keep fighting this. I frantically press the button to the elevator, but of course it doesn't open in time to rescue us from this mess. She catches up just in time to jump in with me.

"We're talking about this," she states firmly. "You wanted that as much as I did. You still do. I know you do!"

I shake my head. "There's nothing else to say." I barely even notice the chill of the air conditioning on my wet body as the ice inside spreads to the surface. I can feel it begin to calm the fire, dissolve the warmth. I'm able to shutdown better than anyone.

"So what, you're just going to deny what's happening between us?"

"No, I'm going to ignore it," I quip.

"What? How can you possibly ignore what just happened?"

I only shrug, knowing it'll upset her. She curses and throws up her hands. "Seriously? God, you're infuriating!"

I study the light moving over each number above the door. One... Two... Three.

"Again, as advertised, right?"

She's about to explode as she turns on me. "No! That's bull-shit and you know it! You're scared. You're scared because I mean something to you. Because I got behind your glass barrier, didn't I? Because our connection is more than sex and you have no clue what to do with that!"

"Yep, that's it. I'm scared. So original, Holland." God, what a dick thing to say, but I need her to hate me. I'll never be strong enough to push her away if she doesn't.

Her glare turns hostile, and I wonder if she's actually going to hit me. She doesn't, but her eyes do it for her.

"Wes is a better match for you anyway. You should stalk him instead," I continue for good measure. It works, and this time I can see her visibly shake in anger.

"Excuse me?"

I offer a casual shrug. "I mean, it's obvious there's some-thing going on there. I bet he doesn't come with the same baggage. Does your rule apply to your own band?"

"You have no idea what the hell you're talking about!"

"No? Come on, Holland. You're lying to yourself if you can't see your guitar player has it bad for you. He's doing every-thing he can to keep me away from you."

Fire burns in her eyes. "Oh, because you know us so damn well? Like I said, you have no idea what you're talking about! Is that what this is about? Wes?"

The elevator arrives at our floor and I get out. She follows, but I don't stop.

"No, this is about us," I call back with devastating nonchalance. I've always been a master at channeling my uncanny ability to read people into the ability to cut them with precision. "You're the one who told me out of the gate it can't happen. I'm just respecting your wishes."

I pull my key out and slide it into my door. But instead of the rage I expect, she softens, her face covered with her sudden desperate plea for me. I can't look. Oh god, I can't look.

"Luke, come on. I know whatever this is right now isn't real. I know this isn't you."

"Oh, it's real," I lie. "I thought you did your research."

"No! It's not. I saw you yesterday with those kids! Your smile! The music! I saw what…"

She takes a step toward my door, and I slam it shut.

"Luke!" she cries, pounding once in frustration. "You asshole!" The wounded tears in her voice are wrecking me. "You're a fucking asshole, you know that?!"

Yes. I know that.

I slide to the floor, head on my knees, and completely shatter.

I'M functional again by dinnertime, but have no interest in seeing Holland or Wes. I return Callie's text letting me know they're back from the outlets, and ask if they want to go out with just the three of us. I miss our time together. Callie, Casey, me. Those few months in my suite were some of the best of my life, and a huge reason why I'm even here to miss them. I need them right now. I need to be just the three of us again.

Callie writes back that they're fine with my plan, and an hour later we find ourselves at a steakhouse. Supposedly, this place is a must for anyone visiting Myrtle Beach, and I like the atmosphere the second we step inside. It's upscale, but still laid-back in its own way, and we're seated fairly quickly. We don't seem to be recognized, which I appreciate. It was a rough day and I'm in the mood to disappear.

"Find anything good at the outlets?" I ask, after we're seated and have placed our drink orders. Casey and Callie exchange a look, and I fold my arms. "What?"

Callie grins, and I swear Casey is blushing.

"Nothing," Callie covers quickly. "No, we didn't buy anything interesting. Just some clothing and stuff."

I give them a skeptical look. "Really. So why's your face about to explode, Case?" I ask.

Casey glares at Callie. "You said we wouldn't tell anyone."

My eyes widen as I lean forward. "Tell anyone what? I don't count as 'anyone,' do I?"

Callie is grinning so broadly I can barely stay seated.

"Wait...No..." I breathe.

She just shrugs and leans into Casey, taking his arm.

"You're not...no..."

"Not officially, no. But we've been talking about it. You know, one day."

My jaw is on the floor and the warmth returns, starting to melt the freshly frozen barrier on my soul. There is nothing better that could be happening at this moment.

I grip the table. "Are you freaking serious?" I whisper, and Casey returns my grin.

"Calm down, man. We're just talking."

"Yeah, but..."

"We may have looked at rings today just for fun," Callie whispers back.

Casey gives her a gentle shove, and she giggles.

"What? Oh my...That's amazing! That's..." I'm totally speechless. "I'm so happy!"

"Like we said, it's not official so don't say anything! We've only been together a few months," Casey explains. "It's just...I don't know. It feels right, you know?" And I seriously think I might lose my shit at the looks on their faces as they gaze into each other's eyes.

"Wow, this is...this is definitely not how I thought this conversation was going to go," I laugh, leaning back in my seat. "You two are so great together. I'm so happy for you, you have no idea."

Callie's smile fades as she searches my eyes. "Thank you, Luke. You mean everything to us. You know that, right? No matter what happens, it's always the three of us against the world, got it?"

I smile and nod. "Callie Roland Straight Talk. Got it."

She laughs, and Casey just looks confused.

"Huh?" he says.

"Nothing, hon. Hey! They have those ribs you like!" she cries, pointing at the menu.

"Those ribs?"

"Yeah! The little ones with the BBQ sauce!"

Casey casts me an amused glance. "Um...you mean baby back ribs?"

"Yes!"

"Cal, I love you, but every place has 'those ribs.'"

She scrunches her nose. "Not every place."

"Most places."

"Ugh, fine! Anyway, you should get them."

Casey laughs. "Why? Because *you* want them? Why don't

you just get them?"

"What if I don't like them?"

"Then I'll eat them."

"What if you don't like them?"

"You already know I do. Isn't that what started this conversation?"

"Oh my gosh! You're so annoying," she groans, glaring back at her menu.

Casey only laughs and tucks his arm around her shoulders. I'm freaking melting inside, and puking, but mostly melting. They just make you think you've got a shot at life. Every. Single. Time.

"What about you? How were the pools?" Callie asks me, immediately slamming a pickax into my contentment.

I force a smile. "Great. The hot tub was great. Didn't do much swimming."

She nods. "Looks like you got a little sun. I'm glad. I worry about you and your vampire tendencies."

I smile again, dreading the moment when she finds out how badly I screwed things up with Holland. I'm still haunted by it all, even though I did the right thing, the humane thing. I did what had to be done. For all of us. But just when I think I've got the pain under control, I remember our song, how the music brought us together and connected us in a way I've never felt before, not even with Elena. I loved Elena so much, but we didn't share the music. I never felt my soul suck another in like it had at that moment with Holland. I didn't even know it was possible and now I'm a hostage.

"You ok?" Callie asks, concerned, and I force myself to refocus.

"Yeah, of course. Why?"

She's still looking at me, as is Casey. I thought it would be a good idea to be alone with them, but now I'm not so sure.

"Your face changed. You look darker all of a sudden."

I laugh, but I doubt anyone believes it. "I'm fine. Just hungry. You know what you're getting?"

They let me off the hook, even though I know I've done a terrible job covering my tracks. They don't believe a word I'm saying, but are willing to let it go.

"Well, I'm getting the ribs, apparently," Casey mutters.

Callie's grin returns. "Yes! Thanks, hon. Love you."

He rolls his eyes and closes his menu. "Just don't get a salad. Because if we're switching meals, there's no way in hell I'm trading ribs for lettuce."

MOST OF THE group wants to hang out at the hot tubs and drink again that night. Since I no longer drink and would rather stab myself in the eye than face Holland right now, I pass in favor of an evening alone with Percy.

I love the view from my balcony and decide to take full advantage of it while I can. Something about the moon reflecting off the ocean appeals to me, and I stare at it for a long time, absently strumming several progressions that have been in my head for a while. The chords are far removed from my usual patterns, but they're beautiful and particularly haunting in the darkness.

I can hear the laughter from the pool deck below and I'm glad they're having such a good time. I'm not jealous of other people's happiness, just confused by it. I guess, deep down, I long for it too, I just don't understand it or how to let myself accept it. Callie's words had struck hard that day at lunch. She was right. I do deny myself, but I don't know how to embrace happiness when it almost always seems to be a zero-sum game for me. My happiness in exchange for someone else's misery.

I'm not doing that anymore. I'm protecting Holland. Our song was beautiful but it shouldn't exist in my universe.

I close my eyes and start humming along with the guitar. Words begin to filter in with the notes, which are becoming clear patterns. There's a song forming, I can sense the pieces snapping into place in my head. My strumming becomes more deliberate, my voice stronger.

> "Guide me toward the light, I swear I'll follow.
> Forgive me for the man I am.
> Fight the hollow ghost I carry.
> I've learned to hide the tears,
> Though they still break me.
>
> Search for me, the broken wanderer
> Find me, deep within my own void
> Save me, from my burning lies
> Don't believe what I am
>
> I'm a fallen angel,
> The disease you can't understand
> I'm the reason you've lost faith, your sin
> But I'm a liar, don't believe me, please don't
>   believe me
>
> Guide me toward the light, I swear I'll follow
> Hold me til the hollowness is gone
> These tears mean nothing in the darkness
> Don't believe what I am.
> I need you to believe when I can't
> That I'm more, more than I am."

It's not until I stop playing, the waves once again filling the darkness with their chorus, that I realize the party below is silent as well.

————

I WAKE up the next morning to a slip of paper under my door. I pick it up and try to calm my racing heart as I scan the elegant text.

> You are a liar, Luke, and a damn good one. But no one can ever believe enough for you, not until you do. I hope you find your peace.
>
> - H

6

CHARLOTTE, NORTH CAROLINA

SEPTEMBER 20

It's going to be another brutal stretch: Charlotte, Richmond, and Baltimore. Three stops in three days. Kenneth started hyperventilating the second we boarded the bus in Myrtle Beach, and Tess is doing her best to keep everyone else from quitting. For my part, I'm content just lying low, trying to survive our schedule and my own twisting brain as best I can. I exhaust *myself.* I can't imagine what it's like for other people to deal with me.

I'm on my way to catering to grab something to eat when I catch a glimpse of Jesse, Limelight's frontman, release an angry curse at his phone before shoving it in his pocket. I change course and approach him, squinting against the mid-day sun.

"Everything ok?" I ask. Jesse seems startled, then embarrassed.

"Oh, hey, Luke. Yeah, fine."

I smile to disarm the moment. "You seemed pretty upset at your phone," I observe, and he grunts, running his hand through his shoulder-length hair. He's a good kid, extremely talented, but he makes Casey seem ancient. I'd be surprised if he's all of twenty-two. It was a huge break for Jesse and the Limelight boys to book this tour with us, but it's also a lot to absorb for your first major spotlight.

Limelight was an up-and-coming local Philly band when the Label stumbled upon them to open for our tour. A regional phenomenon, but relatively unknown nationally. Not anymore. I feel for the kid. I know how seductive instant success can be. I also know how devastating. It nearly destroyed me, and I'll admit, I've been secretly keeping my eye on Jesse since the tour began. He has an epic voice for such a young kid and an enviable instinct for music, but also the same doe-eyed approach to Celebrity that almost put me in the ground. Several times.

"The Label hated my work tape," he mutters, glaring at the pavement. "I really thought this one had something, but they don't even want to pursue it."

I sigh. "Yeah. Been there."

He looks up again, surprised. "Wait, really? They've rejected your stuff?"

I laugh. "Um, yeah. Like, all the time."

"Seriously? They said no to Luke Craven? No way."

I shake my head with a grin and sit on the ledge beside him.

"Ok, well, first off, I wasn't always *Luke Craven*. I used to just be Luke Craven, some dude from some band called Night Shifts Black. And second of all, yeah. They own you, man. Mind, body, and soul. Didn't anyone warn you you were selling your soul when you signed?"

"Hell, no," he spits, and scrapes at a crack in the sidewalk with his shoe. "I just wanted to play music. That's all I ever wanted. I didn't know about all this other shit."

I nod and sigh. "Yeah, that's all any of us wanted in the beginning. But that's not the way it works, unfortunately. Every success comes with a new burden of expectations. Each reward has a higher price. You keep going until you reach the threshold of what you can afford to pay." I smile. "Or at least until you can afford to pay someone else to bear the brunt of it for you."

Jesse laughs. "Is that where you're at?"

I smirk. "I wish."

His smile fades as he stares off into the distance. "It's not what I thought. All of this," he muses, waving his hand in front of him. "I mean, it's like this dream you have forever. And then, bam, it happens, but it doesn't even seem like it's happening. You just keep living the moment, surviving it. It's just another day, like yesterday. I thought there'd be magic or something when it happened. Makes you wonder if it's even real, you know? That sounds stupid."

"No. It's not stupid. I know exactly what you mean." I follow his distant stare as I consider my response. "Look, you have to just stop and take a breath," I continue, surprising myself with my sage tone. He looks over at me, and I can see the respect in his gaze. I meet it, a sudden protectiveness washing over me. "You have to force yourself to stop each day and look around. Give yourself a chance to enjoy the reality of the moment because there are no real endings, no bookmarks for your life to guide you. It just keeps going until it's over, and it's up to you to pick a point in time to stop and consider where you are."

I pause and point at his tour bus. "See that right there? That's all you. You made it, Jess. You made it. So stop for a second and enjoy your dream. Think about what you'd be doing if you weren't here and be grateful you are."

He snickers. "I'd be in prison probably."

I grin and shrug. "Me too. But that's what I'm saying. You're not. You're here. In a few hours you're going to be paid some serious money to do something you'd do for nothing. Forget the rest of this crap. The music is what matters. Forget the Label, the schedule, the press, the criticism, the reviews.

They will devour you alive if you let them. You have to stop the avalanche each day and focus on the one truth that matters: you have the opportunity to spend your life doing what you love. The rest is only important to the extent that it allows you to continue doing that."

He doesn't respond right away, but I can see him considering my words. No one is more surprised than I am by my speech, and I had no idea how much I'd learned, how much I'd grown over the last few years until it came pouring out.

"I know you're right. I do, it's just so hard to have your heart shoved back at you and hear it sucks. That someone hates something you love. It's like people don't think you're real. You're just some idea or something, and they take pleasure in shredding you just because they can. The worst part is, you can't even fight back and defend yourself!"

I sigh. Yeah. If anyone can understand that...

"The more people love you, the more others will hate you. The higher they perceive your pedestal, the more pleasure they take in knocking you down. You've exposed yourself, Jesse, made yourself vulnerable. Whether you thought about what you were doing or not, it doesn't matter. It's too late. By deciding to pursue your dream, you've opened yourself up to the good and the bad. And you're right. You're no longer Jesse Everett, the kid from Philly. You're now a shiny object without feelings, a punching bag for hate and other people's biases and issues.

"But, Jesse, it'll break you if you let it. I'm telling you, from personal experience, you cannot take your worth from what others think, good or bad, because they're not judging *you*, they're displaying themselves, their prejudices, their fears and hopes. All you've done is trigger a reaction in them, and sometimes it's beautiful, and sometimes it backfires, but that doesn't make it a statement about who you are. Criticism isn't about the person who created the art, just about how your art fits into someone else's world."

He closes his eyes, and I smile to myself. I'm not sure if any of this is getting through, but I sense it is. Jesse always seemed like a smart kid, a tough kid from the little I know about him, and I'm betting we have a lot more in common than we even realize at this point. He's got a story, like so many of us, and he's clearly a warrior. A damn talented one from what I've seen.

"Can I hear what you've got?" I ask after a long silence. It's hilarious the way he tries to cover his shock as he glances over at me again.

"Really?"

I laugh. "Yeah, of course. Grab your guitar. Let's see what we can do."

"Oh my...seriously? You're serious."

I roll my eyes. "You want to do this or not?"

I'M ONSTAGE MESSING with one of my amps when I sense someone's attention. I glance up and immediately stiffen at Holland's crooked grin.

"Hey, stranger. Did Gary quit on you or something? Do I need to lend you my guy this time?"

I return her smile with a shy one of my own. "Nah, I'm just fooling around. I wanted to try something for a song I'm working on."

"Oh, so intriguing! Do tell. Is it about a perplexing, super hot rocker who sucks you in with glimpses of vulnerability then acts like a total asshole?"

I stare at her in shock, then grin when she does. I laugh and look away, praying I'm not blushing as I focus back on my amp. And she's not even done with me.

"Ok, so, I wasn't sure how this works. Are we not supposed to talk at all now? Do we have to do the awkward silence thing the rest of the tour or what?" She lowers herself to the drum riser a few feet away. "I'm not used to blatant rejection, so I'm not exactly sure what happens next."

I return her grin again, I can't help it, and I'm terrified I actually am blushing now. "Um...I'm not used to acting like an ass to people I care about, so I don't know either."

"Ok, really? Really... 'Cause there was definitely a stunning display of asshole expertise there."

I laugh again and shake my head, trying to focus, but know there's no chance of that with Holland Drake in my line of sight.

"Well, it is a learned art-form, I'm not gonna lie. I'd teach you, but I doubt you could pull it off."

It's her turn to snicker, and we connect with a quick glance before both looking away. I don't know if this is awkward, but it's not hostile, and that's more than I ever could have hoped for after the way I acted.

"I heard you the other night. On your balcony," she continues.

I swallow, but don't look up. "Yeah? I figured, based on your note."

"You got it then," she observes.

"Yep."

Silence. I can feel her amusement. "That's it? 'Yep'?"

I meet her gaze again. "Yes. Yes, I got it."

She stares at me in disbelief, and finally grins when I do. "You're ridiculous, you know that?"

I smile. "Sometimes. And thanks, Holland. Really. Your note meant a lot." I don't need to tell her I stuffed it in my pocket and actually have it on me now. That I've read it about a hundred times and it still stirs something deep inside that scares the crap out of me.

She shrugs and settles back into her seat. "You're welcome. I meant it, you know. I keep thinking about what happened, and I understand it all I think. I understand you. I know what you're doing. Why you push people away."

I turn back to my amp. It's a lot safer than the look on her face. "Yeah?"

"Yeah. You think you're protecting us or something. From yourself."

It takes everything in me not to react. "If that's really true, I'd highly recommend letting me do that," I say quietly, desperately hoping this amp can counteract the effect of her presence. I'm not optimistic.

"I saw you with Jesse, too. You two looked intense, so I'm guessing you were talking him through something."

"I'm not surprised since you stalk me, apparently."

She laughs, and I offer a quick smile before turning away again.

"I'm just saying, you really suck at being a dick. I mean, like really bad."

I laugh again, resting my forehead on the amp for a second before glancing back at her. "Yeah? Well, I used to be a lot better at it."

"So I've heard. Research and all that."

I shrug. She grows serious and studies me.

"Look, I'm sorry about what happened at the pool. I get it, I do. And I agree, we shouldn't have hooked up, even if you could have been a big boy in how you communicated your feelings instead of acting like a total ass. But I don't buy your final stance for one second. I do think we can be friends. In fact, I think we have to be in order to finish this tour, and I want to make it work. Can we do that? I promise, no sex until you're ready, darling."

"Oh my god," I laugh, amused, warmed, challenged, all at once. This woman... I shake my head. She's freaking amazing. There's no other explanation. "Of course. I'm sorry, too. Whether I was an effective dick or not, I shouldn't have tried, and I'm sorry. We'll make the friend thing work."

She slaps her knees before rising. "Ok, good. Oh, and one more thing. I want to steal some of that new bridge we did for 'Perfect Storm,' if you don't mind. Those incidentals you threw in and the extra couple lines after the verse were sick."

I grin. "Sure. But only if you let me come out for a cameo when you do it."

Her eyes widen, and I love that I'm finally able to shock her in a good way. "Wait, what? Are you serious?"

I shrug. "Yeah, I'd love to do 'Perfect Storm' with you on stage."

"No freaking way!"

I can't help but laugh. "Well, I mean, they're my incidentals so you owe me..."

"I owe *you*? Are you kidding me? Thank you! Luke...thank you!"

I can tell she's about to hug me, but thinks better of it. I'm glad because I'm not ready for that fight again either.

"How about tonight?" I suggest.

"Wait, tonight?"

I shrug. "Sure. Let's run it during your sound check."

She looks ready to explode with excitement and I wish I could capture everything about that moment. It's an amazing feeling. We're both happy at the same time. Who would have thought? Two separate conversations today, two different people, three grinning faces at the end. My vortex may cause pain, but maybe it can also do something else. I have no idea what to do with that thought.

"Just text me when you're ready," I say. "I'm gonna go grab a bite before they shut down catering. Kenneth will flip if I miss it."

TRACING Holland launches into the intro for "Perfect Storm," and the crowd absolutely explodes when I step out on stage. Holland and I exchange a grin before she makes a dramatic show of turning the lead mic over to me, complete with a playful bow.

I accept it with one of my own as she moves to another vocal mic without even missing a note on her guitar. We had decided that I wouldn't play along at tonight's show, although we want to do an acoustic version at a later date with both of us playing and singing. For now, I use all my energy and star-power to boost Tracing Holland into the stratosphere. I know this collaboration is going to be talked about, and love that I can use my influence for her benefit.

We brought the key down so I could sing lead, and Holland's voice once again captivates me with its wicked tone and razor-sharp harmonies. It's like we've been singing together for years, and I'm even able to ignore the tangible tension with Wes who's forced to stand behind me. I know he's despising every minute of this, every echo of the crowd's adulation for a duet that should not be happening. He didn't say a word during the sound check, and I was certain Holland must have warned him ahead of time, only because he didn't punch me in the face when I showed up. Even now, I'd expected the rush of the stage, or at the very least, a microscopic level of professionalism to mask his hatred, but no such luck. I make a point not to turn around again after one glimpse of his harsh glare four measures into the song.

"Luke Craven, everyone!" Holland cries into the mic as the final notes ring out to a symphony of wild cheering. I give Holland a quick hug before waving to the crowd and offering a slight bow. Then, I return the stage to her and try to think of a moment when I've ever felt better about being Luke Craven.

MY JOY DOESN'T last long. Casey and I come down off our high from the night's performance with an abrupt bombshell about Callie. She's not waiting for us backstage like usual, and I glance over at Casey who's scanning his phone with a dark expression.

"Shit!" he mutters.

"What is it? Where's Callie?" I ask, my heart slamming against my chest.

"On the bus," Casey answers, still glaring at his phone. I can see the fire in his eyes, sense the heat radiating from him. There's only one thing that makes him burn with that kind of fury: righteous anger. Injury to those he loves. I draw in a deep breath.

"What happened?"

The phone is now at his ear, and he holds up a finger to silence me for a second as he begins talking.

"Hey, Cal. Yeah, I got your messages. I saw. I know. I know, babe, I do. We just finished up. I'll be right there. It's gonna be ok. I know. Love you. I'll be right there."

He hangs up and meets my gaze.

"They dug up that damn grocery store story," Casey hisses. "You know, the lawsuit against her douchebag boss? It's all over the place...Dammit!"

"Oh shit," I reply, my stomach dropping. "How's she taking it?"

Casey shakes his head. "She's really upset. I saw some of the stuff they're saying. It's brutal, Luke," he whispers, looking back at me. "She doesn't deserve this bullshit." He runs his hand over his face. "Dammit, this is all my fault! They're only going after her because she's with me."

"Whoa, hang on," I interrupt. "Don't even start with that, Case. Do you honestly think Callie would change anything that's happened? That she'd trade you for a little privacy? Please. That girl loves you with all her heart, and you love her. This is nothing compared to the power of what you two have. We knew this would happen eventually. It always does. She knew the risks. Remember the chair mess?"

He curses again, and I know right then I'd do anything to fix this for them.

"No, I know," he says quietly, resignation clear in his voice. "I just hate this. It rips my heart out to see her hurt. Especially since you know this is only because she's dating me."

"Yeah, and because she's dating you, she has an amazing boyfriend she loves, a career, and a life most people would kill for." I place my hand on his shoulder and we exchange a solid glance. "Go be with her. Let me worry about the rest."

"What do you mean? What are you going to do?"

I suck in my breath. "I don't know yet, but don't worry about it. You worry about her right now, ok?"

"Luke, what are you going to do?"

I can't look at him. "Nothing. There's still a few hours before we roll out. I'm just gonna go think for a second."

I sense he's still concerned, but lets it go. He's more worried about Callie, as I want him to be.

"Come back with me. I'm sure Callie would love your support right now, too."

I force a smile. "I'll be there. She needs you first, though. Go be with her. I'll follow in a minute."

MY HEART BREAKS EVEN MORE when I board the bus. I can hear her crying in the back lounge where she's locked herself with Casey. My "thinking" turned out to be less fruitful than I'd hoped, but I'm still not ready to give up. I'm not exactly sure how to fight this, and hope something will come to me when I see her.

I notice Eli and Sweeny are already in their bunks, no doubt respecting Callie's privacy by pretending to sleep. My stakes are higher, however, and I'm not about to give her space right now. Not when she saved my life by butting into my nightmare.

I knock on the partition and the quiet murmuring stops. "It's Luke. Can I come in?"

I wait for a moment, wondering if they'll accept my role, and I'm relieved when the partition opens. I'm devastated at the look on Callie's face, her red eyes and tear-stained cheeks just tearing at my soul.

I close the partition again and lower myself to her other side on the couch.

"Casey told you," she whispers.

I nod. "He did."

I don't ask if she's ok. I know she's not. I always hated that question.

"Luke, it's bad," she whispers, staring at me, completely haunted. "They're saying we did it for the money. They're making *him* look like the victim! It's happening all over again!" She presses her palms against her eyes, and Casey wraps his arms around her. "This is why I left Shelteron in the first place!"

Casey and I exchange a glance over her shoulder, and I can feel the rage building. Casey isn't wired for rage like I am. He's built to be a pillar. I'm a freaking landmine, and I know there's no way we're leaving Charlotte before it explodes. I watch them in silence for a bit, my insides shredding at Callie's pain, but I have no idea what to say. I would do anything to make it stop, which only fuels the wrath at how helpless I feel. I'm not good at the talking part. I act, usually rashly, and in a way that gets me in trouble.

But, I just can't take it anymore. The sound of her tears is destroying me. I have no choice.

"Let me make some calls," I say, rising from the couch.

"What? What are you going to do?" Casey asks, glancing at me in surprise.

I suck in my breath. "I don't know. I'll be back later."

"Luke, what are you going to do? Where are you going?"

I can't look at him, at either of them, as I move from the room. "Nothing. Stop worrying. Just gonna get some air and make a few calls," I lie.

I sense he knows I'm lying, but I will die before letting him bear the burden of what I'm about to do.

"I love you, Callie," I say gently.

She glances up and melts my heart with a weak smile through her tears.

"I love you, too, Luke. Thank you."

I swallow and try not to choke as I close the partition.

7

RICHMOND, VIRGINIA

SEPTEMBER 21

The bigger news doesn't break until Richmond. At least, it doesn't hit our circle until 1:48PM EST. I get the angry call I'd been expecting first, and have no choice but to absorb the livid tirade from the conference room of the Label's headquarters. They don't understand why I'd screw everything up after all the patience and support they've shown me. Why I'd embarrass them, myself, everyone, just as we were starting to get our groove back. They're not going to fire me, we both know they can't, and I'm not sure why they even bother covering that point, except maybe to give themselves a segue into the part where they're extremely disappointed and hope I understand what a grand fuck-up I am.

The truth isn't exactly an option so I take it all in silence. Apologizing a few times, smarting from the blows I can't defend.

The phone call is easy compared to Casey and Callie's reactions.

"I don't understand! Why would you do this? Is it because

of me?" Callie cries, horrified, angry. Casey looks about the same as they confront me outside the bus just as I'm returning from the brutal lashing by the Label.

My stomach is already in knots and I try to brace myself, but I'm not sure how much more I can take. I see the disappointment on their faces, the questions, the betrayal. I'd been prepared for it all, just not for how much it would hurt. I hadn't realized I'd changed so much, that I actually cared enough about other people for their rejection to injure me. Apparently, feelings are actually real, and I have way more than I'd thought.

"No, of course not," I defend. "I don't know. I just ..." I'm not sure how to finish that sentence. I'm so tired of lying. I'm just exhausted in general.

"So what, you decided to 'fix it all' by partying? By throwing everything away, all that we've been fighting for?"

I've never seen Callie so angry.

Casey looks ready to outright punch me. "I can't believe you! Callie needed you last night and you go out and get wasted? What the hell is wrong with you?" Casey hisses, and I can barely breathe.

When the news broke about my wild slip-up last night, it broke violently. Callie's grocery assault faded almost instantly as the photos of me partying hard at a nightclub seemed to grace every entertainment website and news outlet known to humanity. The pictures pretty much speak for themselves, which comes as a relief since I don't have any other words right now.

"I'm sorry," I say quietly.

"You're sorry? What do you mean you're sorry? Luke, stop! At least talk to us! Make us understand!" Callie calls after me as I flee back toward the safety of the cavernous venue. There's no way I'm letting them trap me on the bus right now. I can hear Casey curse as I disappear into the building.

I TRY to avoid them all as much as possible, but apparently that doesn't amount to much in this latest nightmare. There's nowhere to hide. Not today, anyway, and it just keeps getting worse.

"The blonde on the left was cute," Holland quips as she passes me during my solitary journey to catering. "Not into the games, huh? Guess that just applies to beach games."

I glance at her briefly, my stomach constricting in a painful ache. Holland...I hadn't thought of her when I did it. Dammit! My impulse doesn't think. It just acts and leaves the consequences for my brain to sort out. That wasn't a problem when I didn't have a conscience. When I didn't have feelings. Poor choices work fine when you're numb. Now, it's crushing me.

I don't know how to respond. There are no words. I can't tell her the truth. No one can know. Not yet anyway. Not until Callie is safe. It's too soon.

Holland's not retreating as fast as she should be. She's hoping I answer her challenge. I don't know if she wants me to defend myself or fire back at her, but I can't bring myself to do either.

"You know what's funny, Luke? Since the day we met, I thought I was on to you. I thought I saw this good in you that you don't seem to want to acknowledge in yourself. Even now, I can still see something hiding in there, and yet, I'm starting to get it now. Like, really get it. It doesn't matter, does it? It doesn't matter if there's a light locked inside somewhere, because you will never let it shine. You will never let it out and you know it. That's why you pushed me away, why you push everyone away. Because that light is buried so deep, and terrifies you so much, that you'd rather just bask in the darkness by yourself than deal with how hard it is to fight for who you could be."

I can't move. I'm completely paralyzed as I stare at her. Her words have annihilated me. Her resignation. This is it. She's finally giving up for good. I've officially lost her.

"Thanks for not sucking me into your 'disaster,' I guess," she mumbles, but the pain in her expression betrays her. "I definitely didn't want to be 'blonde number three' in that photo. Kind of embarrassed I almost was."

I flinch, stung by the blow, but manage to wait until she disappears to completely dissolve into the shadows. I'm no longer worried about food. There's no way I'd be able to eat now anyway.

DESPITE THE DRAMA and tension behind the scenes, we put on a good show in Richmond. We're professionals, and I doubt there's a single audience member who knows how torn up I am inside. I can hide in plain sight better than any person on this planet.

Holland and I skip the guest appearance that night, however, which I'm sure makes Wes happy. In fact, I don't say another word to Holland after her rant and avoid her as much as possible. I avoid all of them, which proves to be a challenge considering our tight quarters and rigid schedule. Eli and Sweeny turn out to be the most supportive, strangely enough, and I sense it's because they feel the least betrayed. My behavior was stupid, but not the personal affront it was to the others.

Even Jesse is more reserved with me the few times we interact, always just a polite greeting or uncomfortable smile away from total awkwardness. He must have been starting to warm to the idea of me as a mentor. I would have laughed at that thought a few months ago. Now it stabs at me way more than I care to admit. Dammit. Hadn't thought about Jesse either. I don't think. Or think too much, which is why things rarely work out for me.

Ok, so what I'd done was stupid, I'm getting that now, but I'd meant well. And it worked. Messed up or not in its conception, my plan worked. Everyone is talking about me. Everyone hates me again. Callie and her story aren't even a blip on the radar anymore. But yeah, I could have done some more strategizing, more planning. I just hadn't been able to bear the sight of her in pain and knew I'd be able to handle the abuse a lot better than she could.

The plan hatched in my head the second I saw her. My rock, my guardian angel, cut down and broken by the vultures. I didn't know exactly what I was going to do, just that I had to take the attention away from her. I had to protect her any way I could. Casey could be her pillar of strength through the trial, but I was the one who could make it go away. And I had to. God, my brain just stopped functioning until it could think of a way to make her pain stop.

Then it all came crashing in a whirlwind of twisted logic. Since the day I'd come back, everyone from the nosy fan in line at the supermarket to the top Label execs has been waiting for me to screw up. Nobody except Callie, Casey, and maybe Holland, believed for a second that I could make this work, that I'd truly changed. What better way to turn the vultures back on me than give them reason to gloat about their premonitions, their favorite rotting carcass. *Yep, there. Told you. Fucked it up, just like we said.*

And so I did. Last night I leaked a series of old pictures to some prominent tabloids, as well as on my own accounts, and made sure to cover my lying ass by hiding out long enough to lend plausibility before returning to the bus. And yes, I know it'll eventually come out that the pictures are old, that they weren't taken anywhere near where I was last night, that actually we've seen them before. Hell, my hair isn't even quite right, though we can chalk that up to the hazards of unbridled revelry; and those girls, while I'm sure they'd love another night out with me, know they didn't get one. But by the time everyone figures that out, no one will be talking about Callie anymore, only wondering why the hell I'd do something like that. I didn't think it would matter so much, that the lie would hurt like it does, but it's too late. I did it, and now I have to live with the fact that everyone thinks I am the man I'm fighting so hard not to be.

In an impulsive reaction to protect someone I loved, I fell on my sword. And now, now I'm permanently impaled because I can't let the truth burden them with an ounce of responsibility. I definitely don't want them putting themselves back in the spotlight in an attempt to fix my ill-conceived mess. I don't know what story I'll use to explain it away when the truth comes out, especially since right now it's just jumbled chaos in my head. I make bad choices, it's what I do, but the thing is, I can't get a handle on whether this was a bad one or not. I feel this strange mix of regret, relief, and sadness, and I have no idea how to process it all.

I can't even decide if I love or hate myself right now. I just know it's done, and now I'm standing at the edge, staring down into the latest grave I've dug for myself. Luke the Dandelion. Luke the Train-Wreck. Luke the Liar. Luke the Gravedigger.

I'm a freaking Halloween parade.

I SEE I missed a call from Dr. Flynn and sigh in resignation. I know what she wants. She's got a TV and internet connection just like everyone else. I close my eyes and shove my phone back in my pocket, relieved there's no way I can call her back and have that conversation on the bus anyway. She'll just have to wait until we get to Baltimore.

8

BALTIMORE, MARYLAND
SEPTEMBER 22

"Thanks for returning my call," Dr. Flynn says, and I squint at a building across the street as I settle on the bench I'd found a block from the venue.

It's a surprisingly chilly morning and I wish I'd brought my jacket. But that would have required planning and foresight which we all know I avoid at all costs. I grimace.

"I almost didn't, then realized, you might be the only person in existence I can talk to about this. You know, since I literally pay you to keep my secrets."

She's quiet at first. I'm pretty sure it's my "secret" comment. "What kind of secrets are you talking about, Luke?" she asks, confirming I'm way too good at this.

"The truth about those pictures everyone's talking about. I didn't actually slip up in Charlotte. Those pictures are old. I leaked them to take the spotlight off Callie. The media was going after her about her past and I didn't want them talking about her anymore."

This new silence is because she's processing, and I almost roll my eyes but manage to stop myself. I'm the one who called her after all. Not to mention, it's a pretty big bombshell for eight in the morning.

"So you saw your friend in trouble and stepped in to help her by turning the negative attention on yourself."

I sigh. "Yep, pretty much. But of course, as usual, it totally backfired and now everyone hates me, including Callie, and thinks I'm a total fuck-up. Which I guess I am by definition."

"You consider yourself a 'fuck-up' right now?"

"I'm pretty much the poster boy, I think."

"Really. And what's your definition of a 'fuck-up'?"

"Come on, Doc. I see what you're doing. But let's be honest, even you have to admit I've written the book on this. Every time I make a choice, try to do anything, even for the right reasons, it turns to shit."

She's thinking again, and I wait. It's gonna be bad, but there's nothing I can do about it now. "Luke, can I take you up on that offer? To be honest with you?"

"I pay you a fortune for that," I joke.

I can almost hear her smile into the phone. She's a good person. We've always connected well. I had to try three before I found the right fit.

"You're a very intelligent young man. Your self-awareness and ability to self-reflect is astounding in a lot of ways, which is why I feel comfortable asking you to step into that role for a moment and listen to an outside perspective."

I brace myself. Her comfort with a topic rarely translates into the same for me.

"Go ahead. Shoot," I say anyway. Time to get my money's worth.

"If I'm understanding correctly, you are perceiving this latest challenge as a case of good intentions gone awry."

"Yeah. I just wanted to help Callie."

"Luke, that's not what I see."

I suck in my breath. Of course it's not. "No?"

"No. From my perspective, I see a long pattern of self-sabotage, disguised as altruism."

I nearly choke as her words slam into me.

"You still with me?"

I swallow. "Yeah."

Her voice softens as she continues. "I know that may be hard to hear, but I think it might help you make sense of your frustrations at your tendency toward destructive choices. You use altruistic reasoning to justify decisions that isolate and punish you. You believe you need to protect others from yourself because the depression still has you convinced that you're not worthy of love, that they're better off without you. Deep down, part of you still doesn't believe you deserve happiness. You still believe you should be punished."

I can barely breathe. She's right. Dammit, I hate when she's right because it's usually devastating.

I don't respond for a long time and just stare into the distance, her words ricocheting like blinding neon signs in the darkness of my head. I think back over my life, over every relationship I've had that's important to me. When have I ever let someone get close? When have I ever let myself be happy? The second a spark starts to ignite, I do something to snuff it out. Elena, Casey, Callie, and now Holland. I surround myself with shallow and destroy anything that slips beneath the surface and threatens to go deep.

"But Callie. I really did want to help her," I mutter finally, feeling like I need to put up some defense.

She sighs. "I know you did. I know you believe that, but let's look at the other side for a minute. There are many ways a friend can help another friend in need. In this particular situation, you could have stood by her and supported her through the challenge, provided a compassionate ear, a shoulder to lean on, encouragement from your own experience. Instead, your instinct led you to try to 'help' her by lying to her and damaging your relationship at a time when she needed it stronger than ever. You removed yourself from her instead of drawing closer."

That one hurts. Maybe even more than the other. I close my eyes, wanting desperately to argue. That can't be right, but isn't that exactly what happened? Isn't that why I'm here, talking to Dr. Flynn, shunned by everyone else on that bus? Hell, isn't that exactly what I admire about all of them? Casey's unflinching loyalty to those he loves, even in the heat of battle. Callie's compassion, even when she has no reason to love. Holland's inexplicable faith in people. Then there's me who shows love by lying, rejecting, and destroying all of that. That's not love. Oh god, that's what Flynn is saying. That's not love! It's something else. Something dark, something poisonous.

"How are you processing this, Luke? You still there?"

I don't know how to respond. I'm processing it way too well, I think. "You've given me a lot to think about," I mumble after a long pause.

She doesn't respond at first, and I know she recognizes my signal that I'm done with this conversation. She's just going to have to hope she's gotten through. And she has. For the love of all things holy in psychiatrist land, she has. I feel ready to puke.

"I should probably go," I say.

"Luke, this was a very difficult conversation, but we're having it because there are people in your life who love you and whom you love. This wouldn't hurt so much otherwise. You are very close to letting them in. We just made a huge leap. In your language, an 'epic' one, I believe." I actually do crack a smile at that. "So please, just do me one last favor. Put our conversation into action. Test it. Test me and my perspective. Just try telling one of your friends what you told me. Tell them the truth about the photos. Let them in, truly in, and see what happens. Stop showing love by punishing yourself and see what happens to these relationships, to you and your life, when you accept real love and return it in kind."

I let out a dry laugh. I'm sorry, but that sounds ridiculous. There was nothing funny about this conversation until now. "That's it, huh? Just rewire my entire approach to relationships, the very concept of Love embedded in my soul. Just undo twenty-eight years of betrayal, fear, and pain. Yep, that's it? All fixed?"

"Luke, I'm not asking you to do any of that. I'm asking you to take a small step."

"It sounds like a giant, fucking rocket launch to me."

"That's because you're projecting way beyond what I'm actually asking. You're skipping to the end when all I've asked is for you to open the book. All I want is for you to pick one person and tell them the truth about the photos. A simple, tangible, measurable action. Tell them it was a lie, that you didn't go out partying. You were trying to protect Callie. Then just see what happens next. That's it."

"That's it? And when they laugh in my face or explode on me?"

"You can call me back and say 'I told you so,' and rub it in all you want."

"Promise?"

"Promise. But Luke?"

"What?"

"It's not going to happen."

———

ELI SENDS me a text to meet him in catering for lunch. I do think it's strange, but since he's one of the few still talking to me, I make the effort to show up. I'm surprised to find everything looking completely normal. Jesse, Parker, and Reece are seated at a table with Eli who waves me over.

"Hey, Luke! Grab some food," Eli calls. I nod a greeting and pick up a plate. I fill it while they continue their conversation about getting a new front-of-house console.

"What's up, guys?" I say, taking the empty seat across from Eli.

"Hey," they answer.

"I meant to ask, what'd you think of Charlotte? Do you like playing the outdoor venues?" I ask Jesse.

He smiles and shrugs. "Yeah, it was pretty sweet. Fucking hot, though."

I laugh. "Yeah, Charlotte in early September can be a bitch. But you guys sounded great."

"Really?" Jesse asks, and I like that he seems sincere in his appreciation of my praise. Maybe he's starting to forgive me, too.

"Really. You seriously do have a sick sound. I love the vibe. Your vocals are killer, Jess, and rocked that venue."

He's beaming now, and I feel my cloud start to lift.

"Thanks, Luke. That means a lot," he says.

"Did you get a chance to sign the pallet?"

"The pallet?"

"Yeah, above the fireplace in the green room. You saw that, right? With your warehouse background I figured you'd be all over that."

"Wait, the one with all the burnt signatures?"

I nod. "We signed it at our first show there."

"Aw, damn, no. But that Coke fountain was..."

His response is cut off by the sudden shouts of Derrick, their bass player.

"It's gone!" he cries, bursting into the room.

"What's gone?" Jesse asks.

"The bus!" Derrick continues.

We all just stare at him.

"Huh?" Jesse says. "What do you mean?"

"I mean, it's gone! I went to get something just now and it's missing! The NSB bus is there. Tracing Holland, the crew bus, they're all there, but ours is gone!"

"That doesn't make sense. How could it be gone?"

"I don't know! But I'm telling you it's not there!"

They look to us, and we just shrug.

"Maybe Rob noticed an issue and took it in to get it checked out," Eli suggests.

They consider that, but seem skeptical. "Wouldn't they tell us they're taking our bus? I mean, all our shit's on there!" Parker argues.

Eli shakes his head. "I don't know, dude. That's weird."

"This is...shit! What do we do?" Derrick cries, as the other three pale.

"I don't know. I mean, are you absolutely sure it's gone? It's not just hidden behind a tree or something?" Eli asks, totally serious. At least, he looks totally serious. I'm about to lose it.

Just then, Sweeny comes racing in as well.

"Oh good! There you are! Guys, I don't know how to tell you this, but did you leave your bus unlocked or something?"

They all shake their heads, eyes wide. Parker looks ready to pass out.

"Ok, because I just saw some dude pulling around the front of the building in your bus and it definitely was not your driver. You don't leave the keys in the drawer, do you?"

"Wait, by the fridge?" Derrick asks, past pale and nearly transparent at this point.

Sweeny curses. "You idiots!"

I can't move. I can't speak. I can't even look at Sweeny and

Eli. Oh. My. God. I stare at my plate, focusing on taking deep breaths. In. Out.

"What are you still doing here? Go!" Sweeny cries. "Go chase that criminal down before he gets too far!"

"We need to call the cops!" Reece yells, bolting to his feet. "Our manager!"

"Don't worry, we'll take care of that. You just see if you can catch him. It's probably just some superfan taking a joyride. I doubt they'll even leave the parking lot."

"That happens?" Derrick asks in horror.

Eli shrugs again. "Only if you leave your keys in the drawer. Hope you guys have insurance."

The panic is all over their faces as they rush from the room in a flurry of frantic anger.

We're quiet for a moment after they leave, silently processing what just happened, then exchange a look before exploding into laughter.

"Are you serious? You moved their bus?" I cry, laughing so hard tears sting my eyes.

They are too, and we pretty much collapse on the table from our shrieking.

"Oh my god, did you see their faces? Parker was ready to throw up!" Eli snorts, slapping his hand on the surface.

I shake my head, wiping my eyes. "I can't believe you! They are going to beat the shit out of you!" I still can't breathe as I lean back in my chair. "Where's their bus now?"

Sweeny can barely speak as he starts up all over again. "I waited until I was sure one of them noticed then put it back! It's fucking in its spot!"

My eyes widen in disbelief, my stomach in agony from the laughter. "And you just sent them running all over the parking lot looking for it!"

He nods through his own tears, fighting for air.

"You know what this means, don't you?" I warn, still chuckling after we finally gain control of ourselves.

They nod, but don't seem to care. "Yeah, we know. It's on."

I shake my head in amusement. "Oh, it's on."

I FIND Jesse messing around on his acoustic in their dressing room and hold up my hands in a gesture of peace.

"Just stopping by to see how you're doing?" I explain, and he shakes his head with a grin.

"That was fucking genius. Totally messed up, but genius."

I laugh and drop to a chair nearby. "You know they wouldn't have done it if they didn't consider you friends, right?"

He nods, still smiling. "I know. They really had us. I think Parker might need therapy."

"He looked about ready to shit his pants."

"I think he might have a little."

I study him and lean forward with a mischievous look. "So what are you doing to get them back?"

He stares at me and seems confused. "Wait, what?"

"Seriously?" I scoff. "You're just going to let them prank you like that and not retaliate?"

I can tell it hadn't occurred to them and have to hold in my snicker. I'm here to be helpful. "Ok, look, this is how it works. They started it, so yeah, you have every right to get them back. Just keep it funny and safe."

I see his mind already working. "That's going to be hard to beat," he observes.

"Yeah, but trust me, it'll be worth it when you do." I start to rise, feeling a small sense of pride that he's taking it so well.

"Hey, Luke, wait. Before you go, can I ask you something?"

He quiets, and the mood suddenly shifts. "Um, it's a little personal."

I return to my seat. "Sure, what is it?"

He seems nervous, which is never a good sign. "Well, I'm not exactly sure how to ask you this. It's about those photos of you from Charlotte."

I stiffen. "What about them?" I respond, somehow managing to sound casual even though my insides are exploding.

"Well, it's just that, I'm from Philly. You know that, and we've played pretty much all the local spots in the tri-state area."

I nod, my stomach churning. Oh no. "Yeah?"

He looks away, clearly uncomfortable. "I'm trying to figure out how you were in Club Castor in Atlantic City when we were parked in Charlotte, North Carolina."

He meets my gaze again, and I can tell he's not coming from a place of hostility. He's legitimately confused by the photos, by me.

I take a deep breath. Is this it? Dr. Flynn wanted me to tell the truth to a friend. I never in a million years would have thought Jesse Everett would be my first attempt at honesty, but here it goes. It kind of helps that the lie didn't work on him.

"Ok, fine, the truth? It's because I wasn't in Club Castor in Atlantic City while we were parked in Charlotte. I was in Club Castor almost two years ago on our Bittersweet tour."

I can't tell if that cleared anything up. He looks just as confused, if not more so.

"So the pictures are fake?" he asks.

I shake my head. "No, they're real. They're just two years old."

"So your phone got hacked?"

I suck in my breath. Jesse might be a genius. He's just given me an out for the masses, but that doesn't help me now. My instinct is to accept the perfect lie, but I manage to catch it on my tongue. Dr. Flynn would kill me if I screwed this up after having it gift-wrapped and handed to me.

"Well, not exactly," I begin. "It's complicated, but basically, I'm the one who leaked them," I explain, and his face looks about what you'd expect when you politely inform someone you're a total idiot. As the words slip out, it occurs to me that the lie is way more plausible than the truth.

"Um...wow. Ok..."

I sigh. "I know, it's totally messed up, but you saw the shit they were saying about Callie and I figured if they were talking about me, they'd leave her alone. It was stupid, but it kind of worked."

He just stares at me for a moment, eyes wide. "Shit, man. That is totally fucked up."

I laugh. "Yeah. Yeah, it is. Don't ever do something like that. Totally stupid," I warn. Yes, Jesse, don't be a complete moron who leaks your own social death sentence. Mentor of the Year right here.

"Got it. Still, you obviously haven't told anyone else. They're all really upset."

I look away. "Not yet, but I will. And we'll tell the rest of the world that my phone got hacked. Thanks for that."

He smiles. "No problem. You should probably hurry though because it's going to come out soon that those pictures aren't legit. I mean, Club Castor, man? You could have picked a less obvious spot." He laughs and shakes his head. "It's almost like you wanted to get caught."

I shrug with a sheepish grin. He's probably right. I wouldn't put anything past my subconscious at this point. "I was pretty pissed about what was happening to Callie. Wasn't exactly thinking straight."

"Well, I still think that's totally messed up, but kind of awesome in a way. Thanks for letting me know. I got your back."

I start to warm inside a bit. I don't hear that a lot, but I have to admit it feels good. "Hey, thanks, Jess. And remember to think of a way to return the favor to Eli and Sweeny," I respond with a smile.

He grins. "Oh, don't worry. We got this."

I MAKE the difficult phone call to TJ after leaving the Limelight dressing room. The Label needs the truth, well, most of it, and Jesse's brilliance will give them much-needed direction for their PR spin. They'll like that part at least.

I leave Callie and her situation out of the story. I don't need them resenting her for something stupid I did, something that she'd be just as upset about. TJ is shocked, then furious when I tell him I signed my own death warrant for no apparent reason, but he's at least grateful I'm only guilty of being an idiot, not sliding down the cliff again. He agrees the phone-hack defense could work and is going to call the Label next to see what they can do to fix this mess.

I feel better when I hang up. Maybe the truth is turning out to be an improvement over the lie after all. I glance down at my phone and cringe at the string of texts and missed calls from Callie and Casey. They've been trying to get ahold of me for a while now, but I just haven't been ready to face them. Maybe now I can. They need the truth too, probably more than any of the others, but for some reason I'm finding that hurdle the hardest. It went well with Jesse, ok with TJ, but I'm still not ready. I know I haven't totally fractured that relationship beyond repair yet, and I'm afraid of messing up what's left. I'm still skeptical of this honesty thing, transparency. I need to test out the madness on one more person, one more trial in this messed up experiment.

Time to see what this Truth thing does for the one relationship I've totally fucked up.

———

I'M PRETTY sure she won't see me if I give her a warning, so I decide to surprise her with my unwelcome presence. I have to check several locations and make a few inquiries before finally finding myself standing outside of Holland's dressing room. I still can't believe I'm here, and the only thing giving me the courage to knock is the fact that I have nothing left to lose with her.

She seems irritated when she answers the door, but no longer ready to scratch my eyes out, so I take some solace in that.

"Luke, hi," she says, obviously taken aback.

"Can I talk to you for a minute?" I respond, my stomach suddenly turning painfully at what's about to happen. I've officially punched my ticket into unknown territory, and I'm hit more than ever by the fact that I have no clue how to do this.

"Um...I guess. Sure, come in."

She waves me inside and closes the door. I see her belongings organized in neat piles around the large space, and smile that even her toiletries are confident and put-together. Her dressing room is a museum compared to ours, which is just an explosion of our shit dumped on the floor and tables.

I blink and take a deep breath, fully aware I'm just distracting myself. "Look, I know I've screwed up a lot of things with you. You keep giving me chances and I keep blowing it.

I'm not here for another one, I just wanted to tell you one thing and then I'm gone. It's about the pictures."

She stiffens and holds up her hand. "Luke, that's your business. I don't want to know. What you do, who you party with, has nothing to do with me."

I feel every pinch of her statement. I'm not even sure she was trying to cut me, but I realize right then how much it hurts that I've lost her. "They were taken at Club Castor in Atlantic City. Two years ago," I explain quietly.

She stares at me. I can't read her face, but I'm not sure I even want to know what she's thinking right now. The silence is excruciating as her gaze bores into me, and I suddenly can't stand to be here anymore. I did what I came to do. I never promised I'd stay for the fallout.

"Anyway, that's all I came to say. I wanted you to know the truth before it comes out. It will soon," I mumble and head toward the exit. The door seems so far all of a sudden, the air in the room so thin and stagnant. I try to stay calm as I make my escape, but inside my head is screaming. Laughing at me, cursing. Mocking this embarrassing failure of a mission. I've just reached for the handle when she grabs my arm and yanks me around.

I flinch at the fire blazing in her eyes.

"Not good enough!" she hisses, shoving me against the door. Her palm is on my chest, almost painful as she stiff-arms me into submission to her wrath.

"I'm sorry, I just..."

"Stop! Just...stop! It's my turn to talk for once!" she cries, and I can only stare, eyes wide, as her long overdue fury explodes on me.

"Why the hell are you here? You came for what exactly? Huh? To confuse me again with some infuriating glimpse of honesty? To clear your conscience for a second, and then what?

What's next, Luke? I let you back in for five minutes until you get scared again? Push me away and leave that huge gaping hole in your wake? God!"

She lets go and clasps her hands over her head in distress as she steps back. "I can't get you out of my head! Do you know what that's doing to me? I'm a confident woman. I control my life, myself. I set my standards high because I can. Because I know I deserve that!"

She holds her fist over her heart. "I don't need a man to complete me, to give me value. I want one, but I don't need one. Sure, maybe one day I'll find someone who will fit into the box I created for my life, but it's a measured choice, nothing more, nothing less." She stops and meets my gaze, almost angry. "And then you come along."

There are tears in her eyes as she stares at me. I can't move, can't breathe. "You with your drama and your lies and your fucking eyes that haunt me and threaten everything I thought I understood about what I wanted! You're every reason I have my rules in place! You're everything I've fought to avoid for my life, every reason I should be running in the opposite direction!"

She closes her eyes and draws in a deep breath. I can see her visibly soften, change, and it guts me. "But that song, Luke," she whispers, daring to look at me again. "You put that song in me that day at the snack bar and now I can't get it out. In that brief moment, you showed me what it's like to transform from a connection with another person. You're the very reason I have my rules and yet make me want to break them every second we're together. I don't know what to do anymore! I don't know how to fix it, how to make it stop and put things back to the way they're supposed to be. I don't know how to forget the music now that it's ingrained in my soul!"

"Holland..."

"Don't," she says, wiping at her eyes with a rough hand. "You were right. We can't be friends. You should just go. It's better if you just go."

I should, but for one of the first times in my life, I don't. I shake my head. "No. I don't want to. Not this time."

Her eyes meet mine in shock. The words came out on their own, and I'm just as surprised. But I realize they are Truth. They are more Truth than anything about pictures or haunted pasts or reputations. I don't want to leave her. That is the truth. I want to be here with her. I want to let this person inside me.

She's in my arms before I can say another word, and I pull her tight against my chest. Her own arms constrict around my back as though she's afraid I'm not real, that I'll vanish before her eyes if she doesn't hold on tight enough. I rest my cheek on her hair as we hold on, wondering what this moment means, terrified that we're officially breaking every rule we've sepa-rately constructed to protect ourselves from each other. But we don't belong apart, that much is clear. We may not have a clue about how to be together, but there's no more denying we can't seem to separate no matter how hard we try.

"I'm sorry, Holland. So sorry," I whisper, and she pulls tighter. "I don't want to be what I am."

"Just let me in, Luke. Please," she pleads into my shirt. "That's all I've ever wanted from you."

I nod, even though I know she can't see me, and close my eyes. It feels so amazing to be held. To feel the warmth of some-one's body against mine. Not in a gesture of comfort, but in a union. Free of the guilt, the pain, the horror that is usually weighing on my soul when I'm touched. This isn't comfort, it's connection.

My body starts to react to the closeness of hers, and it's everything I can do to control the dizzying rush of blood and longing. The agony is unbearable when she finally pulls back and unveils the same mirrored in her eyes.

"I'm not sure I'm totally ready to break all my rules yet, but I want more than a hug, Luke. I want free access to you. All of you," she whispers, and I find her comfort with her honesty so incredibly hot.

We're done with words, and my lips find hers in an instinctive crash that sends my brain into oblivion. Her hands slide up my back, curving around my shoulders in a desperate attempt to pull me closer. I can feel her fingertips digging into my muscles, completely claiming me in that moment. It's not enough, though, and soon we're backing toward a table in her dressing room. She pushes me against it and I love her confidence. She wants me and has no hesitation in making sure I know it. She grabs the hem of my t-shirt, and I help her yank it over my head. We work together on hers as well, and when it's our skin making contact this time, the eruptions inside me make it impossible to focus on anything else.

"You are a work of art, you know that?" she breathes, tracing her fingers along my chest, down my abs.

I respond by kissing her again, my blood pounding in my veins. I want her, all of her. I want her naked form melted into mine, to fill her completely, to consume her mind, body, and soul. And I want to give her every inch of me that she's willing to take. God, I want everything, even though I'm still not convinced either of us is ready for that. We instinctively know that, for us, this moment, will come with a commitment both of us still fear from each other.

And then it hits me. Crashes down in an avalanche that slams into my lungs, and it's everything I can do to stay standing. There it is in all its vile, eternal glory, the Truth. The rest of it anyway, all the things I haven't told her but she deserves to know to make this choice. I care about her too much to let her break her rules for a man she doesn't know.

"Holland, wait..." I say, pulling away.

She groans. "Are you serious? Not again!"

I smile in spite of myself. "No, it's not that. I want this. I'm not leaving. It's just, you deserve more than this."

She rolls her eyes. "I'm not exactly the rose petals and candles type. I just want you naked. Why is this so confusing for you?"

"I know, it's just..."

"Seriously, you're killing me!"

I laugh and shake my head. "I know. I want that too, believe me, but..." I grow serious. Time for bombshell number two of this encounter. "I haven't had sex in sixteen months."

She stops, her expression changing, and I look away, suddenly embarrassed but not regretting anything. That's not even in the ballpark of the shit she's about to get dumped on her.

She covers her shock with a dismissive laugh. "Um...ok. Well, I can help you if you're confused. I'm sure it's like riding a bike." She reaches for my jeans, and I catch her wrist, chuckling.

"No, that's not what I mean. I'm pretty sure it'll come back to me. I just meant..." I sigh. "Can we sit?"

She's about to protest again, but then seems to sense there's more standing in our way than a little insecurity. Her mood immediately shifts, and I love her dimensions, how comfortable she is navigating them.

"Sure."

We don't let go of each other and move to the small couch against the wall. Once we're seated, she wraps her arm around mine, our fingers laced together. She rests her head on my shoulder, and I close my eyes. I don't deserve this moment, this woman, but she deserves the truth. The problem is, I don't really know where to start. It suddenly occurs to me that this story has never actually been written. Not in a cohesive form, not in any kind of meaningful narrative that can explain the Train-Wreck, Gravedigger, Dandelion that is Luke Craven. Even during the good years with Elena we had been more focused on surviving our present than worrying much about our pasts. She had known details, facts, but no one knew the person who lived them. Not really. And now she's a chapter I'm still trying to survive, one that will never close but will go on forever, even as new ones begin to form.

Holland squeezes my hand, and I force air into my lungs. She needs to know this story.

"I was married before," I begin quietly.

Holland grips harder, as if sensing I'm approaching the vault. "I know. Elena, right? You still wear the ring."

I nod, casting an instinctive glance at my hand. "I'll take it off eventually. I just..." I can't finish. The sudden heaviness rises into my throat, cutting me off. I'm horrified at the display until Holland huddles closer, shattering the little hold I have left on my emotions. The tears move to my eyes and I try to blink them away, but they press harder, threatening to expose me and the weakness that will probably always haunt me at some level. I can't stop thinking about Elena now, which makes me feel like I'm betraying both of these amazing women I don't deserve. Would she forgive me for this moment? For wanting to explore the depths of another soul? For trying to be the man for Holland that I should have been for her?

"You don't ever have to take it off, Luke," Holland whispers. "I want to share you with her."

The tears fall freely now, knocked from their dam by her selfless beauty. I lean forward and cover my face, embarrassed but unable to stop them. All I can do is hide now, hide and hope she can forgive the damage I've inserted into her life. At least she knows. Giving her irrefutable evidence of what I am is maybe the first truly selfless thing I've done in return. But she stuns me again when I feel the pressure and warmth of her arms around me. She settles her head against my shoulder, holding on to everything that's left of me.

"You're not broken, Luke. Just lost," she says softly. I glance up, and she brushes my wet cheek. "Not a 'broken wanderer,' just a wanderer like the rest of us. You just insist on doing it alone, which never works."

I look away and stare at the far wall. She's not wrong, I just don't know how to be anything else. "I've done a lot of terrible things."

"We all have."

"No, but you don't understand. You should know. You need to understand what I am."

I can feel her soft laugh. "I hate to break it to you, but all your terrible things are pretty well-documented."

I close my eyes and can't stop the brief smile. "I know, but it's more than that. I'm hard, Holland. Really hard," I muse into the stillness of the room.

I sense her increased amusement and cast her a wry grin. "What?"

"Um...really?"

"Oh, come on, that's not what I meant!"

She laughs at the look on my face. "I know, but, seriously! After what just happened?"

I shake my head, still grinning. "Get your mind out of the gutter, woman."

She giggles and latches onto my arm again when I lean back on the couch. "Says the badass rockstar. Please. Your minds live in the gutters. "

I grin and shrug. "Used to. Now I'm a fucking Hallmark card, apparently."

"You're thinking about adopting a kitten aren't you?"

"Hilarious. Hey, how about you stop trying to strip my clothes off every time we're together?"

Her eyes widen at the challenge. "Oh, really? Yeah, you definitely haven't been sending signs that you want it too. I'm sorry, Luke, your head may be impossible to read, but this guy is not," she teases, pointing at my crotch.

I laugh and settle into the cushions. "I can't argue with that." She returns my grin and begins tracing the tattoos on my chest, the mood growing serious again.

"Explain your ink," she continues, and I almost flinch.

"What?"

"If you want to talk instead of letting me ravish you, you're going to pay for it. I want details. Start here," she says, moving her fingers to my wrist.

I laugh. "All of it?" I ask in disbelief.

She grins. "Why not? They don't need us for another three hours. Besides, I've learned it's the best way to get the summary of a person. You suck at sharing, so we can do bullet points."

I let out my breath. "Um...how about we talk about you for once. I know even less about you than you do of me at this point. Maybe I'm the one who should be running."

"Only from boredom," she laughs.

"Oh, please. There's no way."

She settles against me. "Seriously, Luke, I'm frighteningly stable. I love my family, I have a college degree, and I'm incredibly happy doing what I love for a living."

I smile. "So everything I'm not?"

"Everything you don't need to be if you'd just accept the truth about what you are."

I try not to roll my eyes. "So that degree is in psychology, I suppose?"

"Biology. Can I be honest with you for a second?"

I'm not even sure how to respond to that. "Haven't you been flogging me with honesty since the day we met?"

She grins and shrugs. "True. That was more of a warning, I guess." She sighs and pulls back so she can face me. I brace myself as she grows serious. "You think you're protecting me from yourself, all the rotten things you are that I don't know about. You've been pushing me away, refusing to let me in, terrified of the truth about who you are and what it would do to me when I found out."

I suck in my breath. "I don't want to hurt you. I've hurt so many people in my life."

She shakes her head and leans forward with an earnestness that immediately silences further protests. "Here's the thing, though, the part you're not getting. All the rotten stuff that you're so afraid of me discovering? All the shit you think you're hiding and protecting us from? That's the crap that's already out there! That's what we all see, plastered all over the tabloids and Internet."

She takes my hands and meets my eyes, refusing to let me look away. "Luke, I'm here right now, pretty much begging for more, because you have it backwards. You're not hiding your darkness. That's the part you've given the masses to label, judge, and punish." She draws in a breath. "I'm here because I've glimpsed the actual part that no one sees. The real part you're holding back from the world. And I'm telling you, Luke, it's fucking beautiful."

HOLLAND and I talk for a long time, nearly until we have to start preparing for the show that night. It's an incredible thing watching the lust that started the encounter transform into something deeper, something neither of us saw coming but instinctively know has changed everything.

Callie was right. Holland is a fascinating woman, incredibly intelligent, kind, and probably the most sincere, confident person I've ever met. I love every "boring" detail she shares, and find it hilarious that her "boring" is completely mesmerizing to me. She's twenty-nine, terrified of alligators even though she's never seen one in person, and has three sisters, including the baby of the family who's sixteen. She's a natural blond, but likes to dye her hair different colors depending on her mood, and was born and raised in Canada. She can't wait until our Toronto stop so she can spend some time at home for a bit. She's had three serious relationships, her last one ending amicably two years ago. No marriages or children, but would like both one day. She despises mushrooms. All kinds, even on pizza.

I absorb it all, sucking it in like air, laughing so hard at times I can barely breathe. I don't remember the last time I've been able to abandon my weighted existence for so long. For the next few hours I'm someone else, someone I don't hate, someone who laughs, and cares, and even dreams a little. Someone who understands peace.

She learns some things too. I'm ambidextrous, find spider plants creepy, and have never been on a boat. I'm not a huge fan of mushrooms either, but I'll at least forgive them on pizza under the right circumstances.

We talk about some of the dark stuff too. About my aunt disowning me, leaving me with no family other than the small one I've created with Callie and the band. How hard it was growing up believing you must have been the reason everyone kept abandoning you. We talk about Elena.

I can't bring myself to discuss this past year yet, the chair, my gross betrayal the night of Elena's death, but I do admit to my struggle with depression and the battle that will probably follow me the rest of my life. She understands and says one of her sisters deals with the same condition.

We're both disappointed by the knock on the door, but not surprised when we glance at the clock on the wall.

"Crap! It's so late!" she laughs, jumping to her feet. She had put her top back on a while ago, and I rise to grab my own shirt off the floor. I've just slipped it over my head when she opens the door to reveal the last person I want to see at that moment.

"Hey, Wes. Did they finish the sound check?"

His eyes sear me from across the room, and I do my best to pretend not to notice.

"Yeah, they're finished. Just checking to see if you wanted to grab something to eat quick from catering." He stops, and this time I decide to face his hatred head-on. "But I guess you're busy."

Holland has to notice the tension, but chooses to let it go. "No, it's fine. We're finishing up. You want to get some food?" she asks, turning to me. I almost say yes just to annoy Wes, but I'm pretty sure I'd regret it once the satisfaction of the "up yours" wore off.

"Actually, I should get going and check in with the others. You go ahead," I say, moving toward the door as if it's not going to take every reserve of strength I have to pass within five feet of Wes without hitting him.

"You sure?" Holland seems disappointed, but I cast her a sincere smile.

"Yeah. We'll catch up later, ok?" I assure her. We exchange a knowing look that I'm sure Wes doesn't miss.

"Hey, man, sorry about your phone getting hacked," he sneers as I move past him. "That's gotta suck. Those girls were pretty hot, though."

I glare at him, but manage to keep my fists from smashing his face as I move into the hallway. I guess the secret's out.

I'VE PUT it off long enough. Now that I know the new false "truth" about the phone hack is public, I don't really have a choice anyway. I have to come clean to Callie and Casey, and I send them a message to meet me at the bus.

I don't have to wait long when they board with concerned looks on their faces.

"Luke, before you begin, please let us say something," Callie blurts as she drops beside me on the lounge. "We've been trying to get you all day! We're sorry, ok? Whatever happened in Charlotte doesn't change anything. We should have been more supportive and understanding."

Her sincerity cuts into me, and I'm filled with a mixture of warmth, regret, and fear. I guess we'll see how sincere they are when they're forced to confront my latest lie.

I swallow and brace myself. "Well, that's why I called you here. I have to confess something about what happened in Charlotte." I can tell they want to interrupt, but I don't give them the chance. "I didn't go out that night. I just walked around a bit and got some air." I suck in a deep breath and finally meet their surprised gazes. "I leaked old photos because I didn't want them talking about you anymore, Cal."

I stop and allow the shock to settle. Even though they're more accustomed to my infuriating, confusing love than anyone, they're still struggling with this one. The silence seems to go on for hours, but I'm sure it's only a few seconds before I'm being tackled against the backrest of the couch.

"What is wrong with you?" Callie cries, nestling into my shoulder.

I chuckle and shake my head. "God, I have no idea. You know that."

She pulls back with a stern look, but the glisten in her eyes gives her away. "Ok, first of all. That was so stupid! You can't do that, Luke! You have got to start worrying about yourself! Taking care of you!" She actually smacks my shoulder, and then sits back to take a breath. "And second of all..." she stops and hugs me again while Casey only shakes his head behind her.

"Are you fucking serious, man?" he mutters in disbelief.

I shrug. "We're going to say my phone was hacked."

"Hacked by its owner, the biggest idiot on this planet! You let us all shred you!" Casey curses again.

I look away. "Yeah, well, maybe it wasn't the best plan."

"It was a freaking idiotic plan! Dude, that is so messed up. Why didn't you at least tell us?"

"I was afraid you'd be upset and try to interfere which would only make things worse."

"Um, yeah, we would have, you dork!" Callie cries, swatting my arm. "What were you thinking?"

I laugh again at the ironic question. "I wasn't, that's the problem. I just...I don't know."

She moves onto the cushion beside me, turning my face to hers and staring me down. "Luke Craven, it's Straight Talk Time. Don't you ever, *ever*, do something like that again, got it? I mean, ever!"

I grin and shrink a bit. "I won't."

"You better not!" She crosses her arms and glares at the

clock. "You're lucky you need to go get ready for the show right now, but don't get too comfortable. I'm not even close to done with you!"

Casey shoots me an amused look. "Wow. This is a whole new level of Callie-fire. Good luck, man."

"Ok, ok! I get it! I'm sorry!" I cry, holding up my hands in surrender.

She continues to glare at me, even as she wraps her arms around me in another hug. "This is what I wanted that night, Luke. I needed a hug, not to watch someone I love and care about self-destruct. Losing you was so much more painful than the silly rumors."

I sigh. "I know. I'm sorry. I'm getting that now."

"Do you?"

I grin and lean back. "Actually, I think I do."

WE'RE NOT ROLLING out to our next stop until the morning, so the consensus is to let off steam at a local club after the show. Even Jesse and the Limelight guys are in, so as much as I dread the thought of an evening with Holland in the seductive atmosphere of a club under the watchful eye of her babysitter Wes, I accept that this is one social obligation I can't avoid.

Still reeling from our afternoon in the dressing room, I had made the mistake of stalking her performance from backstage later that night. Huge error, since now I can't get her out of my head. I watch her in the car to the club, as she moves a few paces ahead on her way to the door, study her arm intertwined with Callie's. She's gorgeous, as always, but it's how she's able to plow right through my epic bullshit and completely stir the dormant core underneath that's got me glued to her every move. It doesn't help that her own eyes keep wandering toward me, plunging deep into my soul before tracing every line of my body through my clothing. We both know what we want. We both know we're not going to be able to have it right now.

We laugh and joke with the others, settling on opposite sides of the table when the hostess shows us to a private area. But that electricity is always there, sparking, waiting for the moment when the hidden glance creeps from a safe conversation with the others to the burning longing for each other just out of reach. My head is a mess, my body fully charged, and when she finally grabs my hand to dance, I'm sure she's lost her mind.

"Are you sure this is a good idea?" I warn as she drags me toward the dance floor.

"It's a terrible idea, but I don't care. I have to touch you and figured this was better than tackling you at the table," she tosses back, sending my hot blood on a rampage.

She turns without warning and throws her arms around my neck, pulling me into her. I immediately feel the tension release and build at the same time, tearing apart anything left of my will. My hands move over her as well, her smooth back, her perfect ass, and when she sucks in her breath to absorb my touch, I don't know how to stop myself from kissing her. I need her. I need us.

She meets my lips with a hunger that ravishes both of us, and for a brief moment there is no club. No dance floor, no music, no dizzying mix of tightly pressed bodies. There's nothing, no one, just Holland and Luke, together, filling each other with something we can't explain and can't get enough of. But we're not alone. We have a huge audience, and part of who we are means we don't get to make our own choices. We both understand that all too well when she quickly pulls back and rests her head against my cheek instead.

She doesn't have to explain further as I hold her against me. We're both thinking the same thing. Hoping no one saw our stolen kiss, forced to finish the heated encounter in our heads as our firm bodies melt into each other, all under the pretense of moving to music we can't even hear.

But we're not as strong as we'd hoped, and soon it's her hands making the exploration, her secret sin. I close my eyes, trying to hold myself together, even as she works to unravel me. Her fingers slip under my shirt, spreading a searing heat up my chest, around my waist, then clinging to the edge of my jeans and eliminating any protective gap between us. My pulse is pounding, my breath short as she tortures me, but there's no way I can bring myself to stop her. I don't want mercy. I want her hands on me as much as she seems determined to take every inch she can get. It's all hers, whatever she wants, whatever she can get away with in this dangerous moment.

Her eyes rise to meet mine, pleading with me, trapped in the same impossible crisis that I am. In this place designed for crowds, we need to be alone. We need...I stop cold.

Holland follows my gaze, and I feel her deflate as she instinctively puts some distance between us. Wes' glare speaks volumes, and we don't need an explanation about how much he saw. Holland gives me an apologetic look, and I can't help but sigh as she fights through the crowd in his direction. I watch them argue for a bit before she takes his arm and they disappear from my line of sight.

I'm not sure how long I stand there staring after them, a solitary stone pillar stationed in the midst of the undulating waves of the dance floor. It's not that I can't move. I want to, desperately. I just have no idea where to go from here.

I'M NOT surprised when Wes corners me in the restroom the first chance he gets, only that he managed to wait this long. I have to assume he's been watching me all night, and my blood chills at the thought of him stalking me, waiting for this moment to unleash whatever punishment he has planned. I'm not afraid of him, only afraid of what this petty confrontation is going to do to the rickety frame of the new life I've just started building. There are a few witnesses in the room, but they seem to have no interest in involving themselves in our drama. I don't blame them.

"I thought I told you to stay away from her, you piece-of-shit!" he hisses, and I manage to stir my glare enough to match his.

"And I thought I told you she was a big girl and could make her own decisions," I spit back, moving to the sink as though washing my hands is infinitely more important than anything he has to say. I know I'm making a mistake by stoking the fire, but I've never done well with people trying to push me around. I'm the only bully allowed to string myself up.

"I'm talking to you!" he cries, shoving me away from the sink, and I turn on him with the same fire.

"Are you fucking serious? We're going to do this? Fight over a girl in a bathroom? You're kidding, right?" I bark at him.

By now, we're alone and I'm not surprised. We're acting like raging assholes. I want nothing to do with this; I can't even imagine how little a random bystander wants to participate.

"Wes, you need to back off, ok? Seriously, just back the fuck off because I'm telling you, this is not going to end well for you. The only reason this has gone on as long as it has is because I have a huge amount of respect for Holland and her band. You're her band, but take this one step further and I don't give a shit about the blowback!"

"I'm not going to let you hurt her. I warned you. She's

special and I'm not going to let you use her and throw her away like another one of your groupie sluts!"

"You don't know a damn thing about me! Get out of my face or this is going to end with us both in the hospital!"

His eyes narrow and his words come out with so much venom I can barely even hear his next phrase.

"Laurel Karns," he spits, inches from my face.

I stare at him in shock. It's the last thing I'd expected to hear at that moment and throws me so off guard, I'm afraid he can tell he's just gained the upper hand.

"Excuse me?" I manage, suddenly unable to draw in enough oxygen.

"You heard me, bitch. Stay away from Holland. I told you, we know what you are!"

"How do you know Laurel?"

"Why does it matter? Laurel isn't important. It's the fact that you're a douchebag who's about to wreck someone I care about that matters! You're a fucking loser! Total scum who doesn't deserve..."

I see red. I'm not even sure what happens next, I just know it's bad. I know it makes my fist hurt, then my cheek, then my fist again, then my stomach, my ribs. I know it's happening again. I know old wounds are ripping open, tearing chunks of flesh out of my consciousness and littering them all over a grimy bathroom floor that's collected so much of my past over the years.

I catch a brief flurry of activity in the mirror, two grown men flying at each other, fighting for, I don't even know what. What am I fighting for? Certainly not my dignity. I threw that away a long time ago. Holland? No. I'm smart enough to understand that this insanity isn't going to win me any points there, only push me further from any chance of convincing her I'm not this kind of monster anymore. No, I'm just fighting because that fucking fuse blew my head apart and let this idiot derail everything I've been working to build. I'm fighting because sometimes no matter how hard you fight it's not enough and all it takes is the tiniest trigger to explode the landmine.

It doesn't last long. I sense neither of us had a clear goal when we started, and at some point I find myself alone again. There's a sharp pain around my eye, blood dripping from my lip. My right knuckles are swollen and throbbing. My ribs are on fire, but Wes is the one who ran. He looked about how I feel, so I don't even know who won. I'm pretty sure we've both lost, considering the coming fallout.

I grip the edge of the sink and stare at myself in the mirror. My fingers instinctively rise to the growing welt around my left eye and I wince from the contact. My bottom lip is cracked and I don't even want to know what my chest looks like. So stupid. Completely ridiculous, and I'm furious about the entire encounter. I know I should be hating that dick Wes right now, and I do, but it's my own battered reflection that's haunting me.

Old Luke woke up bloody and sore on bathroom floors. Old Luke fought over girls and trash-talked puny threats to his manhood. Old Luke embarrassed himself with public displays of primal rage, and here I am, staring into the troubled eyes of Old Luke. The Luke I just fought to prove I wasn't.

The door bursts open, startling me from my critique, and I sigh as Casey rushes toward me.

"What the hell happened? Are you ok? Oh, shit!"

"I'm fine," I mutter, pushing away from the sink and grabbing a paper towel. I wet it and hold it up to the burning bruise on my eye.

Casey collects a couple more and hands me the wad for my lip.

"So are you going to tell me what happened or am I just

supposed to guess," Casey quips, leaning against another sink to face me.

"I told you. I'm fine. Can we just let this go?"

"Let it go? You and Wes just beat the shit out of each other! We're touring with them! It's kind of a big deal!"

I sigh and shake my head. "Seriously, Case, just let it go. We had a misunderstanding. It's worked out now."

He still looks concerned, and I know this placating thing is not going to work on him, but there's no way I'm getting into the story now.

"Do you want me to call TJ? I'm sure we can get them kicked off the tour."

"No!" I blurt way too fast. "I mean, it's fine. I had it coming. We both did. Just let it go. We'll work it out."

We're silenced by a knock on the door, and Casey pulls it open with a wary peek.

"Is Luke in here?"

My stomach drops at Holland's voice.

"Oh, hey, Holland. Yeah, he's here." He lets her in and I brace myself, having no idea what to expect from her.

"Oh my gosh!" she cries, rushing toward me. "Luke, I'm so sorry."

I'm strangely touched by her unexpected apology. "It's fine. I'm fine," I assure her, turning back to face my battered reflection, mostly so I don't have to face her. But she follows and meets my gaze in the mirror.

"Case, do you mind making sure everyone gets back to the buses? I'd rather not have to see anyone right now."

Casey is clearly still concerned. "Are you sure, man? I don't want to leave you alone."

"I told you, I'm fine. I just need a few minutes. Please, Case?"

"Go, Casey. I'll stay with him and make sure he gets back,"

Holland chimes in, and we both glance at her in surprise. She shrugs. "What? I think I can handle a few wet paper towels. I was pre-med after all."

I laugh despite the grave moment, then wince from the pain. "Seriously, I'm fine," I direct back to Casey who rolls his eyes.

"Yeah, you look fine," he mumbles. "You sure you got him?" he confirms with Holland, and I grunt.

"Oh, so you'll trust her, but not me?"

"Have you seen your face?" Casey returns, his grin breaking as I curse at him.

"Shouldn't you be leaving? Oh, and make sure you take care of the tab!" I call after him, unable to stop my own grin when the last thing I see is his middle finger disappearing through the door.

Holland laughs before focusing back on me, the mood settling again as she reaches up and gently examines my cheek. "I can't believe Wes did this."

"It took two of us," I respond quietly, and she meets my gaze.

"Yeah, but I know he started it." She draws in a deep breath. "Luke, I'm sorry. It's partly my fault too. He saw us together on the floor, and I told him to stay out of it and mind his own business. He didn't like that I basically defended our relationship, defended you. He was out for blood. I could have handled it differently, but I just..."

"He's obviously in love with you, Holland," I interrupt. "I'm sorry, I know you don't want to hear that, but look at my face."

She bites her lip and I wonder if I'm finally getting through to her. After a long pause, she sighs and takes my hand. "Can we go find a place to talk that's not the men's bathroom?"

"Please," I agree, eager to escape, and she grabs a few more strips of paper towels.

"For the road," she explains with a smile.

———

I'M NOT OVERLY excited about re-entering the club, but we manage to sneak through the crowds into the cool evening air without any more drama. Holland still hasn't let go of my hand and leads me to a bench about half a block from the entrance.

She settles against me and we're silent for a moment, doing our best to absorb the rollercoaster we've just endured. "There's something you should know," she begins quietly, and I instinctively brace myself. "Wes and I were briefly engaged at one point. The thing is, we realized pretty quickly that we were great friends but terrible lovers. We were young and had grown up together, so the engagement was more of a formality that everyone else expected. Once we had the courage to swear off the expectations, we decided we'd be much better off as buddies and bandmates than spouses. It's been almost six years and he's now one of my best friends. He cares about me like a sister and I know he'd do anything for me."

"Including punch me in the face," I mutter.

"Especially, punch you in the face," she laughs, and I love the way her eyes shine when she glances up at me. She sighs and grows serious again. "He's not in love with me, Luke, he's just protecting me. He believes all the lies about you. He doesn't have the same faith in people and doesn't believe you can possibly be the person I'm defending. He thinks I'm falling into the same trap you've been trying to protect me from. Ironically, in a twisted way, you and he have been on the same side."

I almost smirk. "Careful. You might actually make me not hate the guy."

She chuckles and squeezes my arm. "He's not a bad guy. He's way off base on this one, and believe me, I'm beyond pissed about what just happened, but his intentions are good. He's just worried about me and doesn't trust you. Or, more specifically, my ability to resist you and your legendary charms."

I want to argue, but I'm not sure how. She's right. It is kind of ironic that we've both spent the entire tour fighting me for the same reason. "Well, he's been pretty open about his hatred. He's been making my life hell since the day we met."

"Yeah, I know, and I'm sorry about that, but there's more to it."

I don't like anything about that sentence. Especially when she draws in a deep breath and I know she's conflicted about whatever is coming next. "He's friends with Laurel Karns, Luke," she explains quietly, and I immediately stiffen.

"What?" I don't even know what to do with that statement.

I pull away from her and suddenly don't feel the pain of my injuries anymore, not when the pain of my transgressions is suddenly assaulting my conscience like I'd just committed the heinous crime yesterday, not well over a year and a half ago.

"We were at that after party, too. Geez, everyone was, remember? She sent us messages when you two left together. She was boasting about how she was hooking up with you. When the news broke about Elena the next day...we knew where you were when it happened, what you were doing." She quiets, and I can't look at her. I can't look at anything. I lean on my knees and stare at the sidewalk, completely numb. I don't want to deal with this right now. I can't.

"I'm sorry, I know I should have said something sooner. I started to, a couple times, but then I saw how you'd changed. How much your past already haunts you, and I just couldn't. I didn't want you to think I still held it against you. But I should have warned you about Wes." I can hear her sigh before she takes my hands and forces me to face her again. "I'm the one who broke our agreement, not him. Going on tour with you was huge for us, so we couldn't pass it up, but Wes made me swear to him that I wouldn't get sucked in if we agreed to go. I promised I wouldn't fall for you."

Tears burn my eyes and I'm still not sure how to speak. There's so much I want to say, but the words aren't forming together in any useful combination. I want to explain Laurel, but there is no explanation, none except the one they already have. There's no softer truth, no defense, just the cold, hard reality exposing the depths of the monster that created the worst night of my life. The ache mixes with nausea at the fact that this entire time she's known. She knew the worst of what I was, my darkest secret, and yet she still chose to have faith in me, still fought to bring us to this moment.

I can't possibly accept that.

"Not a second goes by when I don't regret that night," I manage, finally. I can hear the pain in my voice, but it's not enough. It'll never be enough for what I deserve. I search her eyes, willing her to understand. Begging her to forgive me for a crime that had nothing to do with her then, but might be critical now. "I would give my life to take it back and meet Elena that night instead of going to that hotel room. I replay that moment, that horrifying mistake, every single day, Holland. Every day!"

"Yes, but in a way, it did take your life, didn't it," she responds, and I almost choke.

I can't even begin to respond so I focus back on the concrete again. The ugly, pockmarked, stained sidewalk that lives out its days in functional anonymity as a landing place for the soles of shoes. Sentenced to a destiny of being kicked, stomped, spit upon, and covered with vomit. The fate of a sidewalk.

I'm startled from my reverie by a hand on my thigh, and glance over to meet Holland's compassionate gaze. We don't speak, we don't have to, and I capture her fingers in mine. I don't want to let go. I'm tired of fighting her, this, myself. I'm tired of the past weighing down my present, dictating my future. There's something breaking through, hope, maybe. Something that's making this constant effort at punishing myself even more exhausting than usual.

"You know, I could watch you think for hours. It's fascinating," she observes suddenly, and I feel the slightest crack of a smile spread across my lips.

"Yeah?"

"Yeah. Which is probably a good thing because that's pretty much all I get in these conversations."

My smile widens into a grin, and I finally dare a look back at her. Her own eyes are alive with humor, and I actually suck in my breath at the effect of her light on my scarred soul.

"I just gave you an entire paragraph. That was a full-on legitimate speech."

"Yep." She drops the simple word between us for effect, and this time I actually laugh.

"Yep," I echo, sliding my arm around her. It was the right move, and I love how effortlessly she settles against me.

"Hey, Luke?"

"Yeah?"

"I have one more secret."

"What's that?"

She glances up at me. "You should know that I'm going to be taking your newfound virginity as soon as we get to Philly."

9

PHILADELPHIA, PENNSYLVANIA

SEPTEMBER 23-27

I'm at her door the second we receive our room assignments from Kenneth. I barely even drop my hand from knocking.

"Thank god," Holland breathes, pulling me inside and pushing me up against the solid wood.

We attack each other with a hunger that's been building since that first longing glance, the first time our bodies committed to what our brains would fight for days.

My shirt is on the floor before I even realize it's moving, my jeans unbuttoned as we maneuver toward the bed. Sixteen months. Her mouth is tangling all coherent thoughts in my head, blurring them into a blinding white light as her hands slide over me, forcing my body to surrender to her every command. It's hers, every muscle, every nerve, and when we finally make it to the bed, I can't help but wonder how I managed to stop this from happening so many times. I don't know if I should admire or skewer myself for the lunacy.

"You're in your head again," she warns. "Stop thinking."

I smile against her lips and let her shove me down. She tugs at my jeans, and I help kick them off before flipping her over to return the favor. She grins as I work at her straps and clasps, then pulls me back to her once we're both free of the final barriers.

Our kisses are more fervent now, more urgent in their need to connect us in the impossible. We know we can't get close enough, not like this, but it doesn't stop us from trying.

"Damn, you're beautiful. Perfect," I observe, suddenly pulling back and gazing down at the goddess beneath me.

"Not as beautiful as we are together," she returns, lacing her fingers with mine and kissing them.

My heart is ready to explode, along with every other inch of me if I don't do something soon, and I move back to meet her mouth. She hasn't let go of my hand, and I push it above her head, clasped firmly in mine. I won't let go this time. I hold on, even as my other hand freely explores her incredible body.

She clenches her eyes shut as my fingers move over her, gently at first, then more deliberate as I read her reactions. Her slight groan sends my own blood searing through me, and when she arches to receive my touch, the fire nearly consumes me. I need this woman. I need to be inside her, to intertwine my essence with hers. I need...

I freeze.

For one minute and forty-seven seconds, I was with Holland Drake. For one minute and forty-seven seconds, I didn't think about Elena Barrett Craven.

"Luke? Luke, what is it?"

Holland's staring up at me, her beautiful eyes...I blink, completely paralyzed. I'm still on top of her, still present, still desperate for her, but suddenly, I'm somewhere else too. I don't know where, just that my body wants to do something that's tearing my brain apart.

"Luke. Hey!"

I try to shake off whatever is happening and stare back down at Holland. She doesn't seem angry, just concerned.

"I'm sorry, I..." Words start to come out. I hope they make sense. They're...Elena. I can't even think now. Her face has occupied every recess of my head. Elena...oh god, the guilt. The self-hatred. The anger. It all comes rushing back. I'm about to betray her. But it's not a betrayal, is it? It can't be forever, right?

Holland startles me out of my torment with a gentle push to the side. She guides me back to the bed, propping herself up beside me, gazing into my eyes. She doesn't say anything as she studies my face, tracing my chest, my cheek, my lips. I close my eyes, trying to put this moment back together, reclaim some of the sudden chaos.

"I'm sorry," I whisper, unable to look at her. "I don't know what's wrong with me. It's..." I can't finish, and I'm grateful I don't have to.

"You're thinking about her, aren't you?" she guesses, and I glance over at her again.

I feel like shit. I don't even know how to start sorting through all the reasons why. "I want you, Holland. I want you so badly, I just...I don't know. I don't understand what's wrong with me."

She sighs and settles onto the sheets, tucking herself against my side. Her hand climbs my chest, up my neck, and cups my face, gently stroking my cheek. I close my eyes again, allowing every nerve she triggers to react to her touch.

"Tell me about her," Holland murmurs, still running her fingers in a dizzying pattern of chills over my skin.

"Elena?" I ask in surprise.

She turns my face toward hers and gives me a soft, but lingering, kiss. "Yes. Tell me about Elena."

I know I don't deserve this woman and I can't imagine ever

denying her anything again. I swallow hard and stare back at the ceiling.

"Elena was...I don't know how to describe it. A ray of sunshine, I guess, but not the kind people mean when they say that. Not the easy kind."

I stare off as I fight to explain. "You know how on a really sunny day you can look at a full shade tree in the distance and see a few streams of light piercing the gaps in the leaves? That was Elena. She was the ray of sunshine that fought its way through the darkness, through the gaps."

I quiet, haunted by my description, but Holland prevents any need for more when her lips meet mine. I reach up and touch her hair, pushing it from her face as our kiss intensifies.

"I love that you still love her," she breathes. "I love that you let your love for her transform you."

My soul is bursting, so full of emotion that I'm still lost when she moves on top of me. Holland takes my breath away as she claims me, reminding me that while Elena is in my head, Holland's here too, intent on carving out a piece of my heart. But she already has it. God, she has so much of it, I just don't know how to give it over to her.

"You tell me when to stop," she whispers, fighting for our connection again. My heart thuds against my sore ribs, my body reacting exactly how she wants it to as she takes it hostage. It is hers, every inch of it, and I can't breathe as she pushes for more, escalating her seduction to a feverish intensity. I reach for her, intent on taking over, but she stops me with a greedy kiss, locking my arms against the mattress.

"No, you're mine right now," she directs, pressing me into the sheets. Her hands, her skin, her eyes, she's totally captured me, and I doubt I could have moved right then even if I wanted to disobey her, but I don't dream of it. She owns me in this moment, and I suck in my breath at the power she has over me.

She seems to be losing herself too as she grabs the condom from the nightstand, and I'm shocked that there is nothing in me that stops our progress this time. There's no protest, no devastating explanations. Just anticipation, hope.

Unbearable fire.

She kisses me again, hungry, inviting, and finally lets me hold onto her as she slides into perfect union with me. I'm amazed at how we fit, two halves forming a whole, two imperfections transforming into a beautiful masterpiece.

"It's ok, Luke. It's ok to feel something good," she breathes. "It's ok to let go."

Spellbound, any lingering thoughts dissolve when the white light returns, blistering through my body and exploding the darkness of my head. But she has no mercy, she doesn't stop, and I love every beautiful harmony that escapes her in the next few moments, evidence that she's connected too, that she is satisfied with us, with the final testimony of what we do to each other. That the connection of mind, body, and soul has only begun, stranding us with a new, undeniable addiction to each other.

Sixteen months. Sixteen months erased in sixteen minutes.

"SO THAT HAPPENED," Holland sighs, turning towards me.

I match her grin. "It did."

"You know, you weren't nearly as bad as I thought you'd be."

My eyes widen in disbelief. "What?" I cry.

She giggles and nestles against me. "I'm kidding! I think with a little practice..."

"Oh, shut up. I can tell when a woman's faking it," I bark, and she laughs.

She becomes serious as she takes my hand and kisses my fingers. "Luke, I know how hard that was for you. The significance of this moment. I can't tell you how happy I am right now that I got to share it with you. I don't take it lightly."

I close my eyes and draw in a deep breath, reminded yet again how much I don't deserve this woman but I'm certainly going to fight to try.

"Do you know how much I wish I could say she was my last? That you were the first since Elena?" I confess quietly, opening my eyes again to meet her compassionate gaze. "But she wasn't, Holland. She wasn't even in the last twenty probably. We'd degraded way before her death, and then afterwards, I completely self-destructed. I don't even know what happened those first couple months, only that there were lots of girls and substances to keep me numb. And then, I just stopped living altogether. Over a year of complete darkness."

She squeezes my hand. "You're not that person anymore."

"I'm trying not to be anyway."

"Exactly. Which means you're not."

I grin and adjust so I can wrap my arms around her and hold her against me.

"Hey, Luke?"

"Yeah?"

"You know I was kidding, right? That was amazing. You are amazing."

"Wait until I'm back in full form."

She laughs and twists to face me. "Interesting... And how long will that take?"

I shrug with a grin. "I don't know. Depends how much practice I get."

I love her look as she studies me. "Really...well, we don't have a show for four days. Think the others would miss us?"

"Pretty sure Wes would," I tease, and she flinches.

"Yeah, true...how are you feeling, anyway?" she asks, her eyes changing as she traces the bruise on my ribs. "I was afraid I was hurting you. This one looks pretty bad."

"That's funny, because I was loving the fact that I didn't feel it for a brief moment. You're a great doctor."

She laughs and swats at my arm. "For masking pain with sex? Pretty sure they have another name for that."

I roll my eyes. "Oh, whatever. You know I didn't mean that."

"No, but I gotta say, as much as I hate to admit this, because what you and Wes did was totally immature and stupid, badass Luke is pretty damn hot. I can't believe you took a punch and fought for me."

I laugh and shake my head. "It's not like Wes really gave me a choice."

"Who swung first?"

"This feels like a trick question."

"It's not! I just want to know."

I sigh. "I'm pretty sure I did."

"Pretty sure?"

"It happened really fast. I don't know."

"Has it been sixteen months since your last fight too?"

I glance at her in amused disbelief, and she returns a shy smile.

"What? Has it?"

"I have no clue. Probably not," I laugh.

"How can you not know?" she argues, crinkling her nose in an adorable scowl.

"It's not like I keep a diary of this stuff," I cry in exasperation.

"You should. It's fascinating."

"Fascinating?"

"So when guys fight, do you actually do the whole 'I'm

gonna cut you!' 'No, I'm gonna cut you, bitch!' thing first or what? Like, do you try to work it out with empty threats before the fists fly?"

I shake my head with a grin and rub my eyes. "Oh my god, you're relentless."

"So that's a no?"

"Actually, I'm pretty sure Wes did call me a bitch."

"What? No...really?"

I groan. "Can we please not talk about this anymore?"

"Ok, fine! Just one more question."

I sigh and roll my eyes. "Fine, what?"

"I get the whole macho testosterone thing, but did it ever occur to you that maybe throwing punches isn't the best choice for a guy who makes his living playing guitar?"

I laugh and wrestle her against the sheets, responding with a kiss that eliminates any lingering questions.

HOLLAND and I have pretty much decided to test our espionage skills and figure out a way to spend the next four days in this hotel room when I get a text from Callie that uproots my world yet again.

"Shit," I mutter, staring at my phone in disbelief as I balance on the edge of the bed.

"What is it?" Holland asks, coming up behind me and resting her chin on my shoulder.

I rub my hand over my face. "It's Casey this time... Dammit!" I turn and give her a quick kiss before rising to collect my clothes. "I have to go."

"Yeah, of course. Is everything ok? What's wrong? Is Casey ok?"

I sigh as I pull on my jeans. "Have you seen my shirt?"

"By the door, I think."

"Thanks."

"Luke, what is it? What's going on?"

I stop and face her. "Casey's father died. He didn't find out until today and the funeral is Wednesday."

"What? I'm so sorry! Why wouldn't his family have told him?"

I shake my head, suddenly angry more than anything. "It's complicated. I have to go find him."

"Yes, of course!" She joins me by the door. "Hey, wait."

I do, even as my mind races into the hallway. I have to go, I have to...but the frenetic urgency fades into a strange sense of peace when she slips her arms around me and pulls me close.

"Keep me updated, ok?" she whispers, and I know that request means way more than it sounds.

"I will, Holland." I meet her gaze. "I promise."

I kiss her then, loving how that simple action has transformed the anger of the previous moment into a more functional strength. She makes me better, stronger, no question.

"I'll let you know as soon as I learn anything more," I assure her, pulling away.

She nods. "Ok. And I'll get dressed."

I grin. "Good plan."

———

I FIND them in Casey's room, and Callie lets me in with a knowing look. Casey is by the window doing his frantic pacing while he argues with someone on the phone.

"Molly," Callie explains.

I nod and watch him for a second before turning back to Callie. I don't think he even realizes I'm here yet.

"So what's happening? What's the story?"

Callie sighs and leans against the wall by the door, crossing her arms.

"Ok, so apparently his father had been sick for a while but refused any kind of treatment. He didn't do doctors or whatever. Anyway, when he died on Thursday, his mom didn't want Casey to find out until after the funeral."

"What? Why? That's messed up!"

She grunts. "Yeah, tell me about it. He's really upset, as you can imagine. I don't know. I guess since he was the only one still at odds with the man? Who knows, but Molly couldn't keep it from him any longer and called this morning. She claims his mom is just out of it and thought she was helping Casey by not telling him. She's always been kind of misguided and naïve, I guess."

"Yes, she has, but that's..." I shake my head. "Callie, he needs to go to that funeral."

She meets my eyes briefly before turning back to Casey. I can see how concerned she is for him, how much she loves him. "I don't know. Their whole family situation is so screwed up. It might do more harm than good. Besides, I don't know if you'd be able to convince him to go. He's a mess right now."

I sigh and study my friend, my brother, across the room. "I know, but you have to trust me on this. I know Casey. It's not about his father, it's about him and the rest of his family. He needs to be there. Let me try to talk to him."

Callie seems relieved at my involvement. "Thanks, Luke. Actually, he hasn't eaten all day. I'm going to go find us something and give you time alone."

We exchange sad smiles as she exits the room, and Casey looks over at the clatter of the door as he finishes his call.

"Luke, hey," he says, and I make my way toward the main space in the room.

"Hey, man. Callie's going to get you some food. She told me the news. I'm sorry, Case."

He shakes his head with a dark expression. "That my dad is dead or that my bat-shit mom didn't want to tell me."

"Both?"

He returns a weak smile and drops to the edge of the bed. "Yeah, and so now what the hell am I supposed to do? Molly wants me there, Mom clearly doesn't, Nate and Abby want me...this is so messed up."

"You go."

His gaze shoots over to me. "What?"

"Case, you need to be there."

"Really, just like that, huh," he replies skeptically. "My dad and I were not on good terms. Everyone there will know that."

I nod. "No, but you're on good terms with Molly, Nate, Abby, and the rest of your friends and family. You go, Case. You only get one chance to attend your father's funeral." I know that as well as anyone. I suspect Casey is thinking the same thing when he quiets and considers my argument.

"What about Mom?" he says finally.

"She'll change her mind when you show up. And be glad you did, if I had to guess."

"Maybe." He curses again and shakes his head. "I don't know. I don't know if I can do this."

"You can. Besides, you'll have Callie and me there with you."

His expression turns to shock as he stares back at me. "Wait, what? Luke, no..."

I sigh and lower myself beside him. I knew the second I saw Callie's text I'd be going home to support my best friend, even if it meant I'd have to face my own hell.

"You can't, man. It's going to be my whole family! Hell, your aunt will probably even be there. You know what they'll do to you," he warns, searching my eyes. "They don't know you've changed. They probably wouldn't care if they did."

I suck in my breath, instinctively bracing against the coming storm. "I'm not letting you do this alone, Case. I don't care. I'm going, even if they make me sit outside."

He's still staring in stunned disbelief. "You'd do that for me. Put yourself through that?" He shakes his head and waves his hand dismissively. "No. No way. I'm not letting you do that. You've got enough shit to deal with."

I almost laugh. "Case, seriously? After everything you've done for me? All the times you stood by me when there was absolutely no reason you should have? Not a chance in hell I'm backing away when you need me. I'm going."

I actually think I see tears in his eyes as he stares back at the wall, processing my speech. He's my brother, one of the best people I know. He's suffered through multiple wars for me. I'm fighting this battle with him.

"Thanks, man," he says quietly after a long pause. "Really, I..."

"I know," I respond, clasping his arm. "Let me go take care of something quick, and then we'll talk to Tess and Kenneth, ok?"

He nods, and I give him another reassuring smile before heading back to Holland's room.

HOLLAND IS surprised to see me back so soon, and I love how natural our quick kiss works as a greeting.

"How's Casey?" she asks, clearly concerned as we move inside.

"Not great. That's why I'm here. I wanted to let you know that I'm flying back to Houston with him as soon as possible."

She nods as if she expected as much. "Ok, sounds good. I'm going too." She's totally serious, and I can't help but grin at her effortless kindness.

"You're amazing, you know that?" I say quietly, drawing her into my arms. She returns my smile as she gazes up at me.

"I know. You're a lucky guy."

I laugh and kiss her. "I am. Way more than I deserve. But, Holland, you're not going to Houston."

Her eyes narrow. "Um, yes, I am."

I shake my head. "No. You're not." I sigh and take her hand, leading her to the bed. We sit, and I turn to her with an earnest expression. "Look, I know your instinct wants to support Casey and me, but this is way beyond that. It's going to be a lot more complicated than a funeral for his dad. Like, soap opera level complicated."

She just looks irritated. "Please, you don't think I know that? Everything that involves you is a freaking soap opera. I'm going."

"Holland, I'm serious. You know I'd love to have you there under other circumstances, but you just don't understand what's going to happen. Casey's drama is nothing compared to what I'll have waiting for me. I've hidden from it for so long, but it's time for me to go deal with it. I have no idea what that will look like except that it's going to be incredibly ugly."

She shrugs. "Awesome. You should deal with it. I'm proud of you for taking that step. And I'm going."

I shake my head in exasperation. "Holland, you don't understand..."

"No, you don't understand," she says, forcing me to look at her. "I signed up for this, Luke. And so did you. The sex part comes with a plane ticket to Houston. I told you, I want all of you. That includes all the shit from your past."

I don't even know what to say as I stare at her in awe. I

certainly don't know how to argue. It can't be real, she can't be real, but here she is, staring into my eyes, daring me to contradict her.

"You warned me you were hard. I knew what I was getting," she teases gently, and I can't help but smile.

"Yeah, I did, didn't I."

She nods and leans against my shoulder.

"Ok, fine," I say finally. "But how do we explain this to the others?"

"Explain what? That I want to go along to support my friend Casey in his time of loss?"

I grin, and meet her gaze. "True."

She returns it and pulls me in for another kiss, this one more persistent. "You do understand that we will have to tell Callie and Casey, though, right? There's no way I'm going two days without touching you," she explains lightly.

I smile against her lips. "They'll keep our secret," I assure her, letting my desire match her own. I love her irritated groan as the fire starts to consume us again.

"Ugh, what is wrong with me? It's like some Pavlovian response. I see you and immediately want your clothes off," she mutters between kisses. "Do you have any idea how annoying that is?"

I laugh as she tugs at my shirt in frustration. "I have an idea, yeah."

"Isn't it supposed to be the other way around, though?" she whines.

"Ha. Don't worry. You're always naked in my head," I assure her with a grin, pulling her against me. She smacks me before we attack each other again. This time she seems desperate to explore every inch of me as she rakes my body like she didn't just own it for the last couple hours. I love every second of it, love how her touch soothes and burns at the same time, how she stirs my fire and consumes it.

"You probably have arrangements to make, don't you," she breathes, showing no mercy for my plight.

"I do," I manage, my blood searing, my breath coming in gasps as she moves over me. Her mouth. Her skin. Her smile.

"You should go do that." She clearly loves torturing me.

"I should."

When her hand slips past the waist of my jeans, I'm pretty sure my veins are about to explode from the pounding. Her eyes ignite at my reaction, and she only intensifies her unfair raid on my will.

"It seems like you might be ready for another quick round of practice before, though?" she teases, and I flip her over, kissing her hard as I lock her against the sheets.

I pull back and study her beautiful face in amusement. "And it seems like you don't understand how hard it is to get a flight to Houston."

***

WE HAVE to take what we can get in terms of flights, but with Kenneth and Tess' logistics star power behind us, we manage to find four tickets out early Tuesday morning.

There's an outpouring of support and sympathy for Casey and no one questions his leave of absence, or the three of us going with him. Especially, since our fortunate schedule break means we should make it back in plenty of time for Friday's show. Of course, none of them have a clue about the actual complexity of this trip.

I don't know how Wes takes the news about Holland's involvement in our drama, but I can't imagine it went well. She hasn't said a word about it though, and I'm not interested in discussing him any more than we have to at the moment. We haven't told Callie and Casey about our budding relationship either, although it's getting harder and harder to hide our attraction the more time we spend together. Our assigned seats are scattered all over the plane, but we manage to manipulate our way into the same row after we board. I dare anyone to say no to Callie Roland and Holland Drake when they turn on the charm.

It's a small plane with only five rows across. Callie wanted to look out the window, Casey knew he'd be buried in his laptop, and I'm across the aisle with Holland on my other side. An elderly lady has our window seat, but we can't tell if she belongs with anyone else. She's said nine words since takeoff: "Let me know if the air bothers you, honey."

Casey is on his computer the second the flight attendant won't kill him for it, and I can feel Holland's amusement beside me. He has his studio headphones on, eyes locked on the screen, so I have no problem returning her grin.

"Is he ever not working?" she whispers.

I shrug. "Probably, but not that I've seen."

"Penchant for Red, right?"

"Yeah. Their debut went platinum a few months after it released. He's already working on new stuff."

Her eyes widen as she leans forward to give him another look. "Really, wow. Not bad for a side project."

I smirk. "Yeah, right. I'm pretty sure we're his side project at this point."

"Hey, man. Can you listen to this for me?" Casey interrupts, smacking my arm to get my attention. I take the headphones he's shoving in my face and slide them on, giving him a nod when I'm ready.

My jaw nearly hits the tray table as he starts the track, and I stare back at him in disbelief. He's grinning at my expression, and I shake my head before turning again so I can focus on the music. When the song finishes, I pull the headphones down and face him in awe.

"Case, that's phenomenal. What is that?"

He's so excited that I find myself hoping he's buckled into his seat. "I know, right? I just got this sweet new bass module. With that filter and chorus echo, I just about shit my pants. And then the killer drop after the bridge? What do you think?"

"I think it's amazing. And when did you learn to sing like that?" I laugh, handing his headphones back.

He only shrugs with a shy smile and throws them back on. Callie is giving me her fake-irritated look, but I can tell she's as proud of him as I am.

"He never shuts off, does he," I observe with a grin, and she rolls her eyes.

"Never," she mouths.

I feel a sudden pressure on my leg, and glance down at Holland's hand. I instinctively cast a look across the aisle, but the others aren't paying attention to us anymore.

"Living on the edge, huh?" I tease.

"Time for you to meet my wild streak," she returns, matching my grin, and it's everything I can do not to kiss her right then. I know she wants the same thing when her fingers tighten on my thigh, the pressure intensifying as she moves higher. My heart starts to pound.

"I mean, they have a bathroom," I offer with a mischievous look, and she rolls her eyes.

"I can't get you to make love to me in a four-star hotel room, but you'll take me in an airplane port-a-john?"

"Oh, whatever," I return, grabbing her hand from my leg and giving it a playful squeeze. She chuckles, drawing the attention of the lady to our left.

"You two make a sweet couple. How long have you been married?" the lady asks, eyeing my ring.

My stomach drops, but Holland doesn't catch on and only laughs.

"Oh, we're not married," she corrects, glancing at me when I instinctively pull my hand out of sight.

"It's complicated," I mutter.

"I see," the woman replies with clear disapproval, and Holland seems startled, then embarrassed as she finally clues in.

"Oh, no, we're not having an affair or anything," she explains quickly. "He was married, but his wife..." She stops, the woman looks away, and I choke a little. Now, we're all miserable.

"Oh, well, it's certainly none of my business," the woman continues with a stiff smile. She turns back to her window, and I feel Holland's eyes on me. I give her a weak smile of my own to try to reassure her, but my body suddenly goes cold at a whole new thought. I glance at Callie and Casey to make sure they're not paying attention before leaning toward Holland.

"As awkward as that was, she brings up a good point," I say quietly. "Where we're going, Houston...it's just better if none of this comes up, ok? We're going to be surrounded by Casey and Elena's family and friends. There will be enough drama without me showing up with a new girlfriend. They already despise me." I sigh, hating everything about this conversation. "It's not even for my sake. It'll be much better for you, for all of us, if you're just Casey's friend Holland while we're there."

She searches my eyes, and I'm relieved when she nods. "Of course. I totally understand. Casey's buddy Holland. Got it." She pauses as her serious expression turns into a grin. "But girl-friend, huh?"

"What?"

"You said girlfriend."

I return her grin and give her a look. "Please. You know what I meant."

"Actually, I don't know if I do. Did you mean girlfriend?"

"Um, really? Because I'm pretty sure you just want to know if that would entitle you to my J45."

She huffs and sits back. "Dammit." Then, gives me another smile. "Would it?"

I laugh and shake my head in amusement.

WE HAVE a two-hour layover in Chicago and grab coffees and snacks while we're waiting. I know what Holland's thinking as the four of us sit around the small table, nursing our cups, because the thought is plaguing my head too. I just have no clue how to broach the subject with my two best friends whose minds are rightfully elsewhere. Besides, blurting awkward announcements is Holland's area of expertise, not mine.

"How you doing with all of this, Case?" I ask, breaking the initial silence. He shrugs and glances up at me.

"Fine, I guess. Trying to sort it all out in my head."

I nod. "It's a lot to deal with."

He sighs. "Yeah. It is. Distract me," he directs to Callie who rolls her eyes with a smile at his teasing.

"Uh huh. What'll it be, your majesty? A song? A dance?"

He shrugs. "How about both?"

"Right. Like I'm going to sing for Luke Craven, Casey Barrett, and Holland Drake."

"You have a nice voice! It's very sweet," Casey says, and she only grunts.

"Whatever."

"Have you heard her sing?" he asks me, and I cross my arms.

"Actually, no. Really, Callie? Another secret you've kept from me?"

"Ugh, he's lying! I don't sing."

"You sing in the shower all the time," Casey argues.

Her eyes widen in disbelief as she turns a death stare on him. "How about we not talk about my shower habits in front of our friends?"

"What?" he returns defensively. "Who doesn't sing in the shower? It's not like I'm talking about shaving your legs or something."

"Casey!" she cries, smacking him.

"What? What did I do?"

Holland and I exchange an amused look as they argue, and she takes the opportunity to motion toward them with her eyes. I return the look with a shrug, still not convinced it's a good idea to say anything, even though this is probably the best opportunity we'll have on this trip.

I'm still hesitant about it all, and my stomach drops when I turn back to Callie and Casey to find them staring at us. They must have caught our silent exchange, and I'm afraid I actually cringe.

"What was that?" Callie asks, leaning forward with an obvious glint in her eyes.

"What was what?" I ask.

"That!" she cries, motioning between Holland and me. "You just had a moment."

"A moment?" I scoff. "What are you talking about?"

She leans back and crosses her arms, glaring at us. "Come on. We're not stupid. Something is going on between you two."

"Why? Because we exchanged a look?"

"Um, no, because you've been exchanging lots of looks."

"We've become close," Holland explains, and I cast her a quick glance. I don't know if it was the right thing to say, but it's way better than whatever was about to come out of my mouth.

"Close? How close?" Callie asks, clearly getting excited.

I take a deep breath as the two women exchange knowing grins, and Callie claps in excitement when Holland shrugs.

"I knew it! I knew it! Didn't I call that?" she cries, shaking Casey's arm.

Casey rolls his eyes. "She did."

"We're just...I don't know. Just getting close for now. That's all," Holland continues, and I'm struck again by her profound accuracy. I wouldn't have known how to begin to explain what we are, what's happening between us, but "getting close" certainly applies.

I glance at Casey and try to read his expression. While Callie obviously supports our nascent relationship, I don't know if Casey is ready to understand. I wouldn't blame him for being hesitant, but I'm also glad it's out. I don't want to keep things from him either. Not anymore.

"This is just between the four of us. We're not talking about it yet. There's nothing to really say at this point anyway," I explain, and see Casey visibly relax.

He lets out his breath. "Ok, good. Because you know my dad's funeral is probably the worst possible place to make that announcement."

I roll my eyes. "Uh, yeah. I get that, Case."

He shrugs and gives me a sheepish smile. "Ok, just making sure." He quiets and studies us for a moment. His face changes, and I hold my breath for the verdict. "It's good, though. Really good. I'm glad you're 'getting close,'" he says finally, focusing back on me. I return his smile, warmed, and yes, relieved, by his approval.

He pauses to give us a hard stare. "I just hope you kids are being safe," he jokes, then flinches when Callie smacks him again.

Holland and I laugh. "We're good. Thanks."

———

CASEY'S BROTHER Nate had offered to pick us up at the airport and drive us to the hotel, but Casey didn't want to be reliant on others, having no idea how the coming drama would unfold. It's a smart move, and I'm also relieved we're renting a car and making our own accommodations. It's a little awkward as Holland and I check into our separate rooms, but even though Casey and Callie know we're "getting close," we're not exactly at the point of sharing a room yet either. At least we're on the same floor, which seems like a fortunate compromise. Casey waits until we all have our keys before issuing instructions.

"Alright, let's get settled in and cleaned up. I already let Molly and Nate know we're here so I'm sure they're going to want to meet up tonight. You guys good?"

We nod. "Got it. Let us know the plan," I say. Casey and Callie are both looking at us with hidden smiles, and I actually start to feel shy about the whole thing.

"Ok. Well, um...have fun until then, I guess. But not too much. It might not be long. Not sure how much time you need to 'get close,'" Casey teases.

I roll my eyes. "Shut up," I spit back, and he grins. "We shouldn't have said anything."

"No! You absolutely should have!" Callie cries. "Thank you, Luke. It means a lot that you did. I'll keep him in line. Promise." She gives us an apologetic look as she shoves Casey in the direction of the elevators. "What is wrong with you?" she snaps as they move away.

I cast a concerned glance at Holland after they leave, but she only seems amused by the whole thing.

"What about you?" she says, moving toward the elevators as well.

"What about me?" I ask, following her.

"I don't know. Everyone's concerned about Casey, but what about you? You've been pretty quiet since we boarded the flight from Chicago. Well, more so than usual," she adds with a smile. I return a weak one of my own.

"I know. Sorry. A lot on my mind."

"Um, yeah, I know. That was my polite way of saying spill it."

I laugh and follow her onto the elevator.

"I can't believe you're still willing to go on elevators with me after Myrtle Beach."

She casts me an amused glance as she punches our floor number. "It's not without reservation, I'll be honest."

"Well, I promise to never again act like a dick to you in an elevator."

She smirks. "You better not, although I'm not sure I like your qualification."

I grin and shrug as the door opens again and we move into the hallway.

"What's your room?" I ask, and she glances down at her welcome brochure.

"307."

I nod. "Ok. I'm 310."

We start walking in silence and come to an awkward stop before her door.

"Will you stay and talk for a bit?" Holland asks, glancing up at me with a look I can't ignore.

"Are you sure that's a good idea? Casey said we might not have a lot of time," I argue, and she rolls her eyes.

"We can go into a hotel room without having sex," she returns.

I grin. "I don't know. You're the one who has that Pavlovian response to strip me every time we're alone."

"I'll keep my hands to myself, I promise." She cringes. "Ok, I can't promise that. But...you know what I mean." She opens her door and drags me inside, putting an end to the debate.

After parking her suitcase by the dresser, she turns and pulls me close in a tight embrace. "Seriously, Luke. Where are you at right now? Your head is not a place you should be navigating alone."

I swallow and draw in a deep breath. My head is not a place for anyone. She can't possibly understand what she's asking. "Honestly, Holland, I'm scared," I admit quietly into the dim silence. "Really scared."

She pulls me tighter, and I close my eyes, suddenly overwhelmed by what I'm about to do. It seemed like such a necessary decision yesterday. I had to come home. I had to do this for Casey, for me, for Elena, Holland. Everyone needs me to reconcile my past with my present. I can't have a future until I do, but now, standing at the entrance to the gallows, about to face the jury, my sentence, it's all I can do to keep from running back to the airport.

I don't know if I'm strong enough to face my punishment after a year and a half of hiding from it, but that's where I find myself now. Except for our recent evening with Molly, I haven't been in contact with any of them since The Funeral. Since I completely imploded and added a whole new chapter to my list of crimes. I can't even think about that day without getting nauseous.

So yes, I'm scared. No, terrified, but deep down I know that part of claiming responsibility for the humiliation of what I was is to stop hiding from the consequences. I'm here because I know I'll never be able to accept I've changed until I prove it to them, that I'll never be able to forgive myself until I face the punishment for my sins. I thought I came for Casey, but as I stand here in silence, trying to stop the shaking, the truth hits me hard like it so often does. I brace myself as it crashes down, rooting me in a reality I hadn't truly understood until this moment.

I'm not just here for my best friend; I'm here for my execution.

THE PLAN IS to head over to Casey's brother Nate's house for a barbeque. I brace myself at the announcement, which doesn't come as a surprise, just a disappointment, and do my best to project a nonchalant front as we leave the hotel and head to the car.

I hate the somber silence that's settled over us as we drive. I can feel them all watching me, evaluating. They think I haven't noticed that they're acting like this is *my* funeral, not Casey's father's, but I try to remind myself it's only because they care so much.

"It shouldn't be everyone tonight. Just Nate, Abby, Molly. Maybe some others," Casey muses, glancing over at me briefly before focusing back on the road.

I swallow and turn to him. "Ok." I force in more air. "Do they know I'm coming?"

Casey answers with an uncomfortable silence, and I turn back to the window, my stomach dropping.

"I'm sorry, man, I just...Molly will be cool with it."

I nod. "Yeah, ok. It's probably better this way." Suddenly, I feel a hand on my arm and glance back at Holland who's leaning forward from the back seat.

"If we have to sit in the car all night, we sit in the car," she says with a smile. I try to return it.

"Casey and I will run food to you," Callie adds, and my grin finally breaks.

"Thanks. Make sure you bring some of Abby's iced tea too. It's fantastic."

"It's pretty killer," Casey agrees. "Iced tea is the only thing Abby does well in the kitchen."

"Casey!" Callie cries.

"What? It's true. Isn't it true, Luke? Remember that time she made us that vegetable lasagna?"

"With the carrots?" I laugh. "Oh man, that was awful."

"Was that supposed to be carrots? I had no idea what it was. It tasted like dirty chalk. That's all I remember."

"You two are so mean!" Callie chides.

"No, that lasagna was mean," Casey retorts, and I can't help but snicker.

"It was pretty bad, Cal. Even Elena..." I freeze.

Casey glances at me. They all do. I can't move.

"Even Elena hated it and suggested she try a different recipe next time," Casey finishes for me. I give him a weak smile as the heaviness starts to overwhelm me again.

Holland clears her throat. "Well, then, I guess you don't have to bring us any of that," she remarks, squeezing my arm.

And air finally makes its way back into my lungs.

I DON'T KNOW why I even bothered hoping we'd be able to sneak into the gathering unnoticed. I swear every conversation dies as we come into view, every eye converging on us. I've never felt so exposed in my entire life, and my heart sinks as I take in the crowded deck and surrounding patio. It's not just

Nate, Abby, and Molly. It's everyone, all of them, and the panic begins to mount as my brain and body clue in to the fact that hell's about to break loose now, not tomorrow like I'd been bracing for. I wasn't ready for twenty-four hours from now, let alone twenty-four seconds.

"Shit," Casey mutters, and we exchange a quick glance before he plasters his signature grin on his face.

Molly makes the first move and comes running over, throwing herself into her big brother's arms.

"You made it!" she cries. "Thank you." Her huge smile fades when her eyes rest on me. I read every bit of concern in her expression, and try to steady my breathing. "Luke, hey. You came too."

"Of course I did," I manage. She smiles again, sweet, genuine, and gives me a hug as well. "Well, I'm glad you're here, but..." she stops and glances back at our audience. I can't even begin to do the same. "She's here, Luke," she whispers, searching my eyes. "They're all here. I didn't know you were coming or..."

I force a smile. "I know. It's ok. I'm here to face them."

She stares at me, they all are now, and I finally dare a glance at the crowd.

"You sure, man?" Casey asks, clearly hesitant.

"Better here than at the church, right?" I reason. He seems to understand, but neither of us has any illusions that there's a "better" in any of this.

I can't even look at Holland and Callie.

"Hi, everyone," Casey announces, leading us toward the line of gaping stares. "Good to see you all. This is my girlfriend, Callie, for those of you who haven't met her yet. Oh, and my good friend, Holland. Of course you all know Luke." He climbs the stairs of the deck with his animated Casey Barrett spring and surveys one of the well-stocked food tables. "Aunt

Marjorie! Your deviled eggs. Fantastic! Cal, you have to try these," he calls, waving Callie over. She gives me an apologetic shrug before following Casey's lead, and I try to remain steady. I know Holland is watching me, waiting to see what I do next. Hell, they all are, but I have no idea where to go from here. Molly, ever sensitive, loops her arm in mine and leads me forward as well.

"How was your trip in?" she asks, both of us pretending we'll actually succeed at making small talk right now.

"Fine, thanks. No delays."

"That's great. Holland, it's so nice of you to come to support Casey."

Holland's smile looks a lot more vibrant and genuine than anything that could come out of me at the moment. "Casey always seems to be there for those who need him. Of course we had to jump in when he needed us."

Molly is clearly touched and glances back at her older brother. "He has a huge heart."

"So I'm learning. I'm sorry, what was your name again? Are you Molly?" Holland asks as we reach the stairs also.

She laughs and nods. "Yeah, Molly Barrett. Sorry. My brother may have a huge heart, but he sucks at manners."

Holland grins.

"Luke, hey. Been a while, huh?" I turn and meet the new voice as Holland and Molly continue their conversation.

"Oh, hi, Nate. Yeah, it has. How are you doing? How are the kids?"

Nate smiles. "Good, good. Yeah, everyone's good. They're running around here somewhere. Heard you're touring again."

I nod. "Yeah, I am. It was a long road back, but we're getting there."

"Um, yeah...well, hey, that's great. Good luck to..."

A loud crash stops his sentence, and we spin toward the growing vacuum in the center of the gathering.

"No! No way! How dare you?!" The shrieks match the shattered bowl of pasta salad sprayed all over the rough wood, and I don't even need to see the speaker to know the voice. I'd recognize that hatred anywhere.

Casey moves to jump in, but I shake my head, blocking his rescue.

"Aunt Gina," I acknowledge quietly, stepping forward to face her.

The crowd has instinctively begun to back away from our confrontation, and I forget about everything, everyone else.

"You disgusting, son-of-a-bitch! What are you doing here? Why would you think for a second you'd be welcomed here?!"

I start to shake. I hate it, but I can't stop it and draw in a deep breath, trying to control the trembling, the panic.

"Can we talk about this somewhere else so we don't disrupt dinner?"

"Yeah, sure, run and hide! That's just like you!"

"I'm not hiding, Aunt Gina, I just..."

"I told you never to call me that again! I am not your aunt. I am nothing to you."

"Please, can we just..."

"The biggest mistake I ever made was agreeing to take you from your whore of a mother! I should have known you'd end up just like her no matter what I did! You know she's dead, right?" I feel like a club hit me as I stare at her in shock. She must read it, but has no mercy.

"No, of course you wouldn't know that. Why would you? You've never shown an ounce of concern for anyone but yourself. Well, and those sluts who throw themselves at you at your concerts!" Her eyes burn as she charges toward me. "You may have the world fooled, thinking you're some kind of rock god or something, but we know who you are, what you are! We know the sludge that pumps through your veins and oozes out of your cold, dead heart." She shoves me hard as she moves past me toward the stairs.

My vision is blurring, the air suddenly so thick I think I can feel it closing around my throat. Only one phrase slithers through the darkness in my head and it escapes before I can even consider what's happening.

"You're right."

She stops. They all stop, and the silence is heavy as it settles over us.

It's finally interrupted by a bitter laugh, and I flinch. "Oh, I am? I'm right, but...but what, Luke? What hilarious, ridiculous excuse are we getting this time?" She throws up her hands in anger. "I have nothing else to say to you!"

I close my eyes and struggle for words, anything. My heart is racing, my blood pounding so hard in my ears I don't even know if I'll hear whatever comes out of my mouth next, but I have to stop fighting the words. I just have to stop fighting.

"There are no buts this time. No excuses. You don't have to say anything. It's my turn to say something to all of you."

The tears start to rise, heavy in my chest, but I can't do that right now, cry. I need words, not tears, to have any hope of a future. "I do know what I've done, what I was," I begin, standing before them all, the giant eye staring at me, accusing me. "I have to live with that every second of every day. The pain of trying to atone for something that can never be made right. You're right, there will be no justice for my sins, my mistakes. And you're right, I've spent a long time hiding." The trembling has reached my voice and I clench my eyes shut, trying to gain enough control to complete my damning testimony. My self-incrimination.

"I'm not here for forgiveness," I say finally, quietly, but

somehow firm at the same time. I take a deep breath and open my eyes, meeting the jury again. "I'm here to account for what I was."

THE REST IS A BLURRED NIGHTMARE. Those not involved, or who choose an ounce of civility, flee to the house, leaving me alone with the unfiltered hostility. I get pelted with names, dates, places, accusations for things I didn't even know about. Did I know Elena used to call her cousin Marie at least twice a week sobbing because she knew I was cheating on her? Did I know she kept a file of the many pictures that floated around the gossip stratosphere? Did I know she'd cry herself to sleep more often than not, that she lost seven pounds in a month? Did I not understand how much that woman loved me despite what I was, how I hurt her?

My recent phone hack comes up, of course. They remember those pictures of the blond women from the initial social media explosion. Elena was with her sister Lily the night they found their way into the public eye; the night they charred Elena's soul. Lily makes sure I understand the horror of every second of that night. How Elena blamed herself. How she thought she must not have been good enough for me to love her. How she started to believe maybe I never did. Did I actually love her? It would be news to any of them.

I can't breathe the entire time. Can't even think as the horrific words come at me, each revelation slicing the little that's left of my strength, tearing me apart with old memories, gutting me with new ones I will now have to carry on my conscience.

I don't say more than ten words for the next hour, except for answering some of the questions that are barked at me.

Mostly no's. No, I didn't know. No, I hadn't. No, I'm sorry. I'm really sorry. I'm not allowed to speak beyond that anyway.

Early on, I silently begged Casey to take Callie and Holland away. He knew what was coming as well as I did, and I'm sure he agreed only for their sakes. I could see the concern in his eyes as he convinced them to take a tour of the house, his fear of leaving me alone with the firing squad, but I couldn't bear the thought of them witnessing this. Their absence is the only thing I have left to hold onto.

So it's just me here. Alone. Silent. Condemned.

I'm embarrassed by the tears in my eyes, but I don't even bother trying to stop them. I just let them gather and slowly slide down my cheeks as I stare at the ground, listening, holding my breath, waiting for the next bullet point on my rap sheet.

I forgot her birthday twice, anniversary pretty much every year. Oh yeah, and then there was the dog. Reilly. Because clearly I wasn't enough for her. I didn't meet her needs. The dog now lives with Abby. I tried to make up for getting high and missing Christmas dinner by buying her a diamond necklace. What a joke. Great-Aunt Norma doesn't even believe I'm not high right now. Great-Uncle Alan is sure I must have some kind of STD.

I'm called names I haven't heard in a long time, and some I definitely have. Wes' taunts seem downright kind compared to most of what I get as the seconds turn into minutes that seem like days. And throughout it all, my only remaining blood relation is always there, elaborating on some of the comments, echoing others, nodding at the rest.

Mrs. Barrett doesn't have as much to say as I would have thought, but I suspect it's because her silence makes it easier for her to bask in my pain at the bludgeoning by her rallied army. I don't miss the smirks, the satisfaction that each blow brings to her, but I say nothing as I let them land. Flinching a few times, often fighting the urge to throw up.

And then, suddenly, as quickly as it started, it just stops.

It's almost eerie how the horrible choir bleeds into total silence, but it's unmistakable. When it's clear that the distant sound of a lawn mower has replaced the taunts and accusations, I raise my eyes, tentatively at first, and meet theirs. It seems like each gaze is locked on mine, each face waiting to see what I do with the horrifying chaos just dumped on me. They're breathing hard too. Some have tears, some still only display the resurrected fury, but we finally all agree on one thing. There are no more words. The words are out. The words are done.

"I'm sorry," I say quietly. "I'm so sorry," I breathe before disappearing down the steps and back to our car.

———

I BREAK down the second I'm inside. I was probably stunned for most of what just happened, but as the full extent hits, it knocks everything out from under me. I have no idea what's happening outside of this moment, or if I'll even live through it. I can't breathe from the sobs, pounding the seat with every bit of strength I have left in me. I don't want to be here right now. I'd do anything to make this pain stop. I hate. I love. I fear, regret. God, everything is slamming into me all at once.

I just can't fucking breathe!

And then, inexplicably, I'm not alone. A whisper of air slips into the stifling car as the door opens, followed by the soothing scent I'd recognize anywhere. A firm pressure tightens around my back, then my shoulders, then guides me against her. She pulls me tight, allowing my tears to stain her shirt, holding me as I shatter. I can't even begin to speak or acknowledge what's happened, what's happening. I just survive. Survive this moment, like I've somehow managed to survive all the rest.

"I'm not going to say you didn't deserve that, but you're done now, Luke. You're done, ok?" Holland whispers, only making the tears come harder. "Please let this be enough. Please." She buries her head in my shoulder as we both hold on, waiting to see what time does to us. Where it leaves us when, if, it ever shows mercy.

"Why are you still here?" I cry, the words coming out in a muffled sob, but she only holds on tighter. "You shouldn't be here."

"Because that was incredible, Luke. You took your ugly and made it beautiful. You could have let Elena go and instead let her change you. Because I don't know if I could ever be as strong as you've become." She lifts my face and looks into my eyes. "Elena's death is not your fault. She had an illness that took her life, but you still stood there and took their pain."

"Pain I caused."

"Some, maybe. And you've answered for it. You've paid. Now it's time to honor her."

I manage a numb nod, silent, exhausted. I'm just so tired all of a sudden. I close my eyes and concentrate on breathing, remembering, honoring, as I collapse against her again. She absently runs her fingers through my hair as we sit in the stillness, and I wonder if I can find a way to fall asleep and let the unconsciousness give me a brief relief from this nightmare.

I am chaos. Holland is peace.

"This is what I signed up for, Luke," she breathes into the silence. "This is all I've ever wanted from you."

I EVENTUALLY PULL myself back together, though of course I can never undo my complete self-destruction in front of Holland. I expect the moment that follows to be awkward, but she seems as content as I am to sit in silence, cuddled against each other, staring out the window. She's leaning against me now, my arm draped over her as she settles into my chest, my own back against the door of the backseat. It's hard to believe that just a minute ago our universe was a chaotic firestorm and now we're wrapped in a cozy cloud of peace.

Distant laughter slips into our silence, but it's almost comforting in a way. Reminding me that as long as it still exists somewhere it might be real again for me one day. Holland traces my fingers, my hand, my wrist, as we sit, and I close my eyes, resting my head against the warm glass.

"I guess I'm an orphan now," I muse into the stillness, and she squeezes my hand.

"I'm sorry, Luke. And I'm especially sorry that you had to find out that way."

"She didn't know her, Holland. My aunt didn't know my mother. She only knew a baby sister that left thirty years ago."

I can feel Holland react and open my eyes to meet her gaze as she turns. "Your aunt didn't seem to have a lot of room for understanding that reality, what your life was like with your mother."

I'm quiet again as more unwelcome memories return. Maybe it's time for this one person to understand. "You know my mother never contacted me again after I left?"

Holland stiffens, staring at me in disbelief. I can see her look out of the corner of my eye, but I can't return it. I continue focusing on a fly scaling the headrest of the front seat.

"What? Not once?"

I shake my head. "No. Not a birthday card, phone call, nothing."

"Luke..."

I squint through the far window again. "I didn't expect much, and yet she still managed to completely disappoint. She still managed to make sure I understood how little I mattered. I've been an orphan since I was fourteen."

"I'm so sorry."

I shake my head and finally look at her, willing her to understand. "I had music, Holland. That's it. That's all I had."

She kisses me, then. Gently at first, then harder as I cup her face and unleash some of my own pent-up emotion. It feels so good, she feels so good, such a stark contrast to the hell I just went through. Our connection intensifies as we're over-whelmed by our sudden need to heal the fresh wounds, fill the gouges with something beautiful. It's almost like I can sense the pain melting away the more I breathe her in.

"Luke, someone might see us," she whispers, and I sigh.

"I know. You're right." I pull back slightly and rest my fore-head against hers, trying to catch my breath. She lifts my chin so she can meet my gaze.

"Luke?"

"Yeah?"

"You have a family now. You know that, right? The real kind. The kind that loves you and will protect you. The kind that chose you."

She searches my eyes and that strange warmth begins to spread through me again. I can't even respond at first, her words sinking deep into my soul and taking root. The emotion starts to rise and I have to swallow to keep my hold.

"Thank you, Holland."

She gives me another quick kiss before we spot Callie and Casey, the rest of my little family, making their way back to us.

"WE COME BEARING GIFTS," Casey says, climbing into the driver's seat with two giant plastic cups. He passes one to me and one to Holland. "How much do you love me right now?"

I stare at the brown liquid in awe. "Is this...no..."

He grins and nods. "It is, my friend. The nectar of the gods itself, Abby Barrett's lemonade iced tea."

"It's pretty good," Callie assures us.

"Pretty good?" Casey cries, staring at her in disbelief. "Pretty good? It's freaking life-changing!"

Callie rolls her eyes. "Hon, it's extra sweet iced tea."

Casey groans. "You are *such* a tea snob! It's sweet, tart, refreshing and amazing. Seriously, I've been bugging her to bottle it for years. The world needs to know about this."

"Oh my gosh...Casey! It's. Iced. Tea!"

Casey shakes his head sadly and turns to us. "It's so unfortunate. Please try not to pity her. It's because she considers cold tea an affront to the very concept of tea. She can't cope."

Callie shoves him, and he grins. "I already said it was good! Sorry if I'm not ready to trade my firstborn child for it!"

"Really? Don't I get a say in that?" he teases, and she glares at him.

I can feel Holland's eyes and exchange an amused look with her.

"Thanks, guys. This is great. We were thirsty," Holland adds, taking another sip.

When the mood settles abruptly, I suck in my breath.

"We heard what happened, man," Casey begins softly after a pause. "I'm sorry. Nate said it was brutal."

I nod and instinctively stare out the window again. I can't even begin to respond to that right now. "Thanks. Can you just take us back to the hotel?" I plead, meeting Casey's gaze, and I swear ten years pass between us. I hope he understands how much I love him.

"Of course, bro. We got you."

I force a grateful smile and turn back to my window as Casey straps in and starts the car. I feel pressure on my hand and close my eyes as the tension starts to melt from my body. Holland squeezes, and I squeeze back, protecting her hand with everything I have left.

————

I'M NOT up for anything else after we return to the hotel, and Callie and Casey seem just as happy to retire as well. They have the dreaded funeral the next day, and I'm sure they'd appreciate an evening of peace to prepare for that trial. After today's adventure, we all agree I should sit this one out.

Holland follows me into my room and drops to the bed, grabbing the remote in one fluid motion. "So, what's it going to be? Long, involved conversation saturated with feelings and angst, or TV?"

I give her a look, and she chuckles, patting the space beside her.

"Come here."

I lower myself to the soft comforter and close my eyes, suddenly so tired I think I'll fall asleep before she even finds a show to watch. I can hear the channels change and finally stop on what sounds like a cooking competition. The warmth of her body soon follows as she snuggles against me, and I tuck my arm around her, holding her close. She intertwines her fingers with mine and kisses my hand.

"Did you know I wanted to be a chef before a doctor?" she asks.

"No," I mumble from my stupor, amused by the random question.

"Yep. Chef Holland. Has a ring to it, don't you think?"

"Babe, your name is Holland. No matter what you do it would have a ring to it. Dr. Holland. President Holland. Tracing Holland."

She adjusts her position so she's facing me, and I open my eyes to meet her.

"I love music, Luke. I love what I do, but I could have done something else. I could have been a chef, or a doctor, or anything, really, and the world would have been the same." She pauses, studying me with an intensity that always captivates me. That intelligence behind her eyes. That grasp of life. "But not you. You had to be a musician. There was no choice."

I grin. "Well, that's good, because I'm not good at anything else."

She doesn't smile, still considering, still searching my eyes. "No, that's not what I mean. I'm not talking about your job or career. I'm talking about history. I'm talking about the way your music changes the people it touches. The world needs it, Luke. It needs your gift."

My smile fades as her words overwhelm me. I don't know what to do with them. I don't know how to return something so beautiful, so precious. Instead, I find myself doing the only thing I can, giving her my heart with a kiss that unhinges both of us.

A moment ago I was ready to fall asleep and now every cell in my body is blazing with life. I can barely hear the TV blaring behind us as I lean over her, our kiss intensifying from sweet to all-consuming. Every muscle in my body tenses, straining with hunger for this woman, and when she rips at my shirt, I help yank it over my head. Her impatient hands climb my arms, my bare chest, wrapping around my neck and forcing me into her.

She can't get enough, and neither can I when she tortures me further by shrugging off her own clothes.

There is nothing gentle about our contact now. We are fighting for each other, our bodies colliding in that natural rhythm that makes you forget your own existence. She's all there is at this moment. Holland Drake. Beautiful. Talented. Compassionate. Driven. Honest. And completely mine, for no reason I will ever understand.

Her hands grip my hair, pulling me toward her with the same force pushing me. We're completely lost now as I explore her, drawn to every curve, every addictive gasp from her lips that vibrates through me as she reacts to my touch. My mouth finds hers again as she fights the button on my jeans, just wrecking me when she wins. Her merciless grasp only makes me burn hotter, destroying my ability to focus on anything but her. I can't even think straight.

We own each other. We need each other.

"Please tell me you brought protection," she breathes, and I grin against her lips.

"Front section of my suitcase."

"Good. Go!"

I need no more encouragement and love that she can't even wait for me to return. She follows me, nearly driving me to distraction before dragging me back to our desperate contact the second I succeed. Her perfect body is fully exposed now as she pulls me on top of her. She's a dream. She has to be.

"Have I ever mentioned how gorgeous you are?" I murmur, almost paralyzed when her beautiful eyes search mine. But we're in no state for words, and drive back into each other with renewed desperation. This time, I'm ready for the assault on my nerves and surrender to every thud of my pounding blood. It's blistering through my veins now, consuming me, propelling me toward her with an urgency she meets in an agonizing, magnificent, mutual ache. I'm completely abandoned to her.

Her groans, her reckless grip, is gasoline for the fire I already can't control, and I find myself obsessed with taking her wherever she wants to go, with making myself the only presence in her universe. I want her to explode, to make her body plead for mine. To draw her to another place, another level of ecstasy. She's as wrecked as I am, I can see it, sense it in every arch, every surrender of her trembling form. It's devastating my own. I can't think, I can't breathe. I just have to be part of her.

"Luke..." she can't speak as another gasp takes her breath away, then another, but I don't need guidance. I understand this woman. Every line, curve, and cell just makes sense to me. She pulls hard, her hips begging with a force that unleashes everything left of the explosive power reserved for her, this one woman I never saw coming. She meets me in perfect harmony, just as lost as I am. Both of us completely annihilated by the volatile connection. Beautiful, dangerous, breathtaking.

I'm still fighting for air as we finish and I gaze into her face, so beautiful in that moment I can't look away. She grins, releasing a content sigh that echoes deep into my soul.

"Ok, wow," she whispers, curving her hands around my arms as I balance over her, still staring in awe.

I return her grin and give her another kiss.

"Hang on. I have to just stare at you for a moment," she says with a sly look, and I laugh.

"Um..."

She pulls my head down and kisses me again. "Sorry. It's that stupid Pavlovian thing!"

I grin, and collapse on the mattress beside her, completely content for one of the first times I can remember. We're quiet for a long time as we lie close, but it's not awkward, just perfect peace after the raging storm.

"You're getting better, you know," she teases after a moment, interrupting the formerly pleasant silence.

My gaze shoots over to her in disbelief, and she laughs at my expression.

"I'm kidding!" Her eyes dance as she takes my hand and brings it to her perfect lips.

I shake my head with a grin. "You really know how to give a guy a complex, I swear."

She rolls her eyes. "Oh yeah, because I clearly didn't like what just happened."

I laugh again, and lean back on the pillow. "You know, please feel free to tell me how much I rocked your world. Anytime now would be good. My ego can handle it, I promise."

It's her turn to laugh as she turns and props herself up on her elbow. "So that's it, huh? That's what does it for you? To finish and have my big blue eyes stare into yours. Husky, post-sex voice all gravelly and desperate...'Yeah, baby. Thanks for rockin' my world.'"

I almost choke, and she giggles as I wrestle her back against the pillows.

WE HAVE food sent up and are working our way through another cooking competition when Holland's phone buzzes to life. She glances at the display, and there's nothing I like about the way her expression darkens.

"What is it?" I ask, and she almost seems startled at my voice as she glances up. She waves her hand dismissively but I don't buy it for a second.

"Oh, nothing. Just stupid stuff. Ok, so is there any way you would actually eat that sea urchin aioli the bowtie dude is making?"

I don't want to call her out on the lie, but I really couldn't care less about sea urchin aioli at the moment. When her phone starts going again, and again, and again, I've had enough. "Holland, what the hell is going on? It's obviously not nothing."

She bites her lip and glances back at her phone.

"Holland, come on. After everything I've dumped on you?"

She sighs. "It's not that. I'm not hiding anything from you… it's…"

I curse, suddenly so angry I can barely stay seated. "It's Wes, isn't it? He's been harassing you since you left Philly with me!"

She shrinks a bit, and I swear my head's about to explode. "Luke, please, he just doesn't understand!"

"He doesn't understand? What's there to understand? All he needs to understand is that it's none of his damn business and he needs to back the fuck off!"

"Luke, calm down! This is why I didn't say anything. Please don't be upset with me, I just…"

I freeze, immediately softening and moving to her side. "Whoa, hang on. Holland, I'm not upset with you." I take her hands and force her to look at me. "I just can't stand the fact that he's making your life miserable because of me. I don't want you to have to fight this battle on my behalf. He took me on directly at that club, and that's the way it should be if he has a problem with me, ok? That's all. I don't like you being caught in the middle."

I can't tell if she's convinced, but I know I'm not resting until she is. "Holland, please, just give me his number. Let me talk to him."

"What? No. No way."

"Just let me talk to him. Please! Let me do this for you."

She shakes her head. "No, Luke. Thank you, but I really don't think it's a good idea."

I grin and almost laugh. "No, of course it's not. It's a horrible idea. Just, let me try. I have to."

She looks away. "Seriously, Luke, I appreciate it, I just don't see any way out of this one. He hates you because he doesn't understand. He will never see you the way I do."

I sigh. "That's because all I've ever given him is what he expected."

Her eyes shoot to mine, and I hold out my hand. "I know it could be a disaster, but let me try. Please?" I draw in a deep breath. "Just one shot, that's all I'm asking."

"What are you going to do? What could you possible say to fix this?"

I shrug and shake my head. "I don't know yet, but I do know it has to stop." I pause and look in her eyes again. "I'm not giving you up, Holland, so either we deal with this, you let him go, or we continue fighting this battle forever. Ultimately, it's your choice, but I vote for dealing with it."

"Ugh. Fine," she grumbles, logging into her phone. "I hate when you're logical. It's so annoying."

I grin and reach for it, but she hesitates. "You're sure? You're absolutely sure you want to do this? After everything you just went through at that nightmare of a barbeque, you now want to deal with this too? We can tackle it later, Luke."

I shake my head and grab the phone from her. "I'm sure." I click on his name and take a deep breath when the line connects.

"Holland?"

"No, it's Luke."

"What? You bastard! Why do you have her phone?"

"Because it's me you need to be talking to right now, not her."

"That's her choice!"

"Yes, and she's choosing the fact that she wants to have

both of us in her life, so now it's up to you and me to resolve this."

"Never gonna happen."

"Wes, it has to, man, ok? It has to." I sigh and clench my eyes shut for a second, trying to gather myself together. Am I really going to do this? I glance at Holland and realize I have no choice. "Look, I get it. I do. I was an asshole for most of my life. You're right, I would not have deserved a woman like Holland then, and quite frankly, I'm not sure I do now. But all that means is I'm going to fight every second of every day to overcome my shortcomings, to fight toward the goal of being worthy of her, so that maybe one day I will actually be something she deserves." I glance up at her again, and almost lose it at the look on her face. "She makes me want to try, man. She makes me believe that I can be better. That I have to be."

He doesn't respond, and I force my gaze away from Holland so I can focus back on my plea. "Wes, I swear to you, I know what I have here. I know she's too good for me. But I am not the person I was. I'm a person who understands exactly what I was, and why I need to be better. And I sure as hell know why I need to be thankful every single day that Holland Drake is in my life. I will not fuck this up. But, dude, if I do? I will find you, wherever you are, and let you beat the shit out of me. No questions asked."

The line goes dead, and I let out my breath before daring a look back at Holland. I don't even get a chance to say anything before her arms are around my neck, her face buried in my shoulder. I just hold her, both of us locked in silence as we process what just happened.

"That was beautiful, Luke. What you just did was..." she pulls back and stares at me in awe. "I didn't think you could surprise me anymore."

I smile, suddenly shy. "I'm pretty sure the surprises are just starting. I'm going to be surprising both of us a lot from here on out. I better, or Wes just got a license to mess me up."

She shakes her head in disbelief. "Unbelievable."

I'm not really sure what to say next, but I'm glad I did it. It feels so good to have made her happy. To have done the right thing for once. Still, I'm not sure what to do with these new, strange sensations, and she almost seems annoyed that I'm not gushing about my heroics like she is. "You don't even get it, do you?" she continues, and I swallow.

"Um..."

"What you just did... I know every part of you wanted to beat his face in, and instead you did the last thing I ever expected you to do."

"I told the truth."

"You were amazing." She grins and leans forward, rewarding me with a long kiss. "I love sweet Luke. I can't even tell you how hot he is."

Crap, I hope I'm not blushing. "Well, don't get used to it. I have a reputation to maintain," I tease.

"Not unless you want Wes to demolish you. As God is my witness, I now get to let him destroy you if you ever break my heart." She sits back and scrunches her nose. "What did he say anyway?"

I smirk. "Honestly? Nothing. He just hung up."

"Nothing? Not a word?"

"After my speech, no. Nothing."

She shakes her head. "Wonder what that means."

I shrug. "I have no idea, but I'll probably need to sleep with one eye open for the rest of the tour."

"Your eye is still messed up from the last conversation!"

I grin and lean toward her again. "Makes me look like a badass though, right?"

She answers my question with another kiss. A much deeper one than I was expecting. "Maybe."

"I knew it. You talk big about being all evolved and mature, but deep down you just want your boyfriend to beat the shit out of people like everyone else."

Her eyes widen at my teasing. "Oh really? Big tough guy, huh?"

I laugh as she shoves me down and straddles me. The hungry kiss that follows completely erases anything left of my arguments. I don't even remember the topic.

"Wow," I say when we finally come up for air.

"That's one way to get you to shut up," she grins, kissing me again.

"Wait, I thought I'm always in trouble for not talking *enough*."

She rolls her eyes and smacks me before leaning in again and leaving no doubt about who will be winning this debate.

WE HAVE breakfast at the hotel with Callie and Casey the next morning before they take off for the funeral. Casey is unusually quiet, somber certainly, but I'm not convinced it's solely related to the death of his father. I don't think anyone could have dreaded such a gathering as much as I had, but this event will be no picnic for Casey either. His rocky relationship with his father will be the elephant in the room, and that's best-case scenario. Worst case, he becomes the focal point of today's drama, and my heart goes out to him as he prepares to face his own demons that have followed him to Houston. He and I both suspect he was spared their claws yesterday only because I was a more desirable target. There's so much to say, but I can tell he has no interest in talking about it right now. I don't blame him and give him a knowing look when they rise to leave.

"We'll be here when you get back, ok?" I assure him quietly, knowing he'll understand my unspoken message.

"Thanks, man," he replies.

I give him a quick hug and turn to Callie. "Take care of him. I'm putting you in charge today."

She nods and tucks her arm around Casey's waist. "For sure." She squeezes and smiles up at him. "I love you, hon. You got this," she says, and I catch the way he immediately seems to relax.

"Thanks, Cal." He gives her a quick kiss. "You ready?"

She nods again and turns back to us. "Wish us luck," she says with a knowing look, and I almost cringe. They are going to need so much more than that. I'm feeling terrible about abandoning Casey, but realize I would be doing him no favors with my volatile presence.

Holland and I watch them leave before returning to our seats.

"You ok?" Holland asks, searching my eyes. "It had to be hard letting him go."

I give her a weak smile, appreciating her insight. "There's no way I could step foot in that church after yesterday."

She grins and shakes her head. "No. Not unless they want to perform a dozen more funerals this week."

I smirk and lean back. "He's got Callie. Thank god for her. She'll take care of him."

"They're lucky to have found each other."

"You don't even know the half of it," I mutter, leaning forward and rubbing my eyes. I shake off the story. "Anyway, Casey will be ok. He's one of the strongest people I know."

She nods and studies me. I have no idea what she's thinking, which always fascinates and scares the crap out of me at the same time. I don't know how she always seems to get inside me, but man, that's no place for her right now. She has mercy for once. "So what's the plan for today now that the funeral has been removed from the agenda?"

I swallow and look away, having no idea how to respond to that question. It's a simple answer, but completely impossible at the same time. I steady my nerves and force myself to meet her gaze.

"I want to visit Elena while I'm here," I explain quietly, begging her to understand.

Her eyes soften as she reaches for my hand. "Of course," she says, squeezing my fingers. "May I go with you?"

I just stare at her. I'm sure I look ridiculous. Actually, I have no clue what my face looks like because if it's anything like what's going on in my head...

"Holland, I...Really? You'd go with me?"

She almost seems surprised by my question. "Of course I would. She's part of you. She's always going to be a part of you. I understand that."

I look away, fighting the emotion that starts creeping into my chest, my throat. I'm so unprepared for this moment I have no idea how to navigate it.

"When do you want to go?" she continues gently, clearly sensing my struggle.

"Now, probably."

Holland gets up from the table and moves around to my side. She holds out her hands, and I gaze up in awe for a moment before accepting her amazing gift and letting her pull me to my feet.

I KNOW I'm being quiet, even for me, as we climb out of the cab and approach the giant iron gate. Holland takes my hand and squeezes as I draw in a deep breath, bracing for what lies beyond. We start moving again and I can't help but reflect on how much has changed since the last time I passed through this arch just a couple weeks before. I feel like a different person, almost like there is an entirely new path carved for me through this maze of grass and rock.

Neither of us speaks as we walk and I'm grateful for the silence. I have no words for this situation, and I'm beginning to think Holland doesn't either. We both sense our submersion in uncharted territory, but then again, nothing about our relationship has followed the rules so far. I suppose that shouldn't surprise me when my entire life has been one giant "F-U" battle between me and the universe. I have no idea who's winning at this point.

I slow as we approach Elena's grave and lead Holland off the asphalt path, into the grass. Her grip tightens, but I'm no longer certain the pressure is entirely for my benefit. I glance at her face, struck by the glimpse into what this truly means to her for the first time. She has been nothing but supportive, an angel, since the day we met, but this moment, this reality, can't be easy for her either. To know she not only has to share me with a ghost, but a ghost I wronged. A ghost that represents the horror of what I was and will never be appeased. No amount of apologies, counseling, or promises will ever reverse this headstone.

"It's beautiful," she manages finally, staring in awe at the breathtaking ruby granite.

I swallow, trying to steady my breathing. "It was the only beautiful thing I did for her," I whisper before I can stop it.

I sense her gaze but can't look.

"That can't be true," she returns, and I close my eyes. I can feel the hot tears beating against my eyelids and quickly focus back on the headstone.

"It was custom-made," I continue quietly, somehow needing her to understand what Elena never will. "I didn't just want an angel or heart or something. I wanted a work of art, something that no one else would ever have. I wanted everyone who saw it to understand how beautiful she was. How much she was loved. I just..." My voice is quivering too much now. The words stop, and I finally dare a glance at her, even though I know it's a mistake as I let it happen. I know once we see each other in this moment there is no going back from it. The tears are so heavy in my chest now, I'm not sure the words that got stuck will come out.

"Holland, I..." I search her eyes, silently pleading for something I don't even understand. "I made sure everyone who passes this rock knows how amazing she was. I just wish she had known that in life. I'd give anything to have the chance to explain why her headstone is so incredible."

I lose the battle with my tears then, and she wraps her arms around me. I cling to her with a desperation that silences us, the air heavy with emotion we can't even begin to sort through.

"What if she didn't know? It was my job to make sure she understood that!" I charge at the awful, thick cloud around us.

Holland doesn't respond, and I'm grateful. I don't need lies right now; I just need to figure out how to move forward with the crushing reality that sometimes it seems like the wrong person gets the second chance.

"You're not broken, Luke. Just lost like the rest of us," she says softly, and I clench my eyes shut at her familiar mantra. I know she had no idea what she was saying that first time she uttered those words. She couldn't possibly have understood what she'd face if she braved this journey with me. She was being kind then, compassionate. The fact that she can repeat it now changes everything.

"You're amazing, Holland. You're beautiful," I whisper, pulling back and gazing into her eyes. "For as long as I'm alive you will know that."

Her own eyes fill with tears as she stares at me. I can tell she's speechless, and I'm glad because I'm all out of words too. I kiss her gently instead before we turn back to Elena. Slipping my arm around Holland's shoulders, I hold her against me, silent and still as we remember.

IT'S NOT EVEN lunchtime by the time we start to make our way back to the hotel, although it might as well be midnight for how exhausted I feel. I'm surprised, even slightly irritated, when Holland pulls out her phone and begins issuing new directions to the driver.

"Where are we going?" I ask, starting to get nervous. I'm not sure I'm up for another adventure at the moment.

"You'll see."

I don't respond, mostly because I don't want to hurt her with the protest in my head, and stare back out the window. I'm confused when we pull up to a very average-looking shopping complex.

"Want me to wait?" the cab driver asks.

"No, it's fine. We might be a while," she says, paying the fare.

The driver nods, and I hold out my hand to help her from the car.

"I could have paid for the cab," I mutter.

"So could I." Her grin manages to force a smile from my sour face.

"So, what? We're going to the mall?"

"Kind of."

"Forgot your toothbrush or something?"

"Luke, this is one of the few times in our relationship where I give you permission to shut your mouth."

I laugh then, I can't help it, and she tugs my arm. "Let's go!"

I sigh and allow her to lead me toward one of the giant storefronts. I glance up and almost pull to a stop.

"A music store? Holland..."

"What did I just say?"

I grunt as she yanks me toward the entrance.

The store is nearly empty, which is bad enough, but even worse is the fact that we can tell the employees immediately recognize us. I guess we shouldn't be surprised given the fact that our faces are probably plastered all over the wall of screens to the left all day, every day.

"Hi, can you help us for a moment?" Holland asks the first slack-jawed, twenty-something we find in a uniform.

"Uh, yeah. Hi...what..."

"I'm Holland, this is Luke, and we're interested in your acoustic guitars. Can you let us into the display room?"

He manages a nod and fumbles with his keys. "Um, yeah, this way. Do you need help? I mean, probably not. But if you have questions...I'm Tyler. I'll be..." He tucks his hair behind his ears. "Over there." He points to the counter, and Holland gives him a gracious smile.

"Thanks, Tyler. We'll let you know if we need anything."

He nods, but still hasn't moved.

I'm sure Holland notices, and it's everything I can do not to laugh. "Oh, hey, Tyler?" Her smile turns from sweet to down-right stunning, and I suppress my grin. This kid doesn't have a prayer.

"Any chance you could give us the room for an hour or so? Tell people it's a private demo?"

There is nothing on this planet that would make the guy deny her request, that much is obvious, and this time I have to escape to the display room to hide my amusement. Not surprisingly, Tyler is pretty sure that shouldn't be a problem, and Holland is very grateful. She follows me a few seconds later and we exchange a subtle grin. We know we're on camera and don't want to embarrass poor Tyler who's been nothing but accommodating.

"What'll it be, rockstar?" Holland asks, facing the giant wall of acoustic guitar models. "Ooo, check out this Taylor."

"We're buying cheap guitars now? You dragging those on the flight back?"

She rolls her eyes. "Oh, so now suddenly you're a diva? Darling, this baby has an eight-thousand-dollar price tag."

I grunt and have no choice but to take the instrument when she shoves it at me. Even my worst pout wouldn't risk an eight-thousand-dollar guitar. I have to admit it feels really nice in my hands.

"The action is great," I mumble, testing out a few chords.

"It's got a sweet finish."

"Yeah, I can see that. Needs new strings, though. We should go find Tyler."

We don't have to go far since he is hovering right outside the display room, pretending to unload the same three guitar tuners. We catch his eye and wave him in.

"Hi, need something?" he asks.

"Yeah, can you grab us a new pack of medium Elixers? Purple pack," I say.

He seems embarrassed. "Oh, shit, sorry. Those need to be changed?"

"Yeah, man, no big deal. You must have some serious customers testing this out in here."

He smirks. "Yeah, everyone picks that one up, but no one actually buys it. I wish."

I study him for a second. "Why? You get commission or something?"

He seems to blush a bit. "No, that would be awesome, though. Here, I'll change those for you," he adds, reaching for the guitar.

"Thanks, man," I say, handing it to him.

I feel Holland's gaze and glance back at her when Tyler disappears.

"What?" I ask defensively.

She just smiles to herself and shakes her head. "Nothing. I just see your brain working."

"My brain isn't doing anything except trying to figure out why we're locked in the display room of a chain music store."

She grins and grabs another guitar from the wall. "How about a Martin?"

"What about my Taylor?"

"Your Taylor's getting worked on at the moment, relax. Try this one."

I sigh and take it from her. I like the feel of this one too, although both make me long for my '43 Gibson. When we get back I will be craving some serious alone time with my other girlfriend. I love that Holland will be more jealous of me than the guitar.

"Ok, so now what?"

She shrugs. "So now you play."

"Huh?"

"That was confusing?"

I roll my eyes. "Um, this whole thing is pretty damn confusing."

"You need music, Luke."

"I know, but..."

She shakes her head. "No, you don't know. You don't even understand what music is to you. What it does for you. You think you control the music, but it controls you, and you need to let it right now. So play."

"Play what?" I cry in exasperation.

"I don't care! Anything!"

"Holland, come on..."

She gives me a hard look and moves to the door. "Tyler, how are those strings coming?"

"Still have a couple more."

"No problem. What's your favorite Night Shifts Black song?"

We watch Tyler just about drop his eight-thousand-dollar guitar. "Um... 'Better Get Back.'"

"Oh, nice! Hockey fan, huh?"

He grins and nods. "Go Wings!"

"Thanks, Ty."

She closes the door and returns.

"'Better Get Back.' Go."

I'm still staring at her in disbelief. "This is crazy."

"No, what's crazy is the fact that one of the most incredible musicians of our generation is so shut off from his own gift that he's embarrassed to play his own song in front of his girlfriend." She moves to the stool beside me. "Please, Luke, just trust me. You've had a brutal couple days. You need this. You need to let the music be more than music."

I have no idea how to argue with that and finally give up the fight. I adjust the guitar in my hands and grip the neck. Drawing in a deep breath, I stare at the opposite wall and start to play.

As the music comes out, the world begins to melt away like

it so often does. It's not a different reality; it just feels different, more possible. It's the same way I feel when I'm on stage, when I'm writing, when I jammed with Percy alone in my room while my mom and her boyfriend screamed at each other in the kitchen. Like the life that I could have is right there, right at my fingertips, and when I play I actually get to touch it for a few brief seconds.

Then, Holland Drake came along and shoved life right into my soul.

At some point Tyler returns with the guitar, but I don't stop playing. I hardly even notice him as the chords bleed into song which bleeds into art. The expression on Holland's face as she watches me play is just as mesmerizing. It's more than pride, it's pure joy that she gets to be part of a moment. As though I'm giving *her* the gift.

No one moves when I finish, least of all Tyler who looks completely paralyzed. There's the warmth again and I wave him over.

"You play?" I ask.

He nods. "Yeah, but not like that."

I laugh. "Grab a guitar. That my Taylor?"

He hands me the Taylor, and I give the Martin back to Holland.

"What's your favorite Tracing Holland song?" I ask, and love how Holland glows at my question.

"Um, 'Perfect Storm,' probably," he says.

"Yeah, me too."

I strum the new guitar and grin. "This has a nice tone. I like the feel of it."

Tyler nods. "Yeah, it does. It's got that sweet cutaway too. The other model in the series doesn't."

"Have you ever played it?"

"A little."

I hand it to him. "Play something."

"Um..."

"Do you write any original stuff?" I ask, helping him along.

He reddens a bit, but nods. "Some."

"Ok, so play us that."

His eyes shoot to mine in shock. "Seriously?"

"Yeah, why not. I want to hear the guitar store expert play this thing."

He grins at my joke and seems to relax a bit. "Ok, sure."

He moves to one of the other stools, and we settle back to listen.

When he starts to play, Holland and I exchange a surprised look. The kid's not bad. He's actually a whole lot better than not bad.

> "I'm Nowhere Man in nowhere spaces
> Everywhere a thousand faces, places spill from
>   beneath the wreckage
> Oh it's over now
> Oh oh it's over
>
> I'm Forgotten Man in endless races
> Chasing air with futile paces, traces of the craft
>   that made us
> Oh it's over now
> Oh oh it's over
>
> You say you see me, but it's just my shadow
> I'm not waiting, just fading past the time you
>   remember
> I'm Forgotten Man, Nowhere Man
> Light a candle before I'm gone.

I'll run this race, it's still my anthem
Past the shame, the pain is where I fight now
I'm a blaze, a fire, a final hour
Oh it's not over
Oh oh it's not
It's never over"

Tyler glances up with a shy look as he finishes, and I lean back with an approving smile.

"Nice! That was great, man. You write a lot?"

He beams as he hands the guitar back to me. "Yeah. I mean, just for myself mostly. I fool around a little bit with some guys in the area, but we haven't done anything other than play a couple bars. And honestly, they like to do covers more than originals for the most part anyway." He laughs. "We actually cover one of yours all the time."

I grin and cross my arms. "Really. Which song?"

"'Suture.'"

My eyes widen as I stare at him in disbelief. "'Suture?' No kidding."

"Do I even know that one?" Holland chimes in, and I smirk.

"Probably not. That was from our first album. We didn't even put it on the re-release."

"You should have, man! That song is epic."

"Yes. That's what I said. But the Label was not having it. They already said we were too heavy for the mainstream when we signed, so that was it."

"No way! That's what I love about you guys! No bullshit."

I grin and glance at Holland. "Hear that? No bullshit."

She rolls her eyes. "Please."

"What do you play in your band?" I ask, returning to Tyler.

"I lead, for the most part. Jack takes a couple of the songs, but I do the rest."

I nod. "You in school or anything?"

He shakes his head. "No, well, not really. I've taken a couple classes at the community college, but my mom really needs me around. She hasn't been doing well the last couple years. I'm trying to work as much as I can."

He's about to continue when the door opens and a stern man shadows the gap. We know he's the manager from his tie and unfiltered glare.

"Tyler, I thought you were supposed to be working on inventory?"

Tyler deflates, and my good humor gives way to the inevitable boil of my blood when challenged. "Actually, sir, we requested his assistance. We're interested in these guitars," I explain, holding up the Taylor and motioning toward the Martin.

The man gives me a skeptical look. He has no clue who I am, which only encourages me further. Unlike Tyler he doesn't actually pay attention to what happens in his store.

"Is that so? Did Tyler review the price of that guitar?"

"He did, thanks. Seven thousand nine hundred ninety-nine dollars and it comes with a case. He recommended I go with the Platinum Warranty. Considering the abuse it'll take on the road, that's not a bad idea."

"You tour then?" the manager asks, and I force a polite laugh.

"Oh, right, sorry." I slide off the stool and approach, holding out my hand. "Luke Craven with Night Shifts Black. That's my friend Holland Drake from Tracing Holland. We're actually touring together at the moment. I think she's interested in that Martin. Right, Holland?" I ask, addressing her.

She nods to us with a smile and holds it up. "It's a pretty color." I almost snicker at her joke, but manage to hold it in.

The man just stares at us. And stares. And glances at Tyler. He studies my tattoos for a while, then back to Tyler.

"I see. Well..."

"So, can he ring us up here, or do we do that at the counter?" I add, solely to see his face explode.

It does, and there is no doubt in my mind this will be an eight thousand dollars well-spent. I'm pretty sure Tyler is wetting his pants.

"Um...Tyler can ring you up at the counter. Our computer...he needs the computer."

"Great! Oh, hey, he's been great. Does he get credit or anything for this sale?"

The man looks about to pass out before shaking his head. Tyler's eyes are the size of guitar picks.

"No, our employees are hourly."

"Oh, really? Well, that's too bad. Hey, Ty, can you throw in one of those mini clip-on tuners you were showing us earlier? I can't even tell you how many of those damn things I lose. Thanks. Oh, and an extra set of strings and your favorite strap."

The manager has to step from the doorway so we can march past. I know Holland's eyes are glued to me. She has no clue what I'm doing. Hell, I'm not entirely sure at the moment, I just can't shake this sense that a slight shift in the universe is about to occur.

"Well, if you need anything else, please let me know," the manager says, and I wave my hand.

"Thanks, but I think Ty's got it. Right, Ty? We good? You can ring us up?"

"You want the Taylor?"

"That's the one you like, right?"

He nods. "Yeah, she's a beauty."

"You're sure? I shouldn't consider a different one?"

"I mean, the Martin you were looking at is nice too, but if it were me, you struck gold with that Taylor."

I nod. "Perfect. That's all I need to hear."

He's smiling to himself as he processes the transaction, and I cast a quick glance at Holland who's giving me the death stare. She didn't bring me here to buy another eight-thousand-dollar guitar I'll have to fly back to Philadelphia.

"So, it'll take us a little bit to get it ready for you and adjust anything you need, the action or whatever. Will you be able to come back in about an hour? We'll have it all polished up and ready for you," Tyler says as I'm signing the receipt.

I sigh. "Well, I don't think that's going to work for me."

His face falls. "Oh, ok, well, maybe..."

"Tell you what, how about you adjust the action how you like it since you're the one who will be playing it."

He stares at me, completely confused. "I don't understand."

I jot down my e-mail address on the receipt and shove it back at him. "The guitar is yours, man. Let me know how she performs on stage."

HOLLAND DOESN'T EVEN SPEAK to me for the first five minutes after we leave the music store. We walk in silence along the line of storefronts, and the silly grin on her face makes me smile every time I catch a glimpse of it. I can't stop looking.

"You do realize that even after everything, all we've been through, that might be one of sexiest things I've ever seen," she says, finally letting me into her head.

I return her grin and give her a mischievous look. "What? The way I man-handled President Power Trip at the end?"

She laughs. "No, the way you just changed some random kid's life."

Her smile fades when she sees my face. "You get that you not only gave that kid an unbelievable gift, you also gave him hope. You validated his dream. You gave him a story he will now share with every person he knows and will be a part of his narrative for the rest of his life. Whether you want it or not, think you deserve it or not, you have that power, Luke. You touch lives."

Speechless, I can barely even muster a smile as I start walking again, staring at our reflections in the passing store windows. I know I'll be lying awake tonight, fighting my way through that bombshell, but for now, for this second, I can't even hope to start. I draw in a deep breath and turn back to her.

"You hungry?" I ask, finally.

She only grins knowingly and nods her head. "Yeah. I am. I saw a cute Thai place up ahead."

CASEY MEETS me for coffee at the hotel restaurant that night, while the girls check out the in-house spa. I had received a few cryptic texts from Callie throughout the day with updates, but not enough to get a true sense of what to expect when I finally see my friend. He looks drained, defeated, and my heart constricts a bit. I still wish I could have been there to support him, even though I know that wasn't really an option.

"Do you think I can get them to throw a couple shots in here?" Casey mumbles, glaring into his cup.

I smile and cast a glance over at the neighboring bar area. "Maybe we met in the wrong section?"

He smirks before leaning back with a groan. "Can I just say this day sucked? Like, massively sucked."

"So then, how did we get stuck with a coffee date while the ladies got the spa?"

His grin slips out as he shakes his head. "No clue. The plan made perfect sense when Callie laid it out. And then, she walks away, and you're like, wait..."

I laugh. "Yeah, that's usually how it goes."

"How about you? What did you and Holland do?"

"I'm pretty sure we're here to talk about your day."

He grunts and swirls his coffee. "I already told you it sucked."

I almost laugh again. "Uh huh. Well, that's a text message, my friend, not a coffee break. I'm gonna need more than that."

"Geez, dude, when did you get so pushy?" he teases.

"When I started giving a shit about life and other people."

"Funny how that works, huh?"

I roll my eyes. "Spare me the lecture and tell me about your father's funeral, Case."

He shakes his head and settles back into his chair. "They wanted each of us to say something," he begins finally, glancing up at me. "I swear my mom did that just to watch me squirm. They literally stared at me when it was my turn."

"Oh, shit. What did you do?"

He shrugs. "I got up and spoke."

I let out my breath. "Wow...ok..."

His smile starts to poke through the gloom, which always makes it impossible not to join in. "Yeah, it was not the speech they were expecting, I'm sure."

"What did you say?"

"I thanked everyone for coming and then thanked my dad for donating sperm to make such great kids."

My eyes widen. "You did not."

He grins and shrugs. "Yeah, I kinda did. I phrased it better.

At least I think I did. It was such a blur I don't even remember exactly what I said, but it was along those lines."

I breathe a curse and shake my head. "Well, hey, they wanted a speech."

He laughs and rubs his eyes. "Yeah, they did. And they sure got one." He sighs. "It was rough, dude. The whole thing."

I nod. "Did anyone give you a hard time?"

He looks away and seems to focus on the wall behind me. "Not openly. Just a lot of the passive-aggressive shit my family has mastered."

"Aw, I'm sorry. Yeah, your family always rocked the under-handed cut-downs."

He grunts. "Yeah, Great-Uncle Alan actually introduced himself! That bastard. He said he was surprised I still remembered all their names when I told him I knew who he was. Totally serious too, as if I wouldn't see through such an obvious blow."

I smirk, I can't help it. "Um..."

"Yeah, exactly. What a dick."

I laugh, fresh from my own encounter with Great-Uncle Alan. "Well, if it makes you feel any better, he told me I probably had an STD so..."

"What?! No!"

I nod, still chuckling. "Yep. Right after Great-Aunt Norma said I was probably high on 'the dope.'"

"The dope? Oh my god!" Casey roars, laughing so hard we draw stares from other tables.

I'm right there with him, trying to compose myself as the humor of the entire situation begins to chip at the horror.

"Oh, yeah. And you should have seen the flowers the Label sent. Completely ridiculous. Like five times the size of any other display."

I laugh again, not surprised. "They wanted you to know they care, man."

We exchange a wry smile as he shakes his head. "Yeah, whatever. Do you think the Executive Assistant who ordered them even knew who I was?"

"Depends if the Executive who gave the command included the band name in the email," I joke, and Casey laughs again.

He shakes his head with a smile. "Hey, thanks, man. There was nothing funny about it at the time, but some of it is kinda hilarious on the other side," he admits, as if reading my thoughts a moment ago.

I grin. "You know me, always finding the fun in life."

He snickers. "Yeah, you're just a ball of sunshine. Speaking of that, oh man, you should have seen what Uncle Nestor was wearing. Hang on." He pulls out his phone and starts scrolling through pictures.

I just about spit out my coffee when he turns it toward me.

"What is that?" I cry, trying to make sense of the black tuxedo/tracksuit monstrosity.

Casey shakes his head, cracking up so hard he can barely speak. "I have no idea. He walked into the church like that, and even Callie almost lost it. Callie! Unbelievable. I guess it's for when you want to look like you're trying without giving up the comfort of your favorite couch apparel?"

"Wow, that's, uh, something..."

He's still chuckling. "Oh, and then I pretty much choked on my mint when Nate asked him where he got it. You know Nate, totally sincere and polite. Like, just making conversation."

"No way. What did he say?"

"That's the best part. His girlfriend made it for him!"

Casey starts laughing all over again, and I stare at him in disbelief.

"Wait, Uncle Nestor has a girlfriend!"

"Four years, dude! Four fucking years! They met at Sole Barn!"

"The shoe store?"

"I know!" Casey smacks the table. "I guess they share a love of bland, sensible footwear, I don't know."

"Wow..."

He nods. "Exactly." He grows serious. "Hey, so, you should also know that at least ten people came up to me and asked me to tell you how sorry they were for what happened at Nate's house."

Shocked, I'm not even sure how to respond at first. "Seriously?" I manage finally.

He nods. "Yeah, man. They were blown away by you. They feel bad for hiding and not standing up for you at the time, but they couldn't believe you just stood there and took it. That you'd actually come back to take responsibility for your actions. They have a huge amount of respect for you now."

I look away, still not sure what to make of that. "Wow. I..."

Casey shrugs. "Dude, you're legit, and people are seeing it."

I draw in a deep breath and stare into my coffee cup. "Thanks, Case. I needed to hear that." I force my eyes up and meet his gaze. "I went to visit Elena today. Holland went with me."

He's quiet for a moment and I can't begin to read his expression. "Good, I'm glad you did," he says finally, studying me. "Holland's an amazing woman, Luke."

I nod and instinctively glance toward the entrance as if she'll walk in at that moment. It hits me hard how much I want her to. "She is. Incredible." I focus on him again. "You know I didn't ask for any of this. I wasn't looking for someone else."

He meets my eyes. "I know. You have nothing to apologize for. You will always love my sister. We all know that. It doesn't mean you can't love someone else too."

I swallow, doing my best to breathe. Leave it to Casey Barrett to transform his moment of pain into evidence of what an amazing friend he is. I almost smirk at the thought of freaking him out with an impromptu hug but have mercy. I stare back at my mug instead.

"I think I could really love her, man. I think Holland might be it for me," I say after a pause, shocking myself as much as anyone with my confession. I glance up again to test his reaction, but Casey doesn't seem surprised.

"I think so too. But Luke, you should know that Callie and I are going to do everything in our power to keep you from screwing it up this time. You should just know that up front."

He grins, and I return it.

"Thanks. I'm holding you to that."

"Good, because Callie is already planning our double wedding."

I laugh and shake my head. "Wow. Well, don't worry. I think she'll change her mind when she finds out how long she'd have to wait. I don't think Holland's in any kind of rush either."

WE RETURN to Philadelphia different than when we left, but better somehow. The four of us grew individually, as well as together, and it almost feels strange when the car returns us to our tour and the other reality we'd left. I often feel like I'm living multiple lives, but never more so than when I'm reminded of the deep chasm separating my past from my present. I've only complicated the gap further with this new present that I'm still trying to grasp. Still, I can't shake the feeling that the path has changed, that a fragile bridge is now hanging precariously between my islands and I'm starting to catch glimpses of a future where I can navigate them freely. It's a lot easier to imagine that kind of freedom when I watch Holland embrace it with effortless grace.

I linger beside her, holding one of her bags, as she fishes through her purse for her hotel key.

"I'll probably check in with the band tonight for dinner," she announces, almost apologizing, and I grin.

"Yeah, me too. No worries," I respond, following her inside so I can deposit her belongings.

She turns to me and slips her arms around my waist, pulling me against her. "But you know I'd rather spend the night with you."

"Yeah, me too. No worries," I repeat, and she laughs.

I kiss her, surprised when my casual gesture turns much more intense. The magnet of her body starts drawing me forward, locking me against her as she backs into her room.

"We can't. Not now," she groans, but does nothing to help her own cause as she claws at me, her sudden aggression ripping a frenzied blaze through my body. I have no interest in playing fair either.

Her top is on the floor at nearly the same moment my jeans succumb to gravity, and there is nothing refined about our contact. It's one primal need feeding the ravenous hunger of another.

"Luke, don't stop this time. Don't talk. Don't do anything but make me need you," she breathes in the most convincing argument of all time.

And I do.

"I APOLOGIZE in advance for what I'm about to say, but holy shit," Holland sighs, dropping back to what's left of the bed.

I laugh and close my eyes, still trying to catch my breath.

"Unbelievable," she continues and turns toward me. "Pavlov had no freakin' clue. No clue!"

"So I'm getting better then?"

She responds with a kiss that makes me burst with pride at just how satisfied she is. I love that I'm enough for her.

"Seriously. Perfection," she breathes, pulling away, staring into my eyes. I'm not even sure she's talking about the sex.

I return her smile, captivated by the sudden explosion in my heart. Something is happening. Right here. Right now. Something huge, and I take a deep breath, searching her eyes.

"Holland, my entire life people have tried and failed to 'fix' me. You're the first person who's made me believe I'm not broken."

Silence.

I actually think I've stunned her for once. My words settle in the stillness, hanging between us like a promise, a gift, and I wait in agony, wondering what she'll do with it. Her eyes fill as she seems to search every recess of my soul. I don't know what she's looking for this time, but as usual am afraid she won't find it. That I can't be for her, everything she's becoming for me.

I swallow, suddenly nervous, ashamed, maybe even regretting my impulsive confession. I don't deserve her. I'm sure she knows that. "I'm sorry if that scares you. I..."

She shakes her head and cuts me off. "No, you know what scares me, Luke?" she whispers, still staring into my eyes. "I'm terrified I'm not even close to finished falling in love with you."

"DUDE, you killed it tonight! What is up with you?" Sweeny cries as we move off stage. The crowd is still screaming, still calling for us and we've already done two encores. I grin and shrug as I wipe at my forehead with my shirt.

"Just feelin' it, I guess," I return.

"That was amazing!" Callie cries, running toward us. I return her quick hug and catch Holland gazing at me several feet away. She's surrounded by her own band so I know there's no chance to get to her. But my body is pumping with life right now, and it kills me that I can't share this moment with the one person I'm craving. My phone buzzes and I cast a quick glance at the screen.

> Incredible performance. Almost as good as this afternoon's.

My blood sears hot as the grin spreads across my lips. I glance up at her and notice her own attempt to hide a smile.

> Thanks. I was pretty nervous so I just kept picturing you naked in the front row.

She seems to like my joke, and this time gains the attention of her bandmates when she chuckles. I'm careful to look oblivious in my own circle as I sense Wes' gaze. I can't tell if he buys it or not. He has to know she's talking to me.

> When we get to Toronto, you won't have to imagine anything.

I suck in my breath.

10

GREATER METRO NEW YORK CITY
SEPTEMBER 27

"Luke."

"Callie."

Callie grins and drops to the seat across from me at the small table.

"Glad you found it. Thanks for coming," I begin.

"Breakfast with Luke Craven at a local diner? Um, yeah, you dork."

I smile and shrug. "I don't know. It's been a while since we did this."

"I know. Too long."

"I already ordered for you. Hope that's ok."

She seems surprised, maybe even pleased. "You did? Really?"

I nod. "Pancakes, small stack. Fruit cup, no bacon. Oh, and tea of course."

Her grin is priceless. "Perfect. What about you? Rye toast with orange marmalade, coffee?"

"Actually, I went with the French toast. I'm curious about the powdered sugar application at this establishment."

She smirks as the server appears and delivers our drinks. "Your food will be out shortly," he informs us.

We thank him, and Callie stares me down from across the table. "So, what's up with the mysterious breakfast invitation? What's the occasion?"

"No occasion. Just missed this." She looks skeptical, and I shake my head with a sheepish smile. "Seriously!"

I sigh. "Ok, fine. I have some things I want to say to you without everyone else around. Not even Casey."

She puts down her mug and leans back. "Hang on, I'm confused. You actually called me here to talk? Like with real words and stuff?"

I roll my eyes. "Hilarious. I talked at Jemma's."

"Yeah, as long as you didn't actually say anything."

"You kept coming back."

"I sensed you needed someone to care about your life. Plus you were really hot."

I laugh. "Oh, is that it?"

She grins and shrugs. "Kinda. But seriously, Luke, Jemma's changed my life too."

"You completely blew mine apart."

She quiets, and I can tell my confession has touched her. "I've always wondered what went through your head those first few weeks at Jemma's."

I study her for a moment with a mischievous look. "You really want to know?"

She smiles and crosses her arms. "Dying to know. I can take it. Hit me."

I draw in a deep breath. "Ok, honestly? At first I thought you were a little annoying..."

"Annoying?!" she cries.

"But adorable!" I add quickly with a grin.

"Still!"

"Cal, you kept interrupting my breakfasts."

"Uh, you weren't there for breakfast."

"Exactly."

"Ugh," she groans.

"You didn't let me finish," I laugh. "Anyway, you were also sort of fascinating at the same time. That day I walked in and saw you in my chair..."

"It was my chair too!"

"Our chair," I concede. "The point is, I didn't freak you out when I asked you to move. You just scooted across the table like my bizarre request made perfect sense to you. What was I supposed to do with that?"

"Oh, believe me, it made zero sense to me, I just had no reason not to move."

"Well, you did, and it changed everything, Cal. Then when it became obvious that you cared even though you had no clue who I was, you had me. I was hooked."

"You and Casey make fun of me all the time for not knowing who you were!"

"It doesn't mean we didn't love it."

She gives me a mock glare, and I grin before growing serious again. "Cal, you know what I loved about you, what I still love about you? You're just there. Even when you didn't know what to say, what was going on with me, when I pushed you away, you were there. No judgments, no expectations, just present, across from me, reminding me that I was alive and I was important to you." I glance away, still not used to this whole sharing thing. "You probably saved my life, Cal, and I never really thanked you. So thank you."

Her eyes meet mine and the tears there affect me in ways I never could have expected. I'm not finished and search for the rest of the words. "Most didn't even try, and the few who did..." I glare at the table. "God, I was so tired of people trying to fix what they didn't understand, of framing me and my pain with their own experiences." I glance at her again. "But you didn't. You just saw *me*. There was a patience in your gaze that I couldn't ignore no matter how hard I tried. I couldn't let you down. I had to keep coming back because I knew you'd be there waiting for me. You expected something from me after everyone else gave up."

"I think in a lot of ways we needed each other."

I smile and nod. "We did."

She returns my smile and reaches across the table to take my hand. "I just hope you always understand how much Casey and I love you."

I almost laugh. "You make it pretty hard not to."

She grins, and I settle back. "Anyway, that's why I called you here. I wanted you to know all of that. I know I'm not nearly as good at conveying my love for you, but I just really needed you to understand the impact you had. How beautiful you are, Cal. Inside and out."

Her smile makes the whole thing worth it, and I didn't even get to the good part.

"Thanks, Luke. That's..." She wipes her eyes. "Gosh, I don't even know what to say."

"Good, because I'm not done. There's something else I wanted to talk to you about."

She looks surprised. "What's that?"

"I want to send a note to Shauna from us."

Her confusion makes me smile. "What? Shauna, our server from Jemma's?"

I nod. "Yeah, I've always felt badly about the whole chair thing and how it all went down at the end. She helped us out and I never really thanked her. We just kind of disappeared from her life."

Her eyes narrow. "So you want to send a thank you note?"

"Sure, I guess," I chuckle. "Along with a long overdue tip from the two of us."

"A tip? What kind of tip?"

I shrug. "I don't know. I guess, the kind of tip that will give her more choices in life for her and her family."

She stares at me in disbelief. "What?"

"I'll cover that part of it. I just think the note should come from both of us. She always liked you more anyway."

"Um..."

"Just think about it. Maybe after the tour we can deliver it in person. Or mail it, whatever."

She shakes her head, and I'm still not sure what she's thinking.

"Hey, Luke," she says after a long pause. "You know what I thought about you those first few weeks?"

"What's that?"

"I always wondered how amazing it would be to know the rest of you. To see the world react to you when you broke free, when you escaped your prison."

"Yeah? Do you still wonder that?"

She grins. "I'm starting to believe I'm about to find out."

"HOW WAS your date with Callie this morning?"

"Probably much better than your date with Wes," I tease, pulling Holland against me on the couch when I'm sure we're alone in the lounge of my bus. Eli, Sweeny, Jesse and Parker are in the back playing video games, but their enthusiastic hatred for the zombies they're hunting behind the closed partition indicates we should have plenty of privacy for now.

She grins up at me.

"I'm not the one he despises, remember? Not a single punch was thrown."

I smirk. "Has he mentioned anything about our phone call since we've been back?"

She shakes her head. "Not a word, which comes as a relief and scares the crap out of me at the same time..."

"Me too. I guess as long as he doesn't jump me on stage."

She gives me a look, and I grin.

"Don't even joke about that."

"Aw, come on. Chorus two of 'Crash Down,' here comes Wes with a devastating sucker punch to the head? Hopefully to my right side this time. Left eye is still a little sore."

I love the quick transition of her scowl into a smile. "Nah, then he'd have to come out stage right. Too awkward getting past Sweeny."

I laugh. "Good point."

"That's just what your Label wants, more headlines."

"Eh, they're used to it. I'm a permanent headline. I'm pretty sure my name is on the meeting agenda template at this point."

"Wait until news breaks about us." My gaze shoots to hers, and she shrugs. "What? I mean, eventually we'll have to go public, right? I'm not letting you take other girls out for your public appearances, so you're either going to the Grammy's alone, or taking me."

I can't tell if she's joking or not. "You really want to go public with this?"

"Well, not right now, but yeah, after the tour. Why? You don't?"

I almost laugh. "I mean, it's totally your call. You're a lot better for my reputation than I am for yours."

She rolls her eyes and smacks my arm. "So, what was your

plan then, genius? Keep it a secret forever to protect my sweet-heart status?"

I shrug. "I don't know, at least until I save a busload of puppies or something and fix mine."

She laughs. "A busload of puppies? That's your plan?"

"I don't know. It doesn't have to be puppies..."

We're interrupted by a knock on the main door and exchange a brief look before pulling away. I make my way to the stairs and relax.

"Delivery guy," I call back to Holland, opening the door.

"I'm looking for a Jeff Sweeny?"

I nod. "One sec."

Based on the volume still roaring from the back, I know he won't hear me if I call. I pull open the partition and four sets of eyes settle on me.

"Sweeny, your food's here," I say and start moving back to Holland.

"Huh?"

I glance back at them and catch the looks of confusion.

"Yeah, there's a delivery guy here looking for you."

"For me?" Sweeny asks, shaking his head. "No, that can't be right."

I shrug. "I don't know. I'm just telling you."

It's then that I see it. Jesse staring me down, shouting at me with a look, and I just about choke. Oh, shit. Here we go.

"Dude, just see what he wants. Guy's standing there waiting."

Sweeny grunts and pushes himself up from the couch, Eli close behind.

"Are you Jeff Sweeny?"

He nods. "Sweeny, yeah, but..."

"Ok, great. That'll be one thousand six hundred and five dollars."

My jaw hits the floor as Sweeny literally takes a step back.

"Um...I'm sorry...what?"

"Your total for today is one thousand, six hundred, and five dollars. We have two vehicles here with your pies. Thirty pepperoni, thirty plain, thirty meatball, and ten mushroom. Where do you want them? I'm not sure they'll all fit in here."

"Uh, no. I'm pretty sure you made a mistake."

"You're not Jeff Sweeny?"

"No, I am but..."

"Catering event, far north parking lot, black tour bus, phone number 281-3..."

"No, I got it! I mean, I get that it's me it's just..."

"So it is you? Look, seriously, man, I've got a hundred pies here getting cold."

I can't breathe. I'm pretty sure I'm literally dying. I can't even look at another soul right now and focus on the floor.

"I don't have that kind of cash on me!"

"We take credit."

"Ok, but..." Then, he freezes. "Wait....no...no fucking way...." he breathes, his eyes darting toward the back of the bus. I follow his stare and almost lose it completely at Jesse and Parker's perfect disinterest in the events. They're back to zombie-killing, gazes fixed solidly on the TV.

"Seriously, dude. Are you paying for this or what? Do I need to call my manager?"

"Fuck!" Sweeny cries in exasperation, pulling out his wallet. "No, I got it. Fuck! Give him your card too," he barks at Eli who still looks monumentally confused. "We're splitting this."

"What? But..."

Sweeny points to the Limelight boys, and Eli's eyes widen. "No! Those little shits!"

I can't hold it in anymore and the laugh escapes before I

can stop it. They turn on me, eyes blazing, and I hold up my hands.

"Dude, I had nothing to do with this! I swear!"

They curse again and exit the bus to properly confront the delivery guy and claim their bounty. I'm still laughing as I glance back at Holland, startled by her giant grin.

"Wait...you? No..." I whisper in disbelief.

She just shrugs. "I may have helped with the brainstorming session."

All lingering doubts are removed when Jesse and Parker emerge to exchange a casual fist bump with Holland on their way to the door.

"Be prepared to run," she advises them, and they give her a grin.

"We got this," Jesse assures her. They begin their descent, and we rush to the window to watch the coming confrontation.

"Oh, sweet! Is that pizza? I'm starving!"

I had no clue musicians could run so fast.

THE MEET and greet is particularly tiresome tonight. It's this void in my head, normally a vacuum I can fill with whatever present is necessary for survival, but now is increasingly filled with Holland. Her smile, her music, her incredible mind, and yes, the way she feels when my hands slide over her addictive body. The way my own ignites when she claims me every chance she gets. I'm aching for her, and the constant stream of attention from women who aren't her is becoming more than I can bear.

I don't know how many autographs I sign, photos I take, and invitations I turn down, but it can't be more than every other night. It's still an eternity by comparison.

"You ok, man?" Casey asks when it looks like we're finally about to be released for the night.

"Yeah, fine, why?"

"Um, well, for starters you almost made that one girl cry."

My brain does a quick index but comes up with nothing. "What are you talking about? What girl?"

He seems annoyed. "I don't know. The girl with the...the..." His emphatic hand gestures are certainly earnest, but do nothing to turn air into nouns. "I don't know what you call those things. The old man hat."

"Fedora?"

"Sure, whatever. That girl."

"She was upset?" I ask, surprised. I do remember her now. Her name was Evie I think, and she wasn't wearing a fedora, but some newsboy cap looking thing. I made a comment about it, which I feared she misinterpreted as interest when she invited me to a club later with her friends. I thought I nailed the rejection, but maybe not.

Casey shrugs. "She called you an asshole as she walked away."

I wince. "Yeah? Well, sorry I didn't want to go out with her friends. Or any of the other twenty offers I got. I thought I was nice about it."

"Anyway, whatever, you just seem off right now, that's all."

I'm not sure what he means by "off," since my "on" has never exactly been well-documented. But I do know I'm not interested in finding out at the moment. "I'm going to go meet Holland," I say. "You getting Callie?"

He nods. "Yeah, I think we're all heading into the city tonight."

"Oh yeah? Do you know what you're doing yet?"

He shakes his head. "No, I'll check with Callie and the guys but I'm sure Sweeny and Eli will want to hit up Neptune while we're here. When they come up for air with those brunettes, we can ask."

I make a face. "Really? I hate that place."

"Lots of hot models in bikinis."

I roll my eyes. "Exactly. Hot models in bikinis who expect to be acknowledged."

"We don't have to go. We can split up and do something else."

But my brain seems to have even less interest in event planning. It was a long night and I just want to see Holland. "Whatever you want to do is fine. Just text me the details."

I say goodbye to Casey and motion to Eli and Sweeny that I'm leaving. They nod their response, and I'm off in search of Holland. I'm hoping she's finished with her fans and glance at my phone to see if she's sent any updates. There is a message, but it's from an unknown number. I open it and my pulse picks up.

> You were amazing tonight. Can't wait to meet up later. Been a while, huh.

I hope it's a wrong number, but man, those odds are terrible.

CASEY WAS RIGHT. Eli and Sweeny have their horny little hearts set on The Neptune Club, but Casey, Callie, Holland, and I opt for the admittedly less trendy, but much classier Region 3 bar. Sure, our tabs will be identical, but at least the four of us have zero chance of being soaked by bikini-clad models grinding us on the dance floor. That's an undisputed win in my book.

The obvious loss of the evening, however, comes in the

form of Wes and Spence who also choose Region 3 over the Neptune models. This twist surprises everyone but Holland and me, and it's everything I can do to keep the glare in my chest from spilling onto my face as I meet her at the buses to wait for the others.

"You ok?" Holland asks, slipping her arms around my waist.

"Fine," I mutter.

She searches my eyes and sighs. "Is this about Wes going with us to the bar? You know there's absolutely no way he doesn't go."

"Yeah, it doesn't mean I'm not pissed about it. The guy is ridiculous."

"I know. But maybe it's good."

My gaze shoots to hers and the glint in her expression when she smiles seriously threatens my bad mood. "Good? How could being stalked by Nanny Wes possibly be good?"

She shrugs. "I don't know, I guess this is the way I see it. I've had to watch you all night, the way you own that stage, basically enslave everyone else in the stadium to your will. It kind of wrecked me, Luke. You know, filled my dirty mind with a long list of wicked, vile things I want to do to you." Her eyes slide over me, exposing her desire and releasing a violent surge of fire. "And of course, you've been undressing me since the moment I met you by the door. Even now, I can tell my clothes are being scattered all over this shady parking lot." Her tone is so steady, so measured, and making me completely crazy. "So given all of that, yeah, I just don't see any way we go to that bar tonight and leave with our reputations intact without Wes. He's saving our good names. We should be thanking him."

She's only making me hate him more.

I let out my breath in exasperation. "Or we could have found a private place to work through our 'temptations.'" I slip my hand over her ass for good measure and savor her surprised gasp. She glares at me, but I suspect it's because she liked it, not because she didn't.

"Someone is going to see us!" she warns, swatting me away.

I grin and shrug. "If they do, I'll let you give me a very dramatic slap. The press will love it."

She rolls her eyes. "You would too."

"Par for the course, darling. A necessary evil when you have an entire stadium of women lusting after you."

"Oh, please. So now you're going to get all cocky?"

Her grin betrays her, and I have to kiss her. I feel her everywhere inside me, my body screaming for even the slightest drop of relief. I actually curse when I catch the shadow moving toward us, preventing our last chance to release before the brutal night of forced friendship. She sees it too and quickly pulls away.

"Not sure how much longer I can do this," I warn quietly against her ear as we resume our friend stance.

"Neither am I," she tosses back. "But we don't have a choice unless you're ready for the media explosion."

I sigh. I'm so not.

I squint toward the shadow that begins to materialize into hints. It's clearly a woman, but not Callie. Maybe Tess? She seems too tall for Tess, though.

Oh shit, the shadow isn't Tess. My heart just about crashes into my ribs.

I start screaming, wailing, and lashing out with a riot of emotions, but none manage to escape my head as I stare at the approaching figure in horror. I fear I'll be sick, but that would be too merciful of an end to this nightmare.

"Hey, stranger," she purrs, slinking up to us. She casts Holland a quick look, but I don't dare to do the same. I can't breathe. "You're a difficult man to track down. I figured you'd wait for me." She's expecting a response, they both are, I'm sure, and my brain scrambles for words as my pulse thrashes against my veins. This isn't happening. There's no way I'm awake, or alive, or...

"Luke? Hello?" She waves her hand in front of my face which would have been rude even if she wasn't the biggest mistake of my life.

"What are you doing here, Laurel?"

I wanted it to be belted, growled with the fire of the hell-beast chomping at my entrails, but instead it trickles out as an embarrassing drool from my numb lips. I wonder if my face is as contorted as my soul. Hers is... oh god, her demon face that has haunted me for a year and a half is now my present.

She looks surprised, then hurt. "Didn't you get my text?"

My eyes widen. "That was you?"

"Ouch. Wow. Lost my number, I guess?"

"Luke, what is going on? Why is Laurel Karns here?" Holland asks. It's more whimper than anger, which only makes the accusation so much worse. I turn my horrified gaze on her but can't begin to handle the pain in her eyes when my own heart is spiraling into panic.

"I never kept your number..." I bark, focusing back on my first problem. "You need to leave." There's the fire. Thank god!

"Excuse me?"

I'm probably more shocked that she's shocked. "Seriously, I don't know why you're here or why you contacted me but..."

"Um, you're the one who contacted me, babe," she shoots back, whipping out her phone.

"What?"

> Hey, girl. Remember Luke? He asked me to see if you wanted to hook up when we play New York next week.

My brain shuts off. Gone. I no longer see color, hear sound.

"No...No way!" I roar, and take a step toward the building. Holland grabs my arm, and I hate that my instinctive response is to turn my fury on her. One look in her eyes, however, and the inferno simmers into something more manageable. I've never been tempered before. Never. But here we are. Inexplicably under control.

"Luke, what is going on?" Holland asks, searching my eyes. She should be screaming at me. Why isn't she screaming?

"Yeah, Luke, what is going on?" Laurel echoes. "I've been waiting for you forever! You finally reach out and then I can't even get past security after the show to say hello? I had to slip them just to find you now!"

"Waiting for me?" I scoff, returning to the horror show. "What the hell were you waiting for?" I know I'm gutting her but I don't care. I need to go gut someone else right now. This is on him.

"I'm so confused! Luke, talk to me! Did you not tell Wes you wanted to see me?"

"Wes? What does Wes have to do with this?"

I hear Holland's horrified question, but there are too many horrifying interrogations going on at the moment.

I stay focused on Laurel, incredulous. "Of course I didn't tell him that! That was the worst night of my life. The biggest mistake of my life! I can't even think about that night without getting sick, so, no, Laurel, I did not want to 'hook up when we played New York!'"

Tears spring to her eyes as she absorbs my callous outburst but there are no politics left in me, no civility. The void is saturated with something else now, dripping with revulsion transformed into rage.

Laurel shakes her head. "No! Wes wouldn't do that to me."

"He didn't," I spit. "He's doing it to me."

"What?"

I force air into my lungs. I need this woman to remove herself from my life, preferably without a method that lands me in jail.

"Laurel, please. Please." I'm pleading now, searching her eyes, begging her to understand that she's collateral damage on two fronts. I can't call her a victim, though. There is no victim in this, just the one, and she's dead.

I don't even look at Laurel's face as she finally releases a frustrated curse.

"This is bullshit, Luke!" she cries, nearly matching my own disgust. "*You* are bullshit, you know that?"

I don't respond, there's no relationship to save, and turn to confront the one I can't bear to lose.

"Holland, I swear to you, I had nothing to do with her showing up here! Please believe me. Please!" It's amazing how quickly my fire has melted into desperation.

But she doesn't offer much as she studies me, evaluates. "Luke, what's going on? Why was she here? What was on her phone?"

I rip my gaze away, but my response is silenced by Wes making his way toward us with Spence. Their paths are about to intersect with a retreating Laurel, and every fiber of my being longs for her to smack him. It'll be a good warm up for what I'm about to do.

"Ask *him!*" I growl, watching as Laurel unleashes her own verbal assault. He shrinks a bit from her wrath, almost stunned, which catches me off guard more than a punch would have done.

We can hear their conversation in the nearly empty parking lot, and I'm about to join them to offer my own opinions when I feel a soft hand slide into mine.

"I believe you, Luke. I do. Please don't."

Startled, I force myself to meet her gaze. The patience. The forgiveness. The inexplicable trust. It's all there, rooting me by her side when every part of me wants to bash Wes' skull into the pavement.

"Shit..." I mutter, closing my eyes. "I want to kill him, Holland. I might seriously kill him this time."

She tugs my hand and draws me back to her. "I know, but you won't. You know why? Because you've just proven you're a better man than he is."

I suck in a ragged breath and turn back to the scene twenty yards away. Laurel has resumed her furious stomp toward the building, leaving Wes motionless, staring at us as we stare at him. The moment the bulls decide how they're going to slaughter each other.

It's pretty obvious Spence would rather be anywhere else on the planet right now.

"Ok, wait, it's not what you think!" Wes shouts, jump-starting the showdown and moving toward us.

I shake my head, taking a step to meet him but Holland pulls me back. "That's it? That's all you have to say?" I snarl from my place.

"Look, man, just..."

"Wes, what did you do?" Holland cries as he reaches us. "Why did Laurel come after Luke?"

"I...Ok, I know..."

"He contacted Laurel and told her I wanted to meet her tonight," I spit, turning to Holland. "That's what was on her phone. A message from him telling her I wanted to hook up."

"You what?!"

"Ok! I know this looks bad, Hol, I just..."

"Looks bad? It doesn't look bad, Wes, it looks insane! What is wrong with you?!" Holland fires.

"You're falling for him! Everyone can see that and it was

the only thing I could think of to remind you what he is! Nothing else was working!"

"What he is? You don't even know what he is! Nothing was working because you're the one who's not seeing clearly! Luke has done everything he can to prove himself to you because he cares about me enough to do that for me. For me!" Her eyes narrow and I'm just glad I'm not on the receiving end of that fury. "And what did you prove in return? That *you're* the one I should be running from!"

"Holland..."

"Stay away from me. From this point forward, we're coworkers. Nothing more."

"What? Holland, come on, you don't mean that!"

"Let's go, Luke."

"Holland!"

He grabs her arm as we pass, and I instinctively shove him away.

"She told you she was done. That especially means don't touch her," I warn.

"Stay out of it," he returns, and I almost laugh.

"I've wanted nothing more since the beginning! You're the one who keeps making it into something!"

This time there's no doubt he swings first. I duck, but not fast enough to avoid his fist. I can't believe I'm getting hit in the face by Wes Alton for the second time in a week. Spence is running toward us now, Holland's shouting, but I barely notice any of it as I block his next blow and shove him back.

"You're messed up, dude," I mutter, trying to ignore the pulsating patch of skin swelling around my eye. Again.

I could demolish him. I know I could. Hell, his face is still a patchwork of evidence of what I can do when tested. I've done it a hundred times to guys twice his size, but this isn't about him. It's about the woman standing behind me, and right now I know that's not what she wants. I know that love means I have to let that be enough.

"Don't," I warn when he straightens and starts toward me again. "I'm serious, Wes. Just leave. Now. I'm not letting you near her."

"Holland, please! It's only because I care about you! You know that!"

"Coworkers, dude," I quip, blocking his path again. "Got it?" I search his face, making sure he understands how serious I am about protecting the people I love. "One more word and you're off the tour."

"Fuck you," he spits, but at least turns and starts directing his fury in the opposite direction. We watch him go in silence, and it becomes obvious Spence has no clue what to do next.

"We'll get through this," Holland offers gently, acknowledging her drummer's distress as well.

"I've never seen him like that," Spence admits, staring back at Wes' shrinking silhouette. "You ok?" he asks, turning to me.

"I'm fine," I assure him, not missing his concern.

He shakes his head. "I guess I should go check on him. You gonna have him kicked off the tour?"

I sigh and cast a quick glance at Holland. "Only if that's what she wants."

"We'll work it out, Spence, ok?" Holland assures him, squeezing his arm.

He nods, but doesn't seem convinced.

"Can you just do us a favor and let them know we changed our minds about going out tonight? We're going to hang here, I think," Holland continues.

"Sure, no problem. I'll catch up with you later."

We say our goodbyes and wait until he disappears out of sight to turn to each other and begin the debriefing.

"Oh, hey, you dropped this in the skirmish."

She holds out a slip of paper as her face ignites into one of the most beautiful smiles I've ever seen. My heart soars and sinks at the same time. I can't believe I almost lost it. I need to find a more secure place for her note if I'm going to fuse it into my existence.

"You kept it," she whispers, pressing it into my hand. She doesn't let go.

"Of course I did."

"Well, I'm flattered, but I probably should write you a new one."

"Why?"

"Because now I'm the liar. I do believe in you."

"SO HE DIDN'T JUMP you on stage, just the parking lot," Holland teases, handing me a wet cloth for my eye after we're safely back on the bus.

"Seriously. Again with the eye? What the hell..."

"Same spot? Let me see that."

I lower the cloth so she can examine my face. "Well, the good news is the bruising from the first one is hiding the second one."

I grunt and pull away, returning the cloth to try to soothe the pulsating heat.

"I messaged Darlene to see if she can track down some ice for us. There should still be some in the green room."

"I have a better idea. How about you release me to go beat the shit out of Wes."

She rolls her eyes. "You know that's not happening." She takes my other hand and kisses it. "Not a chance we're risking these fingers."

I smirk. "Whatever. Do you know how hard it was not to

hit him back?"

"Do you know how hard it was to watch you get hit in the face and not let you?"

I give her a look. "I'm just saying, you owe me now."

Her eyes widen. "Oh really, is that so?"

"Yep. You should make it up to me."

"Uh-huh, and what do you have in mind?"

I shrug. "I'm flexible as long as it involves you not wearing clothing."

She laughs and shoves me before leaning back and taking my hand again. "Seriously, though. I'm sorry, Luke. You don't deserve this. If it happens again we should press charges."

My gaze shoots to hers in surprise. "Really? You'd support that?"

"Of course. He's way over the line. I'm not going to watch him hurt you again, but I don't think he will. I'm pretty sure he gets it now. Honestly, his face when Laurel was yelling at him? I bet he sent that message before you talked to him on the phone. He probably forgot about it and had an 'oh, shit' moment."

"Yeah, I'm not giving any awards since his change of heart still involved punching me in the face."

She smiles and traces my fingers. "No, I don't blame you. Just pointing out that once the dust settles he'll put all the pieces together and realize what a jackass he's been."

"So you're really not going to let me kick him in the face or off the tour?"

She laughs. "Honestly, right now, I want to let you do both, but I can't do that to Spence and the others. Without Wes, I don't know how we could finish the tour." She sighs. "I'll talk to him after he calms down, though. I really think he'll stop this insanity, but if he pulls anything else, don't even hesitate next time."

"You promise?"

She grins. "I'll be standing by as your second."

I'M jerked awake by my phone in the pitch black of my bunk. Parker's name flashes on my screen for no reason that can possibly be good.

"Parker, what's up?" I mumble, rubbing the sleep from my eyes.

"Luke? Hey, sorry, man. I didn't know who else to call. I didn't want to raise alarms or anything, and I know you and Jesse are close." The urgency in his voice sobers me, and I prop myself up in my bunk. "What is it? What's wrong?"

"I don't know, it's just that we're supposed to roll out in an hour and Jesse's still not back. We don't know where he is."

"What?"

I pull back my phone to glance at the time.

"He left with some girls and that was the last we heard from him."

"Where are you now?"

"In our bus."

"Ok, hang on, I'll be there in a minute."

I hang up and force my feet to the floor. I hadn't been asleep long, but long enough to ensure that my mind and body are not remotely ready for this.

Part of me wonders if this is a prank as I make my way down the stairs, past Holland's bus, the crew's, and all the way to Limelight. But as soon as I see their ashen faces, I know this is no joke.

"Have you contacted your tour manager yet?" I ask, joining them in their lounge.

They shake their heads, clearly out of their depth.

"We're afraid we'll get him in trouble."

"Ok, well, you need to do that first. I'm sure he's fine, but your manager needs to know there may be a change of plans as soon as possible so he can adjust. You don't have to raise alarms, just say Jesse's not back from his night out."

They nod.

"So what exactly happened?"

"We were at this bar and met these girls. They were flirting with him all night and he said he was just going to go to another party for a while. He was supposed to meet us back at the bar a couple hours later so we could ride back together," Parker explains.

"Yeah, we waited for another hour after that," Derrick adds. "We've been calling him and texting and everything, but nothing."

"We're sorry to bother you with this, but if he's ignoring us, we thought he might not ignore you."

"What bar?"

"Chadwick's. 6th and Arch."

"Shit, seriously? Arch Street?" I mutter.

They shrug. "We hang there all the time."

I shake my head. "Fine, whatever. And you didn't know these girls?"

"No. You don't think..." They look ready to puke.

"No, Jesse is fine. I guarantee you, but I'm sure he's not going to take my call either."

"How do you know?"

I give them a look. "I invented this, trust me. Just tell your manager you're not going to be leaving when you thought. We have a long break before the ACC so it shouldn't be a big deal unless you guys had something scheduled in between."

They shake their heads. "I don't think so, but I'm not sure."

"Exactly. So call your manager and work on that. I'll take

care of Jesse."

I'M NOT surprised when Jesse doesn't immediately answer my text, so I try a call next. I expect the same result, but I'm relieved by the click of a connection.

"Hello..."

My heart sinks.

"Shit, are you high, man?"

"Luke?"

"Where are you?"

"Um..."

"Jesse, I need you to focus for a second. Where are you?"

"Flower cave."

"Huh?"

"Flower cave."

The line goes dead and I curse again.

"Hey, guys, does 'flower cave' mean anything to you?" I call over to the others. They glance up and seem relieved.

"You got ahold of him?"

"Yeah, but all I got was 'flower cave.'"

"It's that one park!" Reece cries. "We went there and got wasted after the Underground Masterclass show, remember? There's that tunnel with all the hippie graffiti. We called it a flower cave."

"Where is it?"

"Um...shit, let me think." He pulls out his phone and I wait as he searches. "Ok, here it is. Lewis Park. It's nowhere near Chadwick's. Not sure how he got there."

"Let me see that." I scan the map. "Alright, you guys stay here and put out fires until we get back. I'll go get him. Text me that address."

LEWIS PARK IS ABOUT AS shady and uninviting as I expect. I tell the cab to wait for me, and even he's not thrilled at the prospect, but I promise to reward him for it.

I also send Tess a message letting her know I had to run a quick errand to Newark, thus adding to the train of unhappy people in my wake.

I have no idea how to find a tunnel with hippie flowers on it, but use my phone as a flashlight when the dim path lights aren't enough. My heart is racing, blood pounding in my ears in the unsettling silence, but I try not to show my fear. I've played this game way more than I should have. I know I have to look like I belong if I have any hope of surviving a confrontation. I don't see other midnight loiterers, however; just me, my fear, and another hash mark for my tally of stupid, impulsive decisions. Parker and the others had wanted to come with me, but of course I had refused the most logical option.

I shake off the self-criticism, leaving that for later, and focus back on my present challenge. Suddenly, I can hear voices to the left, and hate that the new direction would take me off the main path. Still, it's my only clue so I change course and shoot Parker a text letting him know I'm here, heard something, and he should call the cops if he doesn't hear from me in ten minutes.

Sure enough, after about a hundred feet, I see a very distinctive tunnel. It's surprisingly better lit than the rest of the park, allowing for the clear illumination of a collection of lethargic bodies strewn over the ground.

I mutter a curse and move toward it, absorbing as much of the scene as I can while still maintaining my casual approach.

"Hey, man," someone calls out. I find the voice, but don't

recognize the speaker. He holds something up to me, and I shake my head, swallowing my disgust.

"No, thanks. Just looking for a friend. Jesse Everett?"

"Jesse?" It's a woman this time, three actually, when I turn toward the new voice sandwiched between a set of groupie clones. "Wow, hello there." She staggers to her feet, and before I know what's happening, collapses against me. I catch her as she giggles and grabs me way beyond what's necessary to establish her balance. Annoyed, but fully aware she may be my best hope at finding Jesse, I let her get her fill.

"Do you know where he is?"

I scan the remaining bodies, but none appear to be a strung-out rocker who's about to get his ass handed to him.

"He was here."

"Ok, and where is he now?"

She gives me a coy look. "We had a blast. He didn't tell us about you, though. We would have waited." There is absolutely no secret in her eyes. "Yeah, definitely would have waited, wow."

I roll my own. "Where is he now?" I repeat, finished with junkie politics.

She points to the other end of the tunnel. I force her hands away from me and start navigating through the maze of zombies. I don't like that I still haven't seen him, and curse when I reach the opening to find a new cluster of passed-out partiers.

"Jesse?" I call into the darkness. "Jesse Everett?"

"Luke?"

This time I recognize the weak voice and turn my flashlight to the right. "Shit..." I mutter when I see him. He's collapsed against a tree, barely conscious.

I step over the others and pull him to his feet, weaving my arm under his shoulders.

"Can you walk?"

"I don't..." His head rolls down, and I can tell he's wrecked. From what, I have no idea. I check for obvious needle marks but don't see any.

"Talk to me, man, or I'm taking you to a hospital."

His head jerks up at that. "No, no, I'm ok," he slurs.

"No, you're definitely not, but you have the walk back to the cab to convince me to take you to the bus instead."

He shakes his head. "No, I'm good."

"What day is it?"

"Um..."

"Jesse, the day."

"Saturday."

I breathe a sigh of relief. "Ok. Well, technically Sunday at this point, but close enough. The date?"

He's quiet again, then gives me a weak smile. "Not sure I would have gotten that one sober."

I grin in spite of myself. "True. What did you take?" I ask, deciding to push my luck while he's lucid.

He shakes his head again. "I don't know. Not sure. Just ended up here."

I curse. "Do you have your wallet?"

We stop so he can pat his jeans. "Shit, no. I don't think so."

I sigh. "Ok, we'll deal with that when we get back. They left your phone, at least. Keep your mouth shut until we get back to the cab, ok?"

He nods, and I brace myself to re-enter the dreaded zombie "Flower Cave."

"Hey, where you going?" my earlier assailant calls as we shuffle past.

"Home," I return in a stern tone.

"Aw, why? It's early."

"He has to work tomorrow. Have a nice night," I mutter.

"Jesse! Call me, babe!" she cries after us.

"Not likely," I return. I give him a look. "You will not," I warn.

He shrinks a bit, but doesn't say a word until we reach the cab.

"LUKE, I'M SORRY," he begins, breaking the uncomfortable silence after we get back on the highway. I'm so relieved he's ok, and even sobering up, that my anger starts to forgive.

"You scared the shit out of a lot of people," I explain, studying him in the rhythmic flashing of passing headlights and street lamps.

"Dammit, I know, I just..." He presses his palms to his eyes, and I soften a bit at his obvious distress.

"Here, drink this," I command, passing him the bottle of water I brought.

He gives me a sheepish look as he accepts it and starts inhaling the contents.

"That was epically idiotic," I continue. "You get that, right? You want to party, fine, but there's a right way and a wrong way. Landing in a fucking tunnel with a crowd of junkies— wrong way."

"I know, it's just..."

"Shut up for a second and listen to me."

I wait until I have his attention and hold up four fingers. "The number of times I ended up in the hospital after a night of partying." Seven fingers. "The number of times I woke up in a completely different place than where I thought I was." Two fingers. "The number of times I was probably drugged and have no idea what happened after that."

I draw in a deep breath. "It's not cool, man. It's not worth it, and it's not you."

He looks away, clearly conflicted, and I sigh. "Look, first thing you do any time you leave the group is tell someone your plan, then you don't veer from it unless you send an update, ok? Second rule, never take a hit you didn't buy yourself. Better to stay away from that shit completely... but I get it." He looks back at me. "Third rule, stay on your turf as much as possible. Bring the girls back to your bus, your dressing room, whatever, but for fuck's sake don't follow them to abandoned tunnels." I shake my head. "And dude, seriously, that chick? You're a freaking epic talent, man. Aim way higher or don't bother. I'm serious. You got nothing from that girl you needed, did you."

I can tell I'm right when he leans back and closes his eyes. "I know. I'm sorry again." He opens them and turns back to me. "Thanks for coming for me, man. I mean it. When I woke up..." His eyes search mine. "I was scared, dude. Really scared."

"Yeah, so were we. Don't do it again, ok?"

He lets out his breath. "Not a chance."

I jab his arm. "Good. And delete that chick's number from your phone. I guarantee it's in there."

I CAN TELL Kenneth is livid when we get back. Our impromptu road trip put us almost two hours behind schedule, but he holds his tongue as I climb back onto my bus after depositing Jesse on his. The Limelight guys were beyond grateful, solemn as they exchanged greetings with their drained and apologetic lead singer.

I have some concerned messages waiting for me from Holland as well, and return them to let her know I'm ok, just helping out a friend. In an update to her drama, Wes has been hiding in his bunk since Holland boarded their bus so she hasn't confronted him yet. Casey is waiting for me on mine.

"Parker told us what happened," he whispers, waving me to the back. We close the partition and I drop to the couch, totally exhausted.

"He's a good kid, he's just got a mountain to climb before he figures this out."

"Really? We don't know anyone like that," he jokes, and I give him a look.

I close my eyes. "I wish I'd kept a journal. I could probably just hand it to him as an instruction manual."

Casey grunts. "More like a violent warning."

I grin. "Exactly."

I open my eyes and glance back at Casey. "Do you think he's got a prayer? I mean, do you believe it's possible to avoid that road for guys like us if you have help?"

"Which road? Your road? Or mine."

"Your road would have been a lot better if I hadn't dragged you down mine."

He shrugs. "Maybe. But we both got through it, right?"

I sigh. "Did we?"

"Your road brought Callie into my life. You won't hear me complaining."

My heart starts to fill as I glance over again at my best friend. "Case, you know how important you are to me, right? You and Callie, and now Holland..." I shake my head. "Anyway, I love you, man. I don't know if I've ever said it, but you need to know that. That's all."

I can feel his grin and let my own slowly spread across my lips. Snide remark in three...two...

"Sorry, dude. You're cute and all, but I'm practically engaged."

11

TORONTO, ONTARIO
SEPTEMBER 29 - OCTOBER 4

Despite our late start, we make good time to the border at that time of the morning. Our driver has to rouse us for a quick inspection of our bus and review of our passports, but nothing like the stop two years ago when the border guard seemed to take pleasure in her power to make our lives miserable. Three hours we waited as they did whatever it is they do with our paperwork and forced us to crowd into the uncomfortable waiting room of the border offices. I was certain we'd be spending the rest of the tour coordinating Kenneth's bail, but by some miracle we managed to keep our tour manager out of prison, even if it required miles of frenetic pacing through the maze of ugly chairs. We never did learn the reason for the hold up. They just handed our passports back and told us to enjoy our stay.

Our delayed start also means we hit Toronto later than planned. Thankfully, it's a Sunday so the legendary Toronto traffic is only a mild nuisance, not a complete 20-kilometer parking lot. You only need to sit through a Toronto rush hour once to learn it's a vicious torture the likes of which we haven't seen since medieval inquisitions. Kenneth probably would have kicked me off the tour himself for sending us into downtown mid-morning, but it turns out to be a pleasant drive on a Sunday. Callie is glued to the windows staring up in awe at the passing landmarks.

"There it is. The ACC," Casey announces, motioning straight ahead. "That's where we're playing Friday and Saturday."

"I can't believe all the Canadian flags everywhere!"

"It's Canada, babe," he points out with a grin.

"I know, but..."

"Wait until we get her some Timbits," I joke. "You can't get tea though, Cal. You've got to go with a mocha or cappuccino or something."

"Huh?"

I point out the window.

"Tim Horton's? Oh, is that a coffee shop?"

"No, it's a way of life here," Casey explains. "Kind of a religion, really."

"I've been known to accept a cappuccino in a crisis," she teases. "We'll make this work." Then, turns to me. "Holland's from this area, isn't she?"

"North York, I think."

"Are you going to meet her family while we're here? We have plenty of time."

I quiet, not sure how to answer a question like that. I woke up dark today so I'm not convinced it's safe to even try. I can't imagine she'd want to bring me home. My own family wanted nothing to do with me. I know hers is close, sweetly dysfunctionally functional, and pretty much the opposite of what should be exposed to my divisive presence. Holland and I never discussed her plan to introduce me into her personal sphere, and to be honest, I hadn't really thought about it since I don't have one. I don't know what I would do if my sweet, intelligent, accomplished, driven, beautiful little girl brought home Luke Craven, but two hundred years ago it probably would have involved a shotgun. Forget about the awkwardness of facing the shadow of Wes, the son-in-law they almost had and probably still mourn. How many frames does he occupy in the upstairs hall gallery? My picture is in the pile of bathroom reads by the toilet.

"I'm guessing that hasn't come up," Callie observes, drawing me back, and I shake my head.

"Not exactly, no."

Her sympathetic look isn't helping right now, and I force my gaze back to the window. I'd been so wrapped up in Holland, in the magic she's inserted into my life, I hadn't given a lot of thought to what I'd do to hers. I hate that the old insecurities are suddenly creeping back, threatening the little shelter we'd begun to build, and I do my best to control the rising chills of panic.

Holland and I were just a story until this moment, until the realization that the story will have to become reality to last beyond the neat little bubble of this tour. Holland threw herself into my baggage; I will have to confront whatever comes with her, even if it's the one thing I will never understand, the one thing that will never understand me.

Family.

I pull out my phone and stare at her name. Everything in me wants to send her a message. That I miss her, that I'm thinking about her, that I can't wait until we park in ten minutes and can steal a touch or two. But my fingers won't move, frozen by sudden images of smiling parents and adoring siblings. Laughter around a Christmas tree, birthday parties, graduations, church choirs, and cheesy beach photos in matching t-shirts. Suddenly, all there is is the world where I don't belong, the world that couldn't accept me even if it wanted to. I see Holland's empty seat at the table because she chose me over them. Because she always chooses me. Because suddenly, it occurs to me that I might love her too much to let her make that choice.

I close my eyes, my chest heavy, aching as the darkness starts to seep from the sewers of my head. The slow mist quickly builds into a suffocating fog, clouding out the light, disguising the recognizable markers I'd planted to maintain my bearings over the last few weeks. I draw in air, but it does nothing to soothe my lungs. Triggers. Triggers. Triggers. I clench my fists. Great, I can label them now. Big fucking deal.

"Luke, hey, you ok?"

Startled, I cast a quick glance at Callie. "Fine, yeah, why?"

I don't like the way she's looking at me. Casey too.

"Just tired. I'm gonna grab something from my bunk. We're pulling in."

I feel their eyes in my back. They're concerned and they should be. Because right now, all I want is to be alone with my darkness.

"LUKE, YOU COMING?"

"Be out in a minute," I lie from the back. I close my eyes and lean against the backrest of the couch, fighting to hold my head together. I hate this sudden meltdown. I hate that the fact that I understand it does nothing to help me stop it. I hate that I'm too weak to control my own thoughts. God, I just hate right now.

I'm not surprised by the backslide, but there's no rejoicing over the few extra seconds you get to study the cliff before you slam into it. These last few weeks have been brutal, and last night's flashback with Jesse wrecked me way more than I'd anticipated. I was rock solid in the moment, but paid dearly the rest of the night as a captive audience to the silent movie replay behind my eyelids. Every dark tunnel and hippie flower graffiti wall that had ever imprisoned me in my protective substance-induced stupor seemed to flash in an endless stream of reminders about why I have no right to be here. I have no right to be here. I have no right to be here. I have no right to...

"Hey, can I come in?"

I force my eyes open at her voice.

Her voice.

"Yeah, sure, sorry. Just taking a break."

She's studying me. I'm sure she knows it's the kind of break that doesn't make sense to most people. The break from life.

She moves beside me and takes my hand, and I fight the urge to pull away. My head knows it would hurt her, not protect her, but the cloud is fighting hard to undermine my head. Empty place settings. Two Christmases alone before the weight of her massive mistake settles in.

"What are we doing, Holland? What are you doing?" I blurt suddenly. It comes out like a cobra strike. She recoils just as strongly.

"What do you mean?"

I face her, I have to, and brace myself even as the pain nearly crushes me. "You know what I mean. This. You and me. We have a connection, great, but what happens when the tour is over? What happens when your family calls you home for dinner? Then what? What happens when you realize that your give is astronomically bigger than your take? That I need you way more than you need me?"

She stares at me, her eyes. I can't look at her eyes and lean forward instead, covering my face with my hands.

"No, Luke. No way."

I still can't look.

"Hey! Look at me! Face me!" she cries, jerking my arm. I do, but wish with all my soul I didn't have to. "I don't know what this is, but it's not happening, ok?"

She gets up and moves toward the partition.

"Where are you going?" I call after her.

Her glare slices into me "You're not breaking this off, Luke Craven. Got it? You're having one of your dark days. Fine. Have a dark day, but I care about you and I'm not letting your bad day ruin the rest of our lives. I'll talk to you later."

She stops. "Oh, and be ready at five tonight because we're having dinner with my parents."

With that she's gone. And it's just me again. Just me and the thick air that never seems quite right for my lungs. Just me and my failed insecurities. Those damn insecurities didn't stand a chance against Holland Drake.

"YOU LOOK AMAZING," I breathe when she meets me at the cab several hours later. She looks more than amazing. She looks like my second biggest regret if I had succeeded in my quest that morning.

"So do you," she returns with a smile. "How are you feeling?"

"Better." Holland had been right. I'd needed time alone to clear my head, not a broken heart.

She gives the driver the address to her parents' house, and the car jumps into motion.

"Holland, about what I said this morning..."

"You don't believe you're good enough for me. Blah blah blah. Yeah, we've been over this," she finishes for me, and I can't stop the slow grin.

"Ok, but your parents..."

"Can't wait to meet you. Anything else?" The clear challenge in her eyes shuts me up, and I shake my head with a shy smile.

"I guess not."

"Good. Because you know what I did this afternoon?"

"What?"

She fishes through her purse and pulls out a piece of folded notebook paper. "Here."

"What's this?"

"A list."

"A list?"

She nods.

"A list of what?"

"Of all the pros and cons of dating you."

I almost choke. "And you want me to read this?"

She shrugs. "Yeah, actually I do. It surprised me, so I think it will surprise you."

I accept the frightening document and unfold it with more than a little apprehension. My heart is beating wildly, thudding against my chest as I glance down at the neat, meticulous strokes. There are actually pros. Shock number one.

> Pros:
> He's deep, intelligent – a lifetime of layers to
>   unravel
> Disgustingly talented – we can grow from each
>   other
> He understands our world, the struggle of the
>   spotlight
> Sexy as hell - duh.
> He fights so hard without knowing it – he fights
>   for me

He touches people without trying
Jesse! How he looks out for him and turns his
    scars into someone else's lifeline
He has no idea how amazing he is, even though
    everyone else can see it
He makes me feel like I'm the most important
    person in his universe
He needs me and I want to be needed

Cons:
He doesn't believe in himself. Maybe he
    never will. Can I believe enough for both
    of us? Do I have a choice when the
    thought of living without him causes
    physical pain?

I stare at the note. Reading, re-reading. I don't know what to do with it. I don't know what words could possibly come next. The fact that she has any pros leaves me speechless. The fact that this is her heart leaves me breathless.

"Keep it," she whispers as I start to fold it back up to return to her. "Let it replace the other one."

I feel the hot prick of tears in my eyes as I nod and grip the priceless treasure in my hand. I still don't know what to say, and do the only thing that makes sense at that moment: take her hand and determine to never let go.

"THAT'S IT THERE. Second house on the left," Holland directs to the driver, and I follow her instructions as well. Sure enough, an adorable brick two-story is packed narrowly among a line of similar structures on the well-kept street. A middle-aged couple rises from their porch chairs at the approach of our cab and Holland is already out of her seat.

"That's them," Holland explains with a grin I know will stay with me for a long time.

"You go. I'll take care of the cab," I offer, and she sheds twenty years as she claps her hands and launches from the car toward her parents.

I pay the fare, barely able to count out the correct change with my eyes constantly wandering toward the reunion on the small porch. I finally complete my assignment and venture from the protective shelter of the car. Holland glances back, and I know the topic has turned to me. She must notice my hesitant approach and bounds toward me with nearly the same enthusiasm.

"Mom, Dad, this is Luke. Luke, this is Annie and James."

I force my best smile. It's not hard when faced with the sincere examples that greet me. "Mr. and Mrs. Drake," I acknowledge, shaking their hands.

"I'm pretty sure she said Annie and James," her father corrects, and my forced smile turns genuine.

"Sorry. Annie and James."

Annie studies me, and I don't miss the look she exchanges with her daughter. Her eyebrows rise in approval, and it's everything I can do to keep a straight face.

"So cute," I hear her whisper as her father waves me inside.

I'm assaulted by the smell of home-cooked food and potpourri as we duck into the foyer, my eyes adjusting to the clean and humble surroundings. Not at all what I was expecting, but then again, I didn't really have expectations.

"You can leave your shoes there by the door," James instructs, and I slide them off to add to the row. Holland does the same and takes my arm, still glowing.

"Are Sylvie and Hannah here yet?" she asks.

"Unfortunately, Hannah couldn't get off work, but she will find another time to see you while you're here. Sylvie's in the basement with Emma. Go tell them you're here."

Holland gives me a conspiratorial look. "Ok, so I should have told you this before, but I know how you get."

I brace myself. "Oh no. What?"

She gives me a sheepish look and leans close. "My sister Sylvie is kind of a huge NSB fan. Like, ridiculously obsessed. Way more than I am," she teases, and I shake my head with a grin.

"Oh, I see. So now you tell me."

"I'm warning you now, right? Can you please do me a favor and just show up in our basement?"

I stare at her in disbelief. "Wait, what? Does she not know I'm coming?"

Holland bites her lip and shakes her head with a mischievous glint. "No. I made my parents swear not to tell her. She thinks she's meeting you after Friday's show."

My eyes widen. "Seriously? Does she know we're...together?"

She shakes her head again and holds her finger to her lips. "No. None of them do. I wanted to talk to them about it in person. I told them we'd become close. They don't know how close."

I sigh. "Ok. Well, hang on then, I have a better idea. Do you have a guitar here?"

She squints at me for a second before nodding. "Yes..."

"Just trust me."

"Ok, be right back."

I wait as she disappears down the hall, and her mother peeks in from the kitchen.

"Did she just leave you there?"

"She's getting something for me," I assure her with a smile.

"Did she tell Sylvie and Emma you're here?"

"We're about to."

Annie nods. "Do you like lasagna?"

"I love it."

"That's a relief because she made way too much like usual," James' voice calls from somewhere behind the wall.

"Oh shush. You like to take it for your lunches."

"For a few days, not a few weeks."

Annie rolls her eyes toward me, and I return a grin. "He loves it," she mouths, then disappears back into the kitchen.

Holland returns with the guitar, a mid-range Martin that's in surprisingly poor condition.

"What happened to this?" I laugh as she hands it to me.

"You have Percy. This is Sam," she explains, beaming. "I just prefer to leave Sam at home for Emma who's starting to get into it."

A sense of reverence washes over me as I take the precious instrument. "Thanks, Holland. It's gorgeous."

She nods. "It was my first real guitar. I had another one before it, but this was from when I first got serious about music." She rubs her hands. "Ok, so what's the plan?"

I clear my head and focus back on the door to the basement. "Well, I don't know. How far down in the basement would they be?"

"There's a small finished section right at the base of the stairs. They're probably watching TV."

"Ok, perfect."

I open the door quietly and work my way down a few steps, careful to make as little sound as possible. Once I find a good spot I lower myself to the carpet and adjust the guitar in my arms. I glance up at Holland and give her a quick smile, loving the look on her face as she begins to comprehend my plan.

Then, without warning, I launch into my favorite acoustic rendition of "Greetings from the Inside."

The volume of the TV drops instantly, followed by literal screams as a young woman who must be Sylvie turns the corner and spots me on her steps. Emma races up behind her big sister and starts grinning as well, although with the shy cool of a self-conscious teenager. The commotion draws Holland's parents, and before I know it, I'm trapped on the stairwell by an adoring Drake family. I cast another glance at Holland and nearly fumble at the glisten in her eyes. I can hear the smile in my own voice as I look away again and finish the song.

"Oh. My. Gosh. No. Freaking. Way." Sylvie cries, rushing up the stairs. I stay rooted in my place so she can reach me and hold out my hand.

"Hi, I'm Luke," I say, and she nods, eyes wide with shock.

"Um. Duh," she replies, and I laugh.

"You must be Sylvie."

"Oh, gosh, that accent!" she blurts to Holland. Now, Holland's laughing.

"Yep."

"You're... Like...on my steps! Why are you on my steps? Why is Luke Craven on my steps?" she demands from her sister.

"He's here for dinner," Holland replies casually.

"Here? Like, with us? Oh, crap, my hair!" She pats her head to hide it, even though I think she looks adorable.

"I like your hair. It's cute," I say, and she just about faints.

"He likes my hair. He..."

"Sylvie. Sentences, darling," Holland counsels. "She speaks fluent English, I swear," Holland assures me.

"Ha. Ha," Sylvie returns, making a face. "I'm sorry, but I bet you reacted the same way when you first met him. Did she tell you what she did when her manager said they were touring with you?"

"Sylvie! Don't you dare!" Holland cries, and now my interest is piqued.

"No, she didn't. Just that it was a good career boost for her."

"Yeah, it was. She also listened to all your albums like a million times for two weeks straight. Morning, noon, and night. Oh! And kept gushing about your genius...blah, blah, blah. Seriously, I've got all the texts to prove it."

"Sylvie!"

I laugh. "Really? Wow. I'm flattered."

"Yeah, she stole them too. Downloaded them from my account. Didn't even pay for them."

"Oh my god, Sylvie!" Holland grabs my arm and starts yanking me up the stairs.

"What? It's the truth. She owes you like fifty bucks!" Sylvie calls after us.

When we reach the top, her parents are doing their best to hide their laughter, and draw to an abrupt stop when they see us. Holland's glare turns on them. "Seriously? I'm home for thirty seconds and you have to embarrass me in front of my boyfriend?"

We all freeze. Their expressions change, and I swallow, the previous butterflies transforming into cyclones in my stomach. Holland realizes her slip as well and blushes.

"Boyfriend?" her father asks, gazing back and forth between us.

She takes my arm and glances up at me briefly before focusing back on her family. "Ok, so, remember how I told you I wanted to talk to you about something?" she begins hesitantly.

They clearly remember. They clearly didn't think this was going to be the topic.

"Luke and I have gotten close. Like, really close. Like bring him home to meet my family close." She gives them a sheepish look. "Surprise."

There's another brief moment of silence before five bodies jump at the sudden, ear-splitting screech erupting from behind us. Sylvie Drake launches herself into my arms, almost knocking me into the wall.

"No way! No freaking way! No way no way no way!" There's no air left in my lungs when she's done with me and turns her passionate approval on her sister.

"Ahh! I can't believe this! This is amazing!" she cries, clinging to her sister. "Luke Craven is going to be my brother-in-law!"

Holland only laughs and returns her embrace. "Um...way ahead of yourself, hon."

Suddenly, the younger woman pulls back and stares at us in horror. "Oh crap...I was kidding about the music! She didn't steal it! I mean, she did, but I'm sure she paid for it later...like, with a donation or something...I...don't be mad at her!"

I just laugh and shake my head. "It's all good," I assure her, before braving a glance back at Holland's parents who are still studying us in silence. I can't read their expressions but her mother doesn't seem happy.

"Holland, I really wish you had told us."

Holland looks away, and my heart sinks. "I know, mom. I knew it would be a shock. I just wanted to be able to talk about it in person. It's good. It's really good, and I wanted you to see for yourself. I knew if you met him..."

Her mother places her hands on her hips and shakes her head. "Well, that may be so, but I really would have wanted to use the good china had we known you were bringing your boyfriend home."

IN A CAREER BUILT ON INTERVIEWS, I've never been asked so many questions in such a short period of time. Most are easy, some are tough, a few are hilarious. My favorite is the barrage about Casey when it turns out Sylvie Drake may love the idea of having me as a brother-in-law, but is a fervent, card-carrying member of Team Casey. Holland snickers as I answer forty percent of the questions and casually deflect the rest. I'm pretty sure Case doesn't want me sharing his underwear preferences with the world. Holland literally spit out her mouthful of water when that one got tacked on to an inquiry about his favorite television show.

"Alright, sweetheart, enough about Casey. Maybe Luke would ask him for an autograph for you?" James says.

"Sure. He'd love it. I'll get a signed stick for you," I assure her, mostly to see Holland's radiant smile again.

"That would be amaaaazing!" Sylvie sighs, melting before our eyes.

"I'll see what I can do."

"More lasagna, Luke? Salad? Bread?" Annie asks. "You sure I can't get you a glass of wine?"

"Oh, no thank you. I'm stuffed. It was delicious."

"Luke doesn't drink, Mom," Holland adds, and I'm not surprised by their surprise.

"Oh! Well, I'm sorry for asking then. Is it bothering you that we are?"

I just smile. "No, it's fine. Really, you all have been great. Thanks for having me."

"You a Jays fan, Luke? You know they have a shot at the Wild Card this year. Just a week left in the season but they're only one and a half games out."

"Dad, he's from South Africa and grew up in Houston. I guarantee you he's not a Jays fan," Holland mutters.

I laugh. "That's true, but I like baseball."

James gives his daughter a triumphant look as he rises from the table. "Well, come watch the game with me and see how real baseball is played."

"Can I help with the dishes or anything, Mrs. Drake?" I ask, picking up my plate as I rise.

"Please, Luke. If you're going to date my daughter you're going to call me Annie. And no. You leave that. Holland and I have a lot of catching up to do. You go relax and watch the game. Can we get you anything else? A bottle of water? Some pop? Coffee?"

"No, thank you, I'm fine."

"Oh, Holland, we have to take him for a poutine while he's here!" Sylvie chimes in.

"Have you ever had a poutine?" Holland asks.

"That's the fries with the gravy, right?"

"And cheese curds, yes. There's a great place over in Scarborough but it's a bit of a trip."

"No, no! They just opened this new place over on Winter Street, Hol," Sylvie corrects. "Just as good!"

"Really? As good as Hendricks?"

"Delicious," James comments. "They do a good burger too. You like burgers, Luke?"

I nod. "Love them."

"Great. We'll take you over there sometime while you're here. How long are you in town again?"

"Through our Saturday show. We'll roll out on Sunday."

"Excellent! That gives us plenty of time to get to know you. Did Holland tell you about Thursday yet?" Annie asks.

I glance at Holland who looks like she wasn't planning to tell me about Thursday.

"No, what's Thursday?"

"You didn't tell him?" Annie directs to Holland who shrugs.

"Geez, Mom. You just asked me about it this morning."

"Still!" She shakes her head and turns back to me. "Anyway, we thought since our daughter is actually home around Thanksgiving time, we'd do an early dinner this year. You're coming as well, of course."

"Um..."

"Canadian Thanksgiving is in a couple weeks," Holland explains. Then glares at her mother. "And you don't have to come if you don't want to. That was an invitation, not a demand, right, Mom?"

"Of course! He's free to turn it down if he wants to insult his future in-laws," James teases from his recliner in the next room.

"Dad! Seriously?" Holland cries in exasperation. Her apologetic look turns outright pleading as she turns it on me. "I'm sorry about them. It's not a Canadian thing, it's a Drake thing."

"HOW'D I DO?" I ask as we make our way back toward the hotel.

"You were amazing," Holland says, taking my hand. "They freaking love you."

"Well, Sylvie anyway."

She laughs. "Not as much as Casey, though."

"Did you know about that?"

"That she's obsessed with Casey Barrett? To be honest, Casey probably knows that. Ask him about Sylvie Drake. I'll show you her room on Thursday."

My grin fades. "About that. Thanksgiving Dinner? I'm honored to be invited, but..." I'm hoping I don't have to finish that sentence. Holland's eyes narrow, informing me that I will.

"But what?"

"I don't know, that's an intimate thing, isn't it? Thanksgiving Dinner? Wouldn't you rather spend that time alone with your family?"

She scoffs, and I know I've lost. "No, I'd rather spend that time watching the most important people in my life get to know each other."

"I know, but I'm sure your parents want to see you."

"Luke, do you have any idea how happy my mom is right now? That she gets to break out her good china? I swear, she will have it out and set by the time we get to our rooms. You also watched six innings of Jays with my dad. He'll date you at this point if I don't. I haven't seen them so happy since Wes and I broke up."

I nearly cough. "Wait, what? I thought you said they wanted you to get married."

"Oh, hell, no," she laughs. "They were always polite to him, but he did not click with my family at all. They thrive on the ribbing and he doesn't have much of a sense of humor anymore if you haven't noticed."

"Yeah, I noticed."

"He used to when we were younger." She sighs and shakes her head. "Anyway, his family was a lot more upset about the breakup than mine, which makes no sense since they also blame me for his 'betrayal.' I think it was more because they were embarrassed than any concern for him...You know they basically disowned him when he chose music and Tracing Holland over the family business?"

"Really? Wow."

"Yeah, he comes from money. Like, *serious* money, and he just walked away from all of it for me, to pursue our dream of music. He's so talented but grew up being shamed for it. They were never fair to him. They didn't get it, or him, for that matter. Gosh, some of the shit they used to say to him?" She sucks in her breath. "I remember this one time back in high school they told him if he played a show with me instead of attending some stupid dinner for his dad's company, not to bother coming home. They actually locked him out. I'm not kidding. He had to sleep at our place for four days before they'd let him back in."

I'm not sure how to respond. I'm sorry for that guy, that version of Wes. But there's another version that's punched me in the face. Twice.

"It means so much to me that you've been so patient with him. I know it's taken a lot for you to show mercy and it hasn't gone unnoticed."

I clench my jaw, still struggling with this whole conversation. I know I'm supposed to be basking in her praise, maybe finding a small ember of forgiveness, but all I'm getting out of it is more evidence of how much I must really love her.

"So Thursday," I continue, preferring that uncomfortable topic over the current one.

"Yes, Thursday. You'll come?"

"Do I have a choice? I mean I don't want to insult my future in-laws," I joke, and she winces.

"Yeah, uh, sorry about that. They were just trying to humiliate me, don't worry."

I laugh. "Your parents yes, not so sure about your sister."

CASEY DOESN'T RECALL the name Sylvie Drake, but loves the fact that my girlfriend's sister is using me to get to him.

"So tell me this story again?"

I roll my eyes and take a sip of my coffee as we walk through downtown Toronto toward today's adventure, some aquarium by the CN Tower. Callie and Holland are grinning, loving this almost as much as Casey.

"None of the details have changed in the last twenty minutes, Case," I mutter.

"Oh, ok, just checking. So she still likes me more than you, then."

"Apparently."

"Even though you're dating her sister."

"Apparently."

"Even though you've had dinner with her and gave her an exclusive, solo performance at her house."

"I shouldn't have said anything."

"You should have invited her to come with us today," Callie adds. "I bet she would have loved to spend the day with you, hon," she says, slinging her arm around his waist.

"Trust me, Cal. I love my sister dearly, but you don't want her anywhere near your boyfriend," Holland laughs. "You should see her room."

"Oh really? Does it have lots of pictures of me and not Luke?" Casey quips, and I shove him forward.

"Concentrate on walking, superstar," I tease, returning his infectious grin in spite of myself.

"I'm just saying, I'm here for you, bro. If you want me to put in a good word for you, I'd be happy to."

I sigh and shake my head, wondering what the fallout would be for tossing someone in the stingray pool.

IT'S ALMOST strange being out in public without Wes, but he must have finally gotten the hint because when the call went out about the aquarium, we had fewer takers than usual. I'm not surprised Eli and Sweeny opted for a trendy bar two blocks from the ACC, or that Jesse is lying low, still smarting from his flower cave embarrassment. I certainly have no complaints about time alone with the three most important people in my life, even though I can't say I'm overly interested in fish and giant algae.

Still, I'm having more fun than I anticipated when Callie and Holland first begged me to go, and have to admit Casey's reaction to the shark tank is probably worth its own television show. He has the entire surrounding crowd of tourists laughing at his commentary and hypothetical conversations between the sharks and fish swimming over our heads as the giant conveyer escorts us through the tunnel.

"Hey, Cal. Why are seahorses such good gamblers?"

"I'm not answering that."

"Aww, come on! You know you want to."

"Nope. Not answering it."

"Why?" Holland chimes in, and yes, part of me is dying to know too after hearing all about how the sea turtle's date had a terrible time at prom because it would only participate in the slow dances.

"Because they know when to let it ride!"

"Casey, that's terrible. That doesn't even make sense," Callie groans, even though she can't hold back her smile for long. Even I'm snickering as he grins and shrugs. The awkward, almost joke barely has time to register, however, before he's pointing out yet another stingray for the eighteenth time. I almost lose it when the eight-year-old in front of us informs him it's the same one he was admiring thirty seconds ago. Also, he's eight, goes to Bradford Elementary, and has a rabbit named Oliver. His sister couldn't come because she has an ear infection.

"I think Casey found a new BFF," Holland observes, taking my hand. I squeeze back and chuckle.

"There's a lot he could learn from an eight-year-old."

"A lot more you could," she returns.

"Eight actually wasn't a bad year for me. The first eight were good."

I feel her glance but don't return it. I'm not really looking for a conversation. I'm not even sure why I said that.

"So what happened at nine? Is that when your dad got sick?"

I nod. "Yeah. And when my mom started not taking it well."

"That makes sense."

I shake my head. "Anyway, how much do you want to bet Casey buys a ticket to suit up and hang with the stingrays?"

"That's a pretty boring bet," she scoffs. "There's no way he doesn't."

"Ok fine. Then how much that he convinces Callie to go with him?"

CASEY DOESN'T CONVINCE Callie to don a wetsuit and Holland owes me a steak dinner. We have fun watching Casey enjoy his private lesson with the stingrays, until the inherent attention on stingray swimmers explodes into a full-on autograph session when we're recognized as quite a bit more than that. Of course, Casey manages to get off with just a few waves and shouted responses from his protected position in the water, but Holland and I end up with crowds that rival the ones we just waded through at the shark tanks. Even Callie signs a few, most likely because our fans aren't sure if they need hers but don't want to take the risk of missing out. Watching her stunned expression as aquarium brochures are waved in her face almost makes the whole thing worth it. A helpful development since we're stuck until Casey finally finishes with his aquatic adventure. The second he joins us we do our best to sneak away from the attention.

"You guys hungry?" Casey asks as we finally step into the freedom of the sunshine. "Let's grab something. What's good, Holland?"

"Hmm...well, there's a nice bar and grill not too far if you like good bar food."

"Bar food! Hear that, Cal? I'm in!" Casey cries.

Callie laughs. "There's a surprise."

"Luke, you good with that?" Holland asks.

"Sure, whatever's fine. You're paying anyway," I tease.

"HEY, man. How are you holding up?" I ask, climbing onto Jesse's bus after we get back from dinner. I'd heard he skipped food again, which makes three missed meals and almost twenty-four hours of self-quarantine: Phase Two of the beating yourself up process. I can tell by his exhausted red eyes that Phase One beat the shit out of him last night.

"Oh, hey, Luke. Doing ok." He's not as good of a liar as I am, but I let it slide. I drop to the other end of the couch as he lowers his guitar. "You want a drink or something?"

"Nah, I'm good."

Jesse nods before shaking his head. "By the way, you were right about that chick. She wouldn't stop texting and calling. I had to block her after the fifth call in two hours."

I sigh. "Yeah. You've got to be careful with your personal info."

"I don't know what I was thinking."

"You weren't," I point out with a smile.

He returns it. "Stupid, I know."

I sigh. "Look, you messed up. It happens."

He studies the far wall. "Yeah, well, my manager was pissed."

"To be fair his meal ticket did end up strung-out in a fucking tunnel."

"I know. Believe me, I know." He lets out a dry laugh and rubs his eyes. "God, what is wrong with me? I mean, I've done some pretty stupid shit, but wow." He shakes his head. "Actually, it's funny, he told me the same thing you did. If I'm gonna party, be smart about it."

"It's good advice."

"Yeah, it just doesn't seem as stupid in the moment, that's the problem. Then later you're like, what the hell was I thinking?"

I laugh. "Story of my life."

He grins. "Yeah, you have some legendary not-so-great moments. So it doesn't go away, huh? It's still a fight, even after you make it?"

"Every damn day, Jess. But that's not being a musician, that's just life, dude. Your screw-ups just happen to be more tempting, accessible, and public. Your stakes are higher now. You're not just some warehouse kid messing around in his parents' garage."

"What if I am, though, you know? I don't want all this shit to change me."

"I'm not saying it should change *you*, just your priorities. The music comes first now."

"It sounds so easy when you say it."

I smirk. "Really? Well, it's not. It's a hell of a battle with all the distractions you've got coming, but I'm telling you, you're gonna need that banner when you fight it. You have no chance otherwise."

"Man, how do you have it so together?" he mumbles,

leaning back against the cushions. "I swear, most days I feel like I'm in way over my head."

He's not trying to be funny, so I hold in my instinctive laugh. But the thought of Luke Craven having anything under control is a joke in itself.

"None of us has it together, man. What we have are our mistakes. I didn't learn all this stuff because I'm some philosopher."

"You messed up."

"Way more than you even know."

He sighs. "You really know how to suck the glamor out of being a rockstar, you know that?"

"Yeah? And how glamorous did it feel passed out against a tree next to a homeless guy who probably stole your wallet?"

He gives me a look and grunts. "Fine. Point made."

"Good. You're gonna figure it out, I promise. But yeah, you're also gonna screw up. A lot."

"You say it like it's fact."

"Do you know where I was when I was your age?" I ask.

"Where?"

"Exactly where you are. Dude, you're not just my friend. You're me."

***

I'M MORE than a little nervous about Thanksgiving Dinner. My last big family event wasn't exactly a cherished memory, and I sense Holland knows where my mind is locked as we pull up to her parents house.

"It's just us, I promise," she says, taking my hand. "I warned my parents in no uncertain terms that our relationship is not public and you are not here to meet every person they've ever spoken to, ok?"

I nod and force a smile, hating this exasperating insecurity. I'm a freaking rockstar. Fucking Luke Craven, and I'm intimidated by roast chicken and fancy napkins at my girlfriend's house.

"You're doing it, Luke…"

"Doing what?"

"That thing you do when you get lost in your head and think things that are going to piss me off."

I can't help but smile when she does and shrug. "As advertised, right?"

She laughs and squeezes my hand as we approach the door.

We don't even have a chance to knock before a young woman I haven't met yet opens it and throws herself into Holland's arms.

"Hey, sis!" Holland cries, squeezing back. "Sorry we missed you Sunday."

"Yeah, stupid partners wouldn't let me off." She pulls away and turns to me. "And you must be Luke. Hi, I'm Hannah, Holland's favorite sister."

"I heard that!" someone calls from the house.

Hannah smirks and waves us inside.

I brace myself for the worst, and I'm actually relieved when the house turns out to be much emptier than I'd expected. True to her word, this really does appear to be an exclusive dinner. Sylvie flies at me, nearly tackling me with a giant hug, and follows it up with one for Holland.

"Hi, Sylvie. Good to see you again. I brought a gift this time," I say, handing her the bag.

Her eyes light up as she grabs it with a screech and starts digging through the contents. Each bit of swag elicits a new sound, and Holland and I exchange several amused glances.

"Wait, there's more," Holland announces. "It's on my

phone, but you have Luke to thank. Hang on, I'll forward it to you."

Sylvie's face is alive with anticipation as she waits for Holland's cryptic gift. I can barely contain my own smile, especially when she literally collapses against the wall the second her display lights up with a video. She stares at us in disbelief, completely frozen.

"Is that...is that..."

"Are you going to watch it or what?"

She squeals and jumps a few times before drawing in a deep breath and pressing play.

"Hey, Sylvie. Casey here. Heard you're into our music. That's awesome. Anyway, just wanted to say hello and thank you for all your support. Hope you like the swag. Enjoy the show tomorrow."

There's no response. She presses play again. And again. And again. Then, Sylvie Drake disappears from view down the hall.

"Geez, Holland. I hope you're happy. As if mom and dad need to spend more money on therapy," Hannah mutters.

"SO LUKE, I hear you've decided to officially brave entrance into this family," Hannah says, selecting a carrot from a tray of snacks on the coffee table.

"Ignore her. She's the moody, sarcastic one," Holland explains, and Hannah makes a face.

"You mean the smart, sane one. Well, minus the meds and shitload of therapy."

"Hannah Marie!" we hear from the kitchen.

"Crap-load of therapy," she corrects. "Crap-load, Mom!"

she shouts. God, I love this girl. "But hey, nothing 1omg of Nilapax and some counseling can't help with."

"1omg? Not bad. I'm in the 20 club," I boast, loving the way her face ignites with a surprised grin.

"2omg? Look at you! Right on. Weekly or biweekly sessions?

"Weekly until the tour. Now, as needed by phone."

"Ha! Weekly for three years, biweekly for the last two."

I warm to the challenge. "Thirty days in an in-patient rehab facility."

"In-patient?" She lets out a low whistle and shakes her head in defeat. "Damn, Holland. Where did you find this god among men?"

She presents her fist, which I tap with a laugh.

"Are you two seriously bonding over antidepressants and treatment plans right now?"

"Well, it beats doing each other's nails...or does it?" She gives me a look. "What kind of rockstar are you exactly?"

Holland smacks her arm as I laugh again.

"The kind that prefers discussing my struggle with mental illness over manicures," I assure her.

She lets out a dramatic breath. "Ok, good. You can keep him," Hannah says to Holland. "Not that the nail painting would have been a problem, it's just we've already got Sylvie so, you know, that's a lot of primping for one house."

"Seriously! I don't know why I ever bring anyone home," Holland mumbles.

"Um, because we're awesome."

"Because you love us," Annie adds, dropping another plate of food between us. "Hannah, I hope you're not tormenting your sister."

"Me? I would never!" she cries, shocked hand to her horrified heart. She exchanges a grin with me as Holland rolls her eyes. "So who's ready for the clarinet recital?"

"You play clarinet?" I ask.

She snickers. "No. But I should totally learn just for moments like these."

"Or you could sit quietly and not scare away my boyfriend."

She scrunches her nose and studies me. "Nah, he's not scared. I'm pretty sure if Sylvie's Casey Barrett obsession hasn't accomplished that, we're good. I mean, are we not going to discuss what happened in the foyer? We're just gonna pretend that was totally healthy?"

"She's got a point, Holland," I admit. "To be fair, I haven't seen 'The Room' yet either."

Hannah laughs. "Ok, whew. Don't let him. He's growing on me," she whispers to Holland. Her phone buzzes and she curses. "Ugh, work again. Hang on, I'll be right back."

"Sorry about her," Holland mutters once we're alone.

"Are you kidding? She's amazing," I say.

"Of course you'd think that. She's the female version of you. Except a lawyer."

I laugh. "So you're dating your own sister? That's not Pavlov, babe. Whole new ballpark right there."

She rolls her eyes, and I give her a quick kiss. The sweet moment turns more urgent when she pulls me in for another one.

"You had to mention Pavlov, didn't you," she breathes. My own pulse starts to pick up, excited by her as much as the stolen moment.

"You just like how much I'm impressing your family."

"You got me. You're killin' the small talk, hon."

"And that veggie platter."

"So hot."

"You know, Holland's old room may be an office now, but I think there's still a futon in there," Hannah quips, and we freeze before exchanging a grin. "That's a thing, right, Hol? Quickies in your childhood room?"

Hannah ducks as a pillow flies toward her head.

DINNER IS DELICIOUS, the conversation flows, and I find myself laughing and joking during a family meal for one of the first times I can remember.

Holland and I are cuddled up on the couch, watching the Jays continue their playoff bid with James, when Annie interrupts the game carrying an armload of equipment. Sylvie and Emma are close behind, neither of whom look thrilled.

"Ok, everyone up!"

Holland groans. "Seriously, Mom? Right now?"

"Oh, I'm sorry. How often do I get my entire family under the same roof? Where's Hannah? Hannah!"

I'm still confused as Holland reluctantly straightens from my arms and starts adjusting her clothing.

"What's going on?" I whisper, and she rolls her eyes.

"Family picture," she explains.

"It's tradition. We've had one every Thanksgiving since Holland was born," Annie explains as she begins unpacking what I can now see is a camera and tripod from its case.

"Well, technically since before she was born, eh?" James corrects, lowering the footrest of the recliner. "You were pregnant with Holland that first year, weren't you?"

"Was I?"

"At least we don't have to wear matching outfits anymore," Hannah snickers, entering the room.

"You girls were so cute in your little matching dresses. We should do that again."

"Over my dead body," Holland mutters.

"Oh, don't be so dramatic, sweetheart," Annie chastises. "A quick shot and you can go back to your game." Her smile grows mischievous. "Or you could try coming home more than twice a year!"

Holland sighs. "Fine. Whatever. Let's get this over with."

"Yes. I'm in the middle of something," Sylvie echoes, joining her sister by the fireplace.

"I'm pretty sure watching an endless loop of Casey Barrett saying your name doesn't count as being in the middle of something," Hannah comments, and Sylvie casts an irritated scowl.

"Ok, girls. We want smiles for the camera! How about that?" Annie chirps.

"I don't know, hon. Maybe this is the year we capture them in their natural state," James teases, earning four sets of eye rolls for that remark.

For my part, I can't get enough. A family photo. No, a long tradition of family photos. Matching dresses. It's too much, and I fight the urge to pull out my phone to film this strange, touching, and hilarious event. I can feel the grin on my face as I take it all in. Studying Holland, my heart exploding at the image of her surrounded by so much love, the thought that she has twenty-nine years of memories like this. I want to know them all right then. Each one, I want to absorb them, let them fill my own void and stabilize the foundation for a future of creating more. I want her, us. I want to give that woman a lifetime of these moments.

"Holland, move closer to Hannah. Hannah! Stop that! Emma, honey, your hair, yes. Perfect. Sylvie, turn more toward me. A little more, oops too much. James, stand to the right, but make sure to leave enough room in front for me..."

Annie stops abruptly. "Wait, where's Luke?"

I had removed myself out of the way against the far wall and straighten at my name.

"Right here," I say, moving toward her. "Would you like me to take the picture?"

Her look of surprise stops my heart.

"Of course not, son. This is a family shot. Go stand next to Holland."

I'M PRETTY sure I'm still smiling from my encounter with the Drake family by the time we reach the hotel, our rooms, and our favorite cooking show while reclining on Holland's bed. And that's without ever gaining access to the Casey shrine in Sylvie's room.

"Oh, hey. Look what my mom just sent," Holland says, shifting so I can see her phone. I mute the TV and glance down at the display. A sudden warmth explodes in my chest at the image.

"Can I see that?" I ask quietly. Her expression softens as she hands me the phone and I study the seven smiling faces in awe.

"I'll forward it to you," she offers gently. "She also said they loved having you over and hope we'll come by again before we leave. Dad wants to take you for burgers."

"I'd love that. Maybe Saturday?"

"Sounds good. I'll let them know." She rests against me and takes my hand. "Thanks, Luke. It meant so much to me to have you there."

"Your family is incredible, Holland. I..." I look away. "I guess I didn't know. I didn't get it." I'm not sure how to explain, how to describe the impact of my first family photo.

"There are going to be a lot more of those, Luke. A lot more of this." She holds up our locked hands.

"Yeah? What about this?" I ask, moving toward her lips instead. I can feel her smile against mine, which only draws me closer.

"Um, yeah. Way, way more of that."

Suddenly, she pulls back with a start, her gaze shooting to my left hand. Tears gather in her eyes, and I swallow the lump developing in my throat.

"Luke..." she whispers, her eyes meeting mine. They're so beautiful in that moment, endless, timeless. I have to blink back my own tears.

She traces the small tan line on my left hand, and I instinctively glance at the ring on my right.

"It felt like it was time tonight," I explain quietly. I have no more words for this, but maybe that's enough when she weaves her fingers with mine and kisses my hand. That vacant spot so full of meaning.

I seem to have stripped her of words as well until finally she settles against me again, gripping my hand, treasuring it. It's her hand now.

"I'm going to be in love with you, Luke Craven," she breathes into the peace.

I smile. "I'm going to be in love with you, too, Holland Drake."

12

BREAKFAST CLUB

OCTOBER 5

"Callie.

"Luke."

We exchange a smile, before I turn to the others.

"Casey. Holland."

"So this is breakfast club," Holland observes, glancing around the small diner.

"Well, I mean, it's not Jemma's, but it'll do for now," Callie explains.

"So what does one do at Breakfast Club?" Holland asks.

"From what I can gather, you awkwardly pick at your food, make even more awkward conversation, and pretend to read menus," Casey quips, and Callie glares at him.

"No, we eat breakfast and make rash judgments about people based on what they order," she corrects, and I laugh.

"All of that is true. We also hang out and spend time with the people most important us," I add.

"Oh, shit, he's feeling sentimental. He's going to recite poetry," Casey mutters.

"Chill out, man. No poems. I'll leave that for Callie."

She gives me a mock glare, before turning to Casey. "Oh my gosh. We should totally have our reception at Jemma's!" she cries. "I'm sure they cater!"

"Uh, that would only make sense if you were marrying Luke, babe," Casey returns, and Callie scrunches her nose.

"Ok, fine. Maybe you're right."

I grin and glance at Holland.

"Not a chance," she snaps before returning my smile. "Does that mean you're engaged?" Holland continues, focusing back on the couple across from us.

"We will be once he asks," Callie answers, and Casey rolls his eyes.

"You act like it's a mystery."

"You haven't asked."

"We looked at rings!"

"Yeah. We also looked at gig bags, athletic shoes, and clearance swim trunks."

"Ugh. Fine. Callie Roland, will you marry me? One day."

Callie leans back and crosses her arms. "That's your speech? You're a freaking songwriter!"

"I didn't plan a speech! You didn't give me time!"

"Ugh! Fine! Yes, Casey Barrett. I will marry you. One day." She turns back to Holland. "Great news. We're engaged. One day."

I can't stop laughing and shake my head. "Oh my god, that's the best proposal I've ever seen. Congratulations, guys. I think."

Their grins are priceless as they exchange a quick kiss, their first as a somewhat engaged couple. One day. Holland finds my hand under the table and laces her fingers with mine. I squeeze, still enjoying the glow of the most unromantic semi-proposal of all time.

"What about you two?" Callie asks, eyeing us next.

Holland and I straighten in unison.

"Engaged? Heck, no," she laughs.

I grin and shove her with my shoulder. "Well, you don't have to be quite so passionate about it."

"Ok, duh," Callie says, rolling her eyes. "But some day?"

"Callie, please," I scoff. "I just figured out yesterday and I'm still trying to work out today. It wasn't so long ago I didn't even have a future to think about."

I glance over at Holland and something moves inside me. Something deep, something strong. Something freaking epic.

I smile. "But for today? Yeah. ...Today."

Holland squeezes my hand and gives me that smile that links my soul with hers. That makes me believe my life might actually be more than a maybe. That turns my future into a conversation instead of a punch-line. The smile that refused to believe my lies.

I steal a solid kiss from that perfect, inspiring, hypnotic smile. Return one of my own.

But I'm Luke Craven.

Dandelion.

Train-Wreck.

Liar.

Gravedigger.

Believer.

Beautiful Moment Destroyer.

"Besides, Holland warned me right from the beginning that she doesn't hook up with other musicians," I tease, ducking away from my girlfriend's indignant swipe.

"Oh really? Hey, Luke."

"Yeah?"

"I said, 'I don't hook up with other musicians.' I never said I wouldn't fall in love with one."

13

THE ENCORE: PART II

It's deafening. I pull out my in-ears so I can truly listen, absorb. I know I should be leading into what's next, but my heart is pounding too fast, the blood searing through my body and blocking all coherent thoughts in my head. I let the screams course through me, spark life in every cell of my being. Stare out over the massive crowd wild with the same excitement bursting in my heart. This moment. I'm living this moment.

I'm living.

So this is it. The comeback I never saw coming. The comeback no one believed. No one except Callie Roland. Casey Barrett. Holland Drake. The comeback I still can't accept I deserved, but have determined to grasp until my last breath anyway. It's a gift, a miracle, and right now it's put me in this place, in this moment. Stolen history for a man who'd given up.

"Let me hear you scream, Toronto!"

I hold my hand to my ear. "I can't hear you!"

"One more time!"

I grin. "Now, that's what I'm talking about!"

I shove my in-ears back in and point to Casey.

It's history time, baby.

1-2-3-4.

Explosion.

FOR UPDATES AND ANNOUNCEMENTS, subscribe to Aly's newsletter.

EXPERIENCE the original song "Greetings from the Inside," along with the rest of Aly's music, wherever you stream music.

Spotify
Apple Music
Amazon Music

MORE FROM ALY

From angsty and dark to snort-laugh funny, Aly writes romance from her soul to yours.

THE SAVE ME SERIES

RISING WEST (available on audiobook)

FALLING NORTH

BREAKING SOUTH

CRASHING EAST

GUARDING SHADOWS

CHASING RIPTIDES

THE WRECK ME SERIES

ASHTON MORGAN: Apartment 17B

CAMDEN WALKER: Apartment 8C

TRISTAN & ISABEL: Apartment 11F

THE HOLD ME SERIES

(Available on audiobook)

NIGHT SHIFTS BLACK

TRACING HOLLAND

VIPER

LIMELIGHT

AN NSB WEDDING

SMARTYPANTS ROMANCE
STREET SMART
PLAY SMART
LOOK SMART

STANDALONES
YOUNG LOVE

PARANORMAL/SUSPENSE
GIFTED (Gifted, Vol 1)
CURSED (Gifted, Vol 2)
SÖREN (Gifted, Vol 3)
HAUNTED MELODY
TRAITOR

STAY IN TOUCH

Thank you for taking this journey with me. I would love to hear from you! For updates, reveals, and more subscribe to my newsletter and join my fun, laidback reader group on Facebook: Aly's Breakfast Club.

You can also follow Aly's original music wherever you stream music:
> Spotify
> Apple Music
> Amazon Music

Find Aly here:
> Amazon
> Facebook Reader Group – Aly's Breakfast Club
> Newsletter
> BookBub
> Spotify
> Apple Music
> Facebook Page – Author Aly Stiles
> Goodreads
> Website
> Instagram
> YouTube
> Blogger sign-up for notifications about future releases

Pinterest

Aly Stiles
PO Box 577
Trexlertown, PA 18087-0577

NOTE FROM ALY

Depression is a serious illness that can go unrecognized by the victim and surrounding loved ones.

If you, or anyone you know, have plans to harm yourself, or you just need someone to talk to, help is available. Dial 988 for the Suicide and Crisis Lifeline, which is a 24-hour, toll-free hotline available to anyone in suicidal crisis or emotional distress.

Please know you are not alone, you are important, and you are loved.

Sincerely,
 Aly

www.ingramcontent.com/pod-product-compliance
Lightning Source LLC
Chambersburg PA
CBHW070630260626
47161CB00007B/2647